REVIVED

by

GINNA MORAN

ISBN 978-1-942073-53-6 (soft cover)
ISBN 978-1-942073-54-3 (epub ebooks)

Cover design by Silver Starlight Designs
Cover images copyright 123RF

For Inquiries Contact:
Sunny Palms Press
9663 Santa Monica Blvd Suite 1158
Beverly Hills, CA 90210, USA
www.sunnypalmspress.com
www.GinnaMoran.com

For Gary Anderson,
Thanks for sharing your fascination of all things supernatural and paranormal with me as I grew up and even now. You've sparked my interest in the genre that has greatly influenced me as a writer. Much love, Dad!

DESTROY THE WORLD

"IT'S GONE." MY words get lost on the breeze with the smell of smoke that wafts up from the ground. Strong arms tighten around me, holding me close. The scent of destruction lingers in the dark night. Bright flames lick over the dozens of buildings below, slowly eating their way through the place that contained some of my best and worst memories.

I stare down, catching the fragrance of death on the icy wind. I can't help but feel satisfied that it has come to this. My demonic blood sends fire through my veins, fighting the heavenly light in my soul in a constant battle of good versus evil within me. And for once, I'm happy to be walking the fragile line between, because it makes me feel more human than I've ever felt, though I'm far from it. A Heaven-bound demon sounds impossible, but I live on impossibilities—it's what pushes me forward.

My heart clenches as Zach, my warrior guardian, descends lower. A sea of bodies covers the ground of the Hunter's Academy, looking like one of the dozens of hellish battle murals that used to decorate the walls. Without having to take a closer look, I know all of them are human—a mixture of hunters and tainted ones alike.

Zach swoops lower, the smoke from a building masking the jasmine scent that clings to my guardian, before he lands on the tall stone wall surrounding the perimeter. His terrifying black wings expand from his back before they disappear with a blink of my eyes. He sets me down next to him, his fingers still locked on my arm, and we silently gaze over the aftermath of the battle between the army of Malicevile—my demonic father—and the Hunter's Alliance. This was one of the few places left untouched by my father's army, but now it's nothing. I almost wish I had been the one to burn it down.

Pushing the thought away, I press my lips together, conflicted. I blame the alliance for the position I'm in, but I didn't want to see so much death. So many lives lost. All because of me. This is my father's way of getting back at the world for my death—one I faked.

But I didn't have a choice. Had my father discovered I willingly gave my soul to an angel, my eternity on earth would've been over, and I'm not ready for that. Though, I'm not ready for this either.

"This wasn't your fault." Being my ever-present shadow and Demon Watcher, Zach's become so in tune with me that I sometimes swear he can read my mind.

"He wouldn't have done it if he knew I was still alive." Apart from self-preservation, I agreed to fake my death because I wanted my death to eat away at Malicevile. He'd always remember me as the seriously faulted daughter who sacrificed it all on his behalf. Who wasted my life for his. Because heavenly light could never kill my father. He's grown too strong. Every soul he collects gives him power, power that protects his life. Power so strong, I'm afraid I won't ever be able to destroy him like Heaven wants, like humanity needs.

"That's not true. He'd have done it regardless, princess. Look around." Zach waves his arm at the smoldering building in front of us, pulling me from my thoughts. "It won't be long before this is what the rest of the world looks like."

"I don't need the reminder." Malicevile is hell-bent on turning the world into his own personal Hell where he's the one who rules. And I've helped him just by being alive. Siphoning my humanity from me has allowed him to gather an army to conquer whoever he pleases—first the alliance and soon the angelic army, and then, the world. Having the weight of the universe on my shoulders does nothing for my confidence. I've failed too many people already. I'm almost sure I'll fail at this, too. But I don't have a choice. I can't stand around and watch as the world burns.

Movement catches my attention, and a tall figure struts from behind the glowing dining hall. Fire ignites in Evan's palms as he steps over and around the fallen bodies of humans caught in the battle between Heaven and my father.

Closing my eyes, I take a deep breath, regretting it immediately. The scent of blood and burning flesh coats my tongue. It does nothing to ease the ache that erupts in my heart after seeing the boy I love strutting among the remnants of what's left of the academy.

After I broke his heart by choosing Heaven, which he assumed was over him, Evan has been setting the world ablaze in my father's honor. And seeing him now, his eyes lit with fire like the depths of Hell, sets my heart racing in a mixture of love and despair. Because our love is the reason he fell.

Without looking at Zach, I jump from the wall and dash forward. My boots thud against the dead, compacted grass, and I levitate a few feet in the air when the bodies become too thick to easily navigate through them.

"Princess!" Zach yells from behind me.

But I don't stop. Instead, I run directly into Evan, knocking him off his feet. We hit the ground with me on top of him, my heart racing so fast I'm sure he can feel it against his own as I press against him.

Our gazes lock, the sneer marring his features softening the moment he recognizes me. He slides his arms around my waist, brushing off the flames that eat away at my shirt that he set ablaze.

"Cami," he whispers.

The sound of my name on his lips sends my whole body trembling as tears burn in my eyes but don't fall.

"I knew you couldn't stay away. I knew you'd be back." His words shoot through my chest, searing my heart like a blessed bullet. Hope shines in his ocean eyes. He reaches up and tucks tendrils of my wild, curly brown hair behind my ear.

I lean into his touch, despite the protests that run through my mind. It's been two weeks since the last time I saw him, but it doesn't feel like time has passed at all. Not with the way he looks at me. "Of course I'm here. Look at what you've done. Evan—" I swallow the burning in my throat caused by the smoky air. Hints of his irresistible patchouli and amber scent trickle through, pushing the putrid air from my senses. "This was once your home."

The softness in his eyes hardens. "Out of everyone, you should be happy."

"But the innocent—"

"No one here was innocent," he says, cutting me off. He might have a point.

I open my mouth to argue, but I can't. Not when the haze of the tainted and Hell-bound souls cloud the air, calling to my demonic blood.

He shifts, pushing up so that I'm sitting in his lap. I can't see anything past the smoke, fire, and bodies—not even Zach.

If he's nearby, I can't smell him. It's just Evan and me alone in a world comparable to Hell, one that feels like we both belong in it. I might be Heaven-bound, but I'm still not innocent.

"This still isn't right," I manage to say.

Evan keeps his arms locked around me, and I find my head leaning closer to his. He studies my face for a moment, like he can somehow read what's on my mind, what I'm not telling him. And then he says, "What you're doing isn't right."

"It's right to me," I whisper. No matter how I try to explain myself, Evan won't be able to see past me betraying him for Heaven.

"You can keep telling yourself that, but it still doesn't make it true. This game you're playing, Cami, it's driving me crazy. You're driving me crazy."

I slide my arms around his neck to meet his eyes dead on. "This isn't a game."

"But isn't it? You're letting the angelic army use you."

"They're not."

"They don't deserve you."

"Neither does my father."

He tilts his head slightly. "What about me?"

"Evan," I whisper.

He leans forward, brushing his lips against mine, sending my mind whirling out of control. I open myself up to everything that he is—what's left of the good, the bad, and the downright infuriating.

"I hate this," he whispers. "I hate knowing you're alive and being unable to tell anyone. I hate that you willingly gave your soul away after everything I gave up so you could keep it. But mostly, I hate that there's nothing I can do to change your mind."

I cut off his words with another kiss. His words slice me open, burrowing inside. "It won't be like this forever," I whisper into his lips.

"Good, because I don't have forever."

Someone clears their throat from behind us. There's only one possible person, because as I sit with Evan among the fiery rubble of the academy, I know that Zach would've never left me unattended. His power shields me from being seen by any threats. I might be willing to risk being seen, but he isn't. The only reason he didn't stop me now is because he knew I'd never have allowed him to. He might be my guardian, but I'm not afraid of blasting the silly smiling sunflowers right off his black cotton shirt.

His jasmine scent trickles into my nose, confirming my suspicions. Evan stiffens, tightening his arms around me, as if Zach will drag me away from him like all the times before. And he might.

"I can't stay," I say, kissing him once more.

"Please, don't leave," he pleads, his words nearly tearing me apart.

"Look around us, Evan. I can't stay. I can't be here and watch you destroy the world alongside my father." I slide from his lap.

He reaches out and locks his fingers around my wrist. "What if I make you stay?"

I close my eyes, a frown pulling my lips downward. "I love you, Evan. Don't you ever forget that."

"Cami."

I tug my hand away and meet Zach's hazel eyes as he stands behind me. His black wings unfurl, expanding wide from his back. Jasmine-scented wind blows away the scent of the alliance's destruction along with the comforting, yet heartbreaking, scent of Evan.

Zach holds his hand out to me, and I take it.

"You're making a mistake, Cami," Evan says, jumping to his feet.

Zach pulls me closer to him. "He'll never see reason, princess. He's too far gone."

Twisting in Zach's arms, I turn to face him. Anger swells in me at his words. I refuse to believe that Evan is hopeless. I don't care if he's at my father's side. I don't care if he led an army against the Hunter's Alliance. I don't even care that he's drenched in the blood of others. Because underneath the influence of my father, Evan is still the powerful demi-demon who'd face the world for me. And I'll face the world for him. I'd fight it, too. It's enough that I know we'll get through this despite everything.

"I don't believe it," I say.

As the words come from my mouth, Evan grabs the back of my shirt and yanks me to him. His wild eyes hold mine as he lifts me off my feet.

I don't protest because I know he won't get far.

As Evan tries to sprint away, Zach drops right in front of us. In one quick motion, Zach reaches out and covers Evan's face with his hand. He tugs me away and into his arms before Evan even drops to the ground. Angelic power washes over him, locking away the memory of me in his mind once again.

Tears line my eyes. "I don't know if I can do this, Zach."

He bends his knees and launches us into the air. "If you don't, then your father has won."

I press my cheek to his chest as he flies us up and away from the Hunter's Academy. Evan's unconscious body blends among the dead masses, and it's enough to force my racing heart into my throat. Because if my father does win, that's exactly where I'll find Evan—dead along with everyone else I love in this world.

I can't let that happen. I won't.

I'll destroy Malicevile.

His life will be mine.

SOULLESS

MY SKIN WARMS with hot electricity coursing through my veins. I face a beautiful demon as she thrashes against the blessed restraints. I managed to snap them on her wrists with a little help from the handy, yet sometimes annoying, shielding power Zach uses on me every second of every day to protect me from my demonic father and the rest of the Veiled Realm.

Cupping an energy orb in my fingers, I hold it in front of me, causing the demonic woman to freeze in her spot. Any demon in the world would recognize my power. It's the same power that flows through Malicevile's veins.

"Your father lied," the demon says, tilting her head to the

side. "He said you perished by the hands of angels. He said the secret of your transformation went to Hell with you."

It's been two months since I was supposedly blasted into oblivion by angelic light. And now it seems that more demons than ever have enlisted in Malicevile's army. All in the name of me. Who knew demons would want to conquer the world on my behalf—the poor pseudo-princess who gave her life trying to protect her dad all while dying with the knowledge of how to transform a demi-demon into a demon. Last I heard, my father was more annoyed about my sacrifice than anything, because the angelic light wouldn't have killed him. He's too powerful. Invincible.

I bare my teeth in a fake smile. "Not to Hell. I'm never returning there again."

Her blue eyes crinkle in the corner. "You mean—"

"Princess," Zach says, coming up behind me. "This isn't a social gathering."

The woman snarls, her true body escaping at the mere sight of Zach as he steps up next to me and slings his arm over my shoulders. The disgust that crosses the woman's face only makes Zach smile while his wings appear, stirring his heavenly scent through the air.

I sigh. "Seeing a demon's reaction to discovering the truth is my favorite thing about these hunts."

"But you're wasting time."

The demon snaps her now sharp teeth. Her face contorts, her true body ripping through her flawless skin, showing off blood-red horns three times the size of my dainty crown of horns that sometimes sneak out of me when I'm feeling extra demonic or angry.

I roll my eyes, turning away from Zach. In one quick motion, I chuck an energy orb at the woman, hitting her squarely in the chest, singeing the front of her cream-colored blouse. The power doesn't settle her down, instead it pisses her off even more. Her wrists and ankles smolder and catch fire as she struggles against the binds tying her to the metal pipe on the wall of this abandoned warehouse.

I hit her with another burst of power. "Knock it off before I cut your heart out."

She stiffens. "Traitor."

I shrug. I've been called worse. If that means trying to stop the demonic world from consuming earth, then I'll wave my traitor flag wildly. Ignoring her, I say, "I heard my father was still hunting demi-demons. Why?"

"Why don't you ask him yourself?" she asks with a smirk.

Anger slithers up my back. I don't know why I bother asking. Demons, especially upper-level demons like this woman, are smart.

Instead of blasting her with another burst of energy, I slide a blessed dagger from my belt. My father always told me how weak human weapons make me look, but I don't care what anyone thinks. Not anymore. It's the only way to steel myself from the world. Demons despise me when they realize who I've sided with—even Evan—and angels, well, they're not exactly as welcoming as I had hoped. Hell makes them nervous, and I'm still a creature of Hell.

Pushing the thoughts away, I hold the dagger up. "Tell me."

She narrows her eyes. "That information comes with a price."

"Name it."

Zach sucks in a breath next to me. "Careful, princess."

I glance at him in the side of my vision. "Go on, demon."

"Release me, and I'll tell you."

"Deal." Studying her for a moment, I waltz closer and untie her ankles before I free her hands. I hold my dagger ready for her next move. I'm not an idiot. "Now tell me."

"He's still attempting to move forward with his plan."

As she speaks, she raises her hands, and a lime-green, slimy looking ball materializes in her fingers. She tosses it at me, and it splashes against the front of my black T-shirt. The moment it touches me, it eats away the fabric, threatening to leave me naked as I quickly try to absorb it.

Then she rushes forward.

Deep crimson blood cascades through the air in an elegant arc, and then washes over me in a sickeningly sweet wave of warmth that smells a lot like the cherry-vanilla ice cream I shared with Cadence at dinner.

I blink through the haze of blood, my knife still raised. With a small laugh, I shake my arms, splattering the demon's blood across the nearby wall. Her sweet scent clings to me, and

I'm pretty sure I won't be eating that ice cream again anytime soon.

"Seriously, princess!" Zach wags his head back and forth, pelting me with the blood that coats his chestnut hair. It drips down his face in disgusting streaks before staining the T-shirt I bought him for ruining three of his shirts last week. Using the back of his hand, he swipes the blood from the picture of a cute black cat with demon horns, only to smear it worse. "I'm starting to think you just want me to follow you around shirtless."

I wipe the blood dripping from my face and smile. "Cadence would appreciate it."

He shakes his head, his cheeks turning red. Before he has a chance to respond, a low moan erupts through the quiet warehouse. My skin crawls at the noise, and I summon power from within my soul. My hands glow a bright green before a small ball appears. The power feels different than all the other times I've absorbed power to protect myself. This power isn't foreign or strange. It feels like it belongs within me unlike the power of my father.

The last time this happened was when my demonic father set me up to be kidnapped by demons as a way to punish me. I killed an upper-level demon and suddenly absorbed his power. And now, it seems that another power has taken permanent residency in my soul, becoming my own. My demonic blood warms at the thought of how awesome it is.

"Whoa," I say.

"Is it?"

I nod. "All mine."

"Princess, you really are extraordinary. It shouldn't be long."

I don't have to ask Zach what he means. He's referring to my new destiny, one scary enough to make me want to put it off for another century. Facing my father is the last thing I want to do. Life's been so nice without him, though he's turning the world into his own personal Hell to rule. Because my father has tilted the balance and gone against what he was intended to do, which was only to punish souls and send them to Hell. Instead, he's keeping souls for himself.

I still can't imagine my father as anything less than all-powerful. To think his sole existence was to deliver souls to Hell seems beneath him. He thought so, too. It's why he started his collection. It's why many demons collect souls.

According to Zach, when a soul becomes demon-bound and remains on earth after the mortal body dies, it upsets the balance between Heaven and Hell. And balance is what keeps the universe in order. Constant chaos will destroy the world, and then there will be nothing left. It's a thought I never want to imagine.

Another groan sounds out and cuts off my thoughts. I take an automatic step forward with Zach behind me. Slowly making our way through the rundown warehouse, I search each aisle created by the junk left behind, following the scented trail.

Zach follows behind me to the back of the warehouse where the groan came from. We pass aisles of junk, remnants from the humans who used to run this place before demons took over.

The scent of smoked paprika and something stronger, fouler, more disgusting, stops me in my tracks. Zach's hand flies out and pulls me back as he blocks me from taking in more of our surroundings. His wings expand out, preventing me from peering over his shoulder.

"What are you doing?" I ask. "What is it?"

His hazel eyes hold mine. "Let's go out the front."

I shove him out of the way and search the area before my eyes land on a cage the size of a large dog kennel positioned against the back wall. Within the cage lies the body of a familiar girl with ratty hair, torn clothes, and small mounds of smooth rocks surrounding her. She's definitely a demi-demon and a hunter. But this girl didn't fall with the academy. I basically handed her over to my father myself after the first time I met Zach.

And she's alive.

I race forward, my heart pounding in my ears.

Strong hands grab me from behind as Zach pulls me against his chest. He's not fast enough though, because I get a clear view of the girl and her milky-white, empty eyes. They blink slowly every few seconds before she releases another moan.

I spin and look at Zach. "What's wrong with her?"

He frowns, his hazel eyes shining. "I'm sorry, princess. Her soul belonged to that demon you just killed."

My mouth falls open. "You mean I—" My voice catches in

my throat as I gag, my stomach rolling as the thought grabs hold of me. This is my fault. I was too concerned about the demon to check the area. I wanted answers, and those answers were the only thing that mattered to me. But now, as I stand here, staring at the shell of the demi-demon, I realize how wrong my world is.

I've known what happens to the tainted once their demonic masters are returned to Hell, but seeing it in person, seeing this girl without a soul, shreds me apart and threatens to make me give up what I've been planning to do: kill my father. Because how can I do this? How can I damn so many to such a fate? And Evan?

"This isn't your fault. She made her choice," Zach says.

My stomach heaves again, and I get sick all over the floor. I cough and spit while Zach pulls my wild mane of dark curls out of the way. It was so easy to ignore the truth when it wasn't sitting in front of me, gaping at me in the creepiest of manners. And now, all I can imagine is seeing Evan sitting before me in a cage, his blue eyes cold, colorless, and empty.

I take a deep breath. "I need to leave."

"Princess, we need to talk about this."

I throw my hands up. "Why? Talking this over isn't going to change the fact that you're expecting me to damn—"

"You're not damning anyone. They're already lost. You know this."

"I can't do this anymore." Tears prickle my eyes.

"This is about Evan," he says.

I hold myself, turning away. "Of course it's about Evan."

"I'm trying really hard to understand, princess, but humanity depends on you completing your task. If you don't, then all will be lost. You and me, Cadence, Dylan—everyone you know. Is that what you want? Evan chose his side. He'll protect your father until the end."

"I can save him," I whisper.

"But you have to accept that he might not want to be saved."

Rubbing my hands into my teary eyes, I strut away from Zach. I can't talk to him anymore, not when I'm feeling like this. Not when it feels like I have to choose between the universe and the boy I love.

Surprisingly, Zach lets me go.

Cool night air steams from my skin as I exit the warehouse and tilt my head toward the sky. The stars fade as the sky lightens, the rising sun pushing away the darkness. If only it could push away the devastating thoughts that cling to me.

What's worse? The demon's words still resonate with me. She said my father was still going to attempt to follow through with his plan. He's going to try to recreate what happened to me even though only I—and Heaven—have the answers. I'm afraid Evan will try. I'm afraid he'll willingly allow himself to be sent to Hell. And then what? There would be no saving him.

God, I miss him. I need to talk to him, make sure he doesn't do anything crazy before I figure things out.

Tugging my cell phone from my pocket, I pull it out and

call one of the few people who has stood by my side through everything. Cadence picks up on the first ring, her perky voice easing the pain pulling my heart apart.

"I need a ride," I say quietly.

"I thought Zach was your ride."

"I don't want to fly with him."

"I'll be there in a few." Cadence hangs up without asking me why I'm upset or why I don't want to ride with Zach. Her loyalty and love is one of the reasons I'm so torn between my life and what Heaven has asked me to do.

The fragrant scent of jasmine permeates the air behind me. Zach hovers next to me, invading my space all over again. I should be used to it, but sometimes I just need to be alone.

"I'm sorry, Cami," he says without touching me. He rarely says my name. "I can't imagine what you're going through, but know that I'll be here for you every step of the way."

I blink the tears away. I'm not going to cry. Not now. "I miss him."

"I know."

"I'm not going to kill my father unless his soul is his own," I say.

Zach sighs. "Even at the expense of others?"

"You must think I'm some monster."

"Never. But I want you to think about what you're considering."

"I have."

The flash of headlights draws our attention to Cadence's

blue Jaguar as she enters the parking lot from the street. She parks at the curb without turning off the engine and waves to Zach.

Without another word to Zach, I slide into the front seat of the Jag and close the door. A moment later, Zach bends his knees and launches into the air and out of sight. Cadence reaches out and touches my knee without a word.

"You okay?" Cadence asks.

I shrug. "Been better. Take me somewhere?"

"Where?"

"It's better if you don't know."

She smiles. "Why do I have a feeling you want to see a certain demon boy?"

"Because you're my best friend."

"Zach's going to flip out."

"Good."

AS THE WORLD BURNS

BRIGHT SUNSHINE TRICKLES through the windshield as we sit in the Jag, idling in the middle of the street not far from the one place I should be nowhere near. I can't help it, though. Last night rattled me so much that I'm willing to risk everything I worked for to make sure Evan still walks and talks and breathes with his soul, no matter how tainted it is.

I vowed I'd stay away from him. I vowed that I'd keep my thoughts locked away. Because every time I see him, I find myself falling under his charm. I'm reminded of how much he doesn't understand. I'll fight all of Hell to see to it that he's okay in the end, but I'm not even sure if that'll be enough. He doesn't want to be saved. He wants an eternity with me. I wish I could give it to him.

I lick my dry lips, run my hands over my crusty, half-missing shirt, and then open the door. Cadence remains in her seat behind the wheel. Where I'm going, I don't want her to follow. I don't want her to see what Zach sees. What everyone sees. Except me.

I half smile. "If I'm not back in twenty minutes, leave without me."

"Cami," she says.

"I'll be fine. I just don't want you to get caught up if I need more time." Like there could ever be enough time, though.

Without waiting for her response, I slam the door a little too hard and jog toward the small unmarked road that leads in the direction of my father's house. There's no possible way he can be around in the daylight, and I won't get close enough to get caught by one of his relentless minions. Either way, I still need to be careful.

Levitating just within the tree line, I travel along the winding road that'll take me directly to the boy I need to see. The sound of tires crunching gravel echoes through the quiet air, causing me to freeze in place.

My red Mustang comes into view at the top of the hill that leads to my father's mansion. This couldn't have been more perfect. I knew Evan ran errands for my father in the day, but I was half expecting to have to sneak onto the property. Maybe someone besides Zach is looking out for me after all.

"Cami," a voice sounds out from behind me.

I spin in my place, energy orb ready in my hand even though I know I'm not going to use it.

Dylan stands a dozen feet away, leaning against a large palm tree, arms crossed over his chest. He looks me up and down, his eyes lingering a little too long on my bare stomach. I turn away from him even as I hear him stroll closer. His apple and rain scent encompasses me, sending my heart beating faster.

"Let me guess. Zach sent you to keep an eye on me. I didn't even know you were back in town." I might've built a wall to protect myself from Evan, but I built an entire fortress to protect me from everything that is Dylan. It wasn't until I had to willingly give up Evan that I knew deep down in my heart that he was the one I never wanted to live without again. Despite the evil tainting him, the constant struggle of wills we face, all the heartache we've put each other through, he's never lied to me, never hid things from me. Even under the influence of my father, he still manages to think of me first.

Dylan closes the distance and puts his cool hands on my shoulders. "I heard about the soulless one you saw."

I shrug away. "So."

"So, I know you're not okay."

"I'm fine."

"Then why are you here."

"Why do you think?" As the words come out of my mouth, the Mustang rolls past, traveling at a surprisingly leisurely pace. It's slow enough to almost stop me in my tracks. But then anger sneaks up on me, because if anyone other than Evan is driving my car, they won't be driving it for long.

Raising my hand, I send a small burst of energy at Dylan, knocking him back before he tries to restrain me. It'd be like him to drag me away kicking and screaming to keep me hidden from the world.

Using levitation, I propel forward into the road before I break out into a full blown sprint. Rocks fly when the Mustang skids to a stop, and the driver's door flies open before Evan hops out, fire bursting in his fingers.

He meets my eyes.

I let out a long, ragged breath. He just stares at me, fire-light in his eyes, a sexy smile leering at me. My feet take on a mind of their own. I saunter closer, an arm slung over my chest in a half hug like the gesture will somehow comfort me or keep me together.

"Come any closer, and I'll throw you over my shoulder and stop you from leaving," he says, closing the distance between us.

I consider letting him. "I had to see you."

"It's been weeks."

I pout my bottom lip. "I know. I—"

His arms slide around me, and he leans forward, cutting off my words with a kiss. His lips, soft and inviting, brush against mine. I find my own arms sliding up and around his neck until I hook him to me so he won't be able to pull away even if he tries. His patchouli and amber scent drifts over me, washing away the rest of the world until it feels like we're alone, and the world isn't counting on me—only Evan is.

"Tell me you've come to your senses," he whispers into my lips. "Tell me you're done playing games."

Slowly, I pull away and meet his ocean blue eyes. I just want to drown myself in them so I don't have to answer his comments. So I don't have to prolong the suffering we're both experiencing all because of my demonic father.

"I can't," I finally say, leaning my head forward until I'm resting on his shoulder.

"You can."

"You don't understand."

"Then make me."

But how can I? The angelic light within me only shines so bright. It's not powerful enough to cut through his darkness. It's barely enough to keep me anchored to this world that wants so badly to cast me out and into the sunlight prison realm where I belong.

Instead of responding to him, I snuggle my face into his shirt. He holds me against him, his fingers locked together on my lower back, caressing the sliver of skin between my shirt and jeans.

"Cami," Evan whispers, his warm breath tickling my knotted hair. "If you're not here to stay, then why are you here?"

"To see you," I say without meeting his eyes.

"It's more than that. I doubt that brainwashing shadow of yours would allow you this close to home without good reason. I swear, if you're trying to do som—"

"I'm not." Pulling away, I meet his hardened gaze. "It's just—I saw something last night. It scared me."

His forehead crinkles as he furrows his brows. He doesn't comment, just waits for me to finish.

I inhale a deep breath through my nose and say, "I sent a demon home."

"You're not afraid of demons."

"But the demon—the demon had a demi-demon."

"Oh."

"Yeah. And now I'm terrified for you."

He tilts his head up and releases a long, loud laugh. It startles me, and I levitate a foot into the air before Evan tugs me back down.

He smiles as he says, "I'm sorry you saw the consequences of what you've done firsthand, Cami, but your fears are unwarranted. Your father isn't going anywhere no matter what the angelic army prays for. I'm alive, and I'm safe."

I don't laugh or smile. He has no idea what I'm dealing with. How could he? "Evan," I whisper. "The angels, they want me to—"

"Cami, it's time to go."

Evan stiffens in my arms, peering over my shoulder. Dylan's scent trickles through Evan's, and I force myself to pull away and spin to face him.

"She's not going with you." Evan doesn't let go of my hand, twining his fingers around mine even tighter. Fire burns in the palm of his free hand as he prepares to launch a fireball at

Dylan, the one Evan thinks is responsible for everything—which he kind of is. I can't blame him for wanting to obliterate him, but there's no way I'll allow it.

My heart aches as I pull myself away from Evan. "I'm sorry, Evan. I can't stay."

A scowl crosses his face, and he glances between me and Dylan. "If you leave now, I don't want you to come back unless it's for good. You coming around tortures me, and I've been through enough of that. It kills me that you willingly go. That you willingly choose to be somewhere I can't be."

"That's unfair. I can't just stand by as the world burns. I can't stand by and watch you set the fire."

"Then why bother with me at all?"

I swallow. "Because I want to save you, Evan. Because if I don't, I know I'll be responsible for the destruction of the world. All because I love you. And then what?"

"There's only one way you can save me," Evan says.

I heave a sigh. "I can't. Not like you want me to. And even if I could, your soul belongs to Malicevile." If by some miracle I could convince someone to fetch Evan from Hell, I still have to kill my father, and in doing so, Evan's soul would follow him to Hell again, leaving Evan as a soulless demon on earth. He'd be no different than my father and just as ruthless.

"Please, Cami." His warm hand cups my chin, and he runs the pad of his thumb over my lips. I look away before he can burrow himself beneath my skin to break me apart.

My lips quiver, and I kiss him once more before whispering, "I can't." Stepping away from him freezes my fiery heart so that every passing beat threatens to shatter it into a million pieces. "I have to go."

He snatches my arm and holds it. "Please, don't."

I turn my gaze to Dylan, who stands there with mixed emotions splattered across his face. He releases a breath when I step away from Evan. "I've stayed too long already. I'll be missed."

"More than you know." His words eat away at me because he's showing the most emotion I've seen on him since he traded his soul. He almost feels like he did when he wasn't Hellbound, but I can't be certain. My mind has warped every part of my past. I can't tell if what I remember is truly real or just how I want to remember it. Maybe a little of both.

"I love you, Evan," I say. "I'll figure things out. I won't let it end like this."

He turns his back on me and struts to the Mustang without another word of protest. It's all I need to hold onto what little hope I have.

After slamming the door and revving the engine, he disappears in a cloud of dust without saying goodbye. I'm glad he didn't. I never want him to again.

"You can't save those who don't want to be saved," Dylan says, coming up next to me.

I glare at the dust cloud instead of him. "He's only saying that because his soul doesn't belong to him. I'll make him see. I'm going to get his soul back, Dylan."

"And how do you plan to do that?"

"You'll see." I hold out my hand to him. "Now come on. Cadence is waiting, and I have a guardian to find."

LIFE ISN'T FAIR

"I'M GOING TO be honest with you, Cami. I don't think your plan will work. Even if you manage to find something Malicevile's willing to trade Evan's soul for, I don't think Evan is just going to drop everything and turn his back on Hell." Jazmin, my former instructor from the Hunter's Academy, sits across from me on the couch, her hands tucked in her lap.

Cadence and Dylan talk quietly in the corner, glancing in my direction every so often. And Zach? He's nowhere to be found, which worries me. Not because he's missing, but because I'm afraid he might reconsider my involvement in the grand scheme of things.

"I did," I say.

She scratches her arm before adjusting her sleeve. "That was different. You might be a demon, but even before you gave your soul to your watcher, you still had some good left in you. I could tell how distraught you were before the angelic army intervened in my deal with Malicevile. And that's something you never see in someone on Hell's side."

Collecting Jazmin was the last thing I had done for my father before Zach decided he wasn't going to allow me to continue down the path I was heading. The only reason he hadn't intervened before that moment was because I was already turning away from Hell. But when I discovered that he was pretending to be a demon, I had assumed the worst. I had assumed he was there to destroy me like Malicevile said the angelic army would do. And honestly, I think he would've tried if I hadn't given in—hadn't let him manipulate me.

I should be angry—furious even—but now that my vision is no longer constantly red-tinted and my emotions have settled, I know that my half human self, the self I sometimes think about, would have wanted this. I want this. I fell by Malicevile's side because I was out of options. What was I supposed to do? My sudden transformation stole me from everything I knew. The people I cared about, the people who had always been there for me, had no idea how to handle me or they turned their backs on me. And Evan was so welcoming.

Jazmin watches me as I process her words. After another long moment of silence, I finally say, "Evan still has good left in him."

"You think so?" Zach appears out of nowhere, interrupting me right in the middle of our conversation. He frowns as he looks at me, and it's enough for me to flick a small burst of energy in his direction.

"You've been following me this whole time?" I ask, annoyed.

"Of course I have. I never leave your side, princess. How else am I supposed to keep you out of trouble?"

"And you didn't stop me from seeing Evan?"

"Would you have let me?"

"No."

Jazmin leans over and squeezes my shoulder, quietly moving from her spot. I wouldn't want to get in the middle of this argument either, because while I know Zach is only doing his job, he's worse than when my father required Evan to babysit me. At least with Evan there was a lot of fun. With Zach? He's like the annoying brother I never had or wanted.

"Okay, then. I hope you found whatever it was that you were looking for, because the next time you get within a mile of any of Malicevile's estates it better be because you're ready to send him back where he belongs."

I slowly nod, curling my fingers into my palms. "I did, but you're not going to like what I've decided."

"Princess."

"The only way I'm going to go on this insane mission on Heaven's behalf is if I get something in return."

"It doesn't work like that, Cami."

Uh-oh. He's using my name. It's enough to make me worry about what I'm about to say next. I know I'm walking a fine line between my demonic nature and my heavenly soul, but what if Heaven decides that I'm not the right one for the job and not only takes my soul away, but also sends me straight to Hell? Or worse, straight into oblivion?

I suck in a deep breath. "It's going to have to, Zach. Because if it can't, then you can count me out."

I feel three pairs of eyes staring at me, and I turn and glance at Dylan, Cadence, and Jazmin from the corner of the living room. Sunlight trickles through the rainbow-colored, stained-glass windows, and the small converted church starts to feel suffocating. So does the sun.

My friends look as worried as I feel.

Zach's shoulders slump. I thought he'd give more of a fight. "Fine, be the one responsible for the destruction of humanity."

His words cut right through me, and I snap. "Hey! That's not fair!"

He unfurls his frightening large black wings. "When will you get it? Life isn't fair. If it was fair, you wouldn't be in this position. It's your job to make it fair again. Restoring the balance will do that."

"But at the cost of Evan's soul? Of so many others?"

"Yes! Everything comes with a price! You can thank demons for that." His voice bellows through the room. He's never raised his voice to me like this, and I can't help flinching.

"I *am* a demon!" Power erupts in my fingers, and I throw it at the carpet in frustration, singeing the scratchy fibers.

Zach punches the air, surprising me. Both our emotions run so hot that I'm afraid we'll cause an explosion that'll be seen by the rest of the world. He's acting like I'm asking to go home to my father. All I want is help acquiring one soul in exchange to save billions. He wants me to save the world, but he just doesn't—either he can't or won't—understand that Evan is my world.

My chest heaves as I take in angry breaths. Cool hands grip my shoulders and pull me back away from my guardian. Power sizzles from my skin, shocking Dylan, but he doesn't let go of me or back down.

Zach expands his black wings through the room, and then suddenly, a bright figure flashes into view next to him. Ethereal hands lock onto his shoulders as a familiar angel, a woman with golden hair that cascades over her shoulders in soft waves, covers him in her own heavenly light. Dani, one of the angels who helps Zach out, whispers something into Zach's ear that makes his eyes widen.

It's enough to cool the heat flowing through my veins.

I reach up and cover Dylan's hands as they still hold my shoulders. A tremble crawls through me, leaving me shaking to my very soul.

All I can think of is that whatever Dani told Zach was enough to change my world. What if something happened to

Evan? What if she's come to deliver heartbreaking news?

Dani lets go of Zach after a second and crosses the room to whisper something to Jazmin. Jazmin takes the angel's hand, and they suddenly disappear together. Ever since Heaven intervened in Jazmin's demonic bargain, I'm pretty sure Dani has been watching out for her. Remaining out of view is an angel thing—except for Zach. Most of the time his presence takes up all the room around me.

Now's one of those times.

As he stands there in place, eyes swirling with thoughts he might never put into words for me to hear, I can't help wondering if he actually cares about me as a person and not just some demon with a soul that helps get the job done. That he actually doesn't want me to spend my existence in constant turmoil.

"Princess," he finally manages to say. "The demon was right last night."

My heart sinks into my stomach as the memory of her words come back to haunt me. I was so caught up with Evan that I didn't even bother to ask him about it, about my father's plan. And now I regret it. Because I want to run right back to him and beg him to not do anything crazy. I know he wants me to help him, but what if he gets desperate and takes it upon himself? *Calm down. He was fine. He'll be fine. You'll make sure of it.*

"I don't understand," I whisper.

"A body of a demi-demon was discovered this morning with a message. Your father's pretty sure he'll be able to recreate your transformation. Are you sure you didn't tell anyone?"

"He's bluffing," I manage to say. He has to be. Because if he's so certain, Evan might put his trust in him.

"You sure?"

"Yes."

Zach relaxes, closing his wings before they disappear. "Okay, because that information—"

"Is priceless." My words hang in the air. My father didn't care about transforming demons until I was already almost pushed back into Purgatory territory. By the time he would've wanted that information, it was too late. But now? I bet he'd give anything...

"Love," Dylan whispers into my ear. He knows exactly where my mind is wandering. "You wouldn't only be putting the world in danger."

His soft voice wraps around my heart, squeezing it so hard that I'm sure it'll turn to dust. If I gave that kind of information to my father in exchange for Evan's soul, it would not only put the angelic army at risk, it'd put Dylan at risk. Could I trade his safety for Evan?

No. I don't even have to think about it.

"I know," I whisper, leaning back until his arms embrace me before I sink to the floor to curl in on myself. The world doesn't feel so heavy when someone else is holding me.

Zach watches us quietly for a moment, his expression indiscernible, and I wish I could tell what he was thinking. But he gives nothing away. He crosses the room and sits down on the couch before propping his feet up. I frown as I watch him. He's gone from intense angel to easy-going guardian in a matter of seconds. And it makes me nervous.

"What are you doing?" I ask.

"What does it look like? Relaxing."

"You never relax."

"Well, until you figure out what's going on, we're not leaving this church. Maybe a night off is what you need."

I sigh. "Stop telling me what I need."

He sighs, shaking his head. "I don't want to fight anymore."

I don't either, but I don't want to stay here. Pulling myself from Dylan, I cross the room to the door. As I swing it open, I nearly collide with Alana, who's about to come inside. She jumps back before I topple into her, and then her eyes widen.

"Sorry, princess," Zach says, covering my eyes with his hands. "I'm not letting you leave."

"Zach, don't you dare!"

But it's too late.

Once again, Zach stops me from facing the world on my own terms, leaving me in a state of nothingness.

SUCH A LIFE

I JOLT UPRIGHT on my bed. Night hangs heavy over me with only the light from the hallway breaking through the darkness of my bedroom. The scent of apples and rain hangs in the air, and I don't even have to search around to know that Dylan sleeps on the floor next to me. I've been out for hours. So long that I can almost feel the sun about to rise in a new day all over again.

And I'm pissed.

Swinging my legs off the bed, I stand next to Dylan's sleeping form before I levitate up and over him. I don't get far. His cool fingers lock onto my bare ankle, and he yanks me sideways until I fall back onto my bed.

"Zach grounded you, love," he says. A smirk crosses his face when I narrow my eyes and glower at him. "Said you were being a thorn in his side."

"One, Zach can't ground me. And two, he better watch out because I'm about to be a dagger in his side."

Dylan chuckles as he moves to sit next to me on the edge of the bed. "You're cute when you're threatening."

I bat his arm. "Only you would call an angry demon cute."

He laughs again, and I bump my shoulder with his before he slides his arm around me. Despite my better judgment, I rest my head on him and allow him to hug me. I know my closeness drives him crazy and wild and all sorts of other things, but a part of me still can't help myself. Even though my soul belongs to Heaven, I'm still quite devilish. I'm a demon after all.

"What would it take for you to sneak out with me?" I ask, running my fingers over his knee. This church is the one place Zach actually doesn't hover in the shadows, so I might have a chance to escape just to annoy him.

"Breakfast," Dylan says, grinning.

"Only if you fly."

He smiles as he pulls me to my feet. His brilliant wings flash on his back once before they disappear, and I lead him through the utterly quiet church toward the front door. The cool early morning air steams my hot skin, and I shiver as Dylan rubs his hand up and down my arm, smoothing the goose bumps away.

We cross the sprawling lawn that ends at an empty street with a hill that dips down into a valley below. From here, we can watch the sunrise, and most mornings I do. Sunrises never get old. I used to love them because it meant that the demons would hide away for the day. But now, it means that I actually get to enjoy the day even as a demon.

Fog hovers over the valley as the sun peaks from somewhere behind us, and I swear I can hear the entire world take a breath in relief. Dylan watches me, his chocolaty eyes boring into the side of my face like he's trying to read my mind. All I do is offer him a small smile, but I never take my eyes from the world as it awakens before me. In this moment, it's easy to forget that somewhere not far from here, smoke wafts through the air as my father leaves another burning night in his unforgiving wake.

The scent of jasmine sneaks through the air, and I quickly turn and hook my arms around Dylan's neck. "If you plan on trying to sweep me off my feet, now might be a good time."

He chuckles as he circles his arms around me to lift me from my feet.

"Breakfast is going to have to wait, princess." Zach's voice sounds from behind us before Dylan has a chance to launch into the air.

I reluctantly unhook my hands from Dylan. "You can't keep me here," I say, peering at my Demon Watcher from over Dylan's shoulder.

Dylan spins, but he doesn't let me go. I didn't expect he

would either. We have our ups and downs and loops and explosions. Things tend to be more often complicated than they are simple, and no matter what I do or say or how mad I get, he has this unconditional devotion to me that I can't comprehend. If I decide to fight Zach's decision, Dylan will fly away with me if I ask. Even after everything, he's still one-hundred percent here for me. And I've accepted Dylan's place in my life as he's taken up permanent residency in part of my heart. But we both know we'll never be together.

Even if it weren't for Evan, I'll always be guarded with Dylan, and he knows it. I just can't handle knowing how easy it is for him to keep secrets from me or how he's manipulated me. Sure I was an uncaring demon, but he cut me open and left me to bleed on my own. When I needed him, when I asked for help, he basically covered his ears so he wouldn't hear me scream, all because the angelic army had other plans. And because of all that, I think it's why he's willing to risk his place in line siding with me now.

A flick to my shoulder draws my attention to Zach as he stands in front of me with his arms crossed. "Is she only this stubborn with me?" he asks Dylan. "I swear brick walls listen better than she does."

I grin at my guardian. I'm thankful he's in a better mood since yesterday. "Did you say something, Zachy-poo?" I ask, stopping Dylan from answering.

We smile at each other, and Dylan flashes his brilliant wings for a second.

Zach snaps his fingers in my face, and I snatch him by the wrist and dig my nails into his skin before he can attempt to boop my nose in the incredibly annoying way he tries to grab my attention.

"You must not like that hand," I say.

We play a short game of tug-of-war until he yanks me from Dylan and throws me over his shoulder. "And you must like being treated like a toddler. Come on, thorn in my side. We have things to do."

Using levitation, I flip over his shoulder and crash into Dylan who wraps me in his arms with a laugh. I wag my eyebrows at him before glaring at Zach. I'm in an extra mess-with-Zach mood after last night, and I don't feel like making things easy.

"Seriously, Cami." Uh-oh. He used my name. He's getting into business mode.

I turn my gaze to Dylan. "You should probably put me down before Zach tries to hold me to his grounding and makes me spend the day with him in the daylight prison realm." Dylan rights me on my feet. I place my hands on my hips and focus on Zach for a long moment. "Well, what's so important that you're making me skip breakfast?"

He looks like he might not tell me because I didn't listen to him the first time, but then he sighs and says, "We have a lead on some demi-demons."

"Live ones?" I hate that I have to ask, but after hearing about the body found yesterday, I need to.

He nods.

Ever since I was proclaimed dead, the leads the angelic army had acquired about demi-demons turned harder to come by, even with the help of Jazmin, who specializes in tracking not only humans but creatures. It's why Malicevile wanted her in the first place and why she was never an active hunter. She doesn't have physical power like most demi-demons. But I'm sure she could still kick butt.

Last Jazmin had heard, Malicevile had split up the demi-demons and sold them off to other demons. It explains why the demon I killed last night had the girl I knew Malicevile had captured. Just the thought of the fates of the poor halfies makes my stomach sour. I couldn't imagine such a life.

"So I'm not going to have to kill another demon?" I manage to ask. I can't help the hesitation I feel toward killing my kin now. I'm terrified of creating more soulless ones.

"As long as we get going."

I swing my gaze from Zach to Dylan. "Want to give me a ride?" I ask without even checking to see if Zach's cool with it. I know he'd much rather fly me himself. He's twice as fast as Dylan. He also uses our travel time to discuss strategy that I never actually follow through with.

"I'm sure Dylan has other things to do, princess," Zach says. Called it.

"I'm pretty sure all those things involved hanging out with me," I say with a smile. "Come on, you owe me for last night."

Zach blushes. I'm sure he had already felt guilty since he's such a softy, but I won't tell him that. "Fine. If Dylan wants to join us, he can, but you need to focus. We can't afford for you to be distracted."

I nod. "I won't be. Promise."

Zach scopes the area for a second for onlookers even though our street is empty as usual. Wind gusts through my hair as he launches into the sky and circles for a moment.

I jump into Dylan's arms and nestle my face into his neck. "You can tell me no, you know."

He brushes his lips against my cheek. "And miss out on all the fun?"

He doesn't give me a chance to respond as he launches us into the air, and we're carried away on the wind.

<hr>

The moment Dylan touches down on the cracked parking lot outside a small office building, I gag. My stomach heaves, and Dylan sets me down and steps back so I don't throw up all over him. This is ten times worse than usual, and I've smelled a lot of disgusting things over my life. You'd think I'd have a stomach of steel, but unfortunately, some things just can't be helped.

I gag again, shifting my eyes around the parking lot. The air is so putrid, it makes my eyes water. There's no denying this place was crawling with all sorts of demons while it was dark out, mostly mid- and lower-level ones at that.

Zach pats my back from my side and chuckles as I try hard to get my gag reflex under control. Without breakfast, my stomach is empty. Dry heaving is just as bad as throwing up, if not worse.

I pull my shirt over my face, but it doesn't do much to filter out the rankness. "If you—" I pause for a moment. "If you want me anywhere near that—that building, one of you better give me your shirt." The rancid air coats my tongue with every word.

"I knew I was right about why you always mess up my shirts," Zach says with a grin that I consider knocking off his face with my new slime power.

I glare as I clutch my churning stomach. "Fine. I'm—I'm leaving."

Zach and Dylan both look at each other expectantly, and I zap a small bolt of power near their feet before I gag again.

Dylan relents first and tugs his shirt over his head and tosses it to me while Zach folds his arms over his silly black shirt with a rainbow unicorn on the front. I slide Dylan's shirt over my own and pull it over my nose, sucking in his irresistible apple and rain scent.

Both boys notice my small sigh, but I play it off as relief even though I'm sure neither believes it. It's not my fault angels—even half angels—smell heavenly.

"Better, princess?" Zach asks with an arched brow. He knows of my love/hate relationship with Dylan but refrains from pointing out the obvious most days. Mortal relationships aren't his thing, though only Dylan is mortal. A thought I don't like to dwell on.

I draw my gaze to Dylan and take in his taut chest and

tight stomach for a second. The lean muscles on his arms bunch when he curls and uncurls his fingers. "Much. Thanks, Angel Boy. I'm glad I can always count on you, unlike *some* people."

I don't give Zach a chance to fire back with a witty remark and instead stroll toward the tinted glass door of the building directly in front of us. I don't even have to guess to know that the stench is emanating from it.

The handle doesn't budge when I give it a few good shakes. I'm not a master at picking locks, so I stroll a foot away, hold my hands close to my chest for a second before sending an energy orb big enough to fissure the door. All it takes is a few swift kicks to punch out the plexiglass with my boot.

The smell intensifies, but I don't have a chance to step forward, because a woman stands on the other side of the door, pointing a gun directly at me. She pulls the trigger, the sound piercing my ears the moment the bullet hits me right in the stomach.

All I do is stand in surprise as the woman pulls the trigger again. It takes another bullet, this time right in my collarbone, to kick me into action. I open my mouth and let out a frustrated scream enhanced with my demonic wind-like ability I acquired from the demon who had kidnapped me. The force knocks her back into the building, where she hits the far wall.

While being shot is not nearly as bad as it was before when I was shot with blessed bullets, it still freaking hurts like Hell. Not to mention I'm pouring blood everywhere, though the moment it leaves my wounds, it smokes, disappearing into the sunlight. My soul is what keeps me grounded to the earth realm, not my demonic blood. I wonder if it's just evaporating or if a bunch of demons are watching the ground in the sunlight realm as it suddenly bleeds.

"Cami?" A hand shakes my shoulder. I turn to look at Zach. His mouth moves again, but the sound of his voice is lost due to the pounding in my head. This is the most injured I've been since leaving my father's side.

I blink a few times, trying to let things register. The edges of my vision blur. *This is so not the time to pass out.*

Sudden movement in the corner of my eye draws my attention away from my nearly black blood as it burns away. The woman within the office is scrambling to grab the gun she dropped a few feet away from her. Zach's too busy focusing on me to notice as she pulls the trigger.

With a forceful shove, I push him back and hold my hand up, blasting the woman with my new slime power. I didn't mean to do it, but it's what came to the surface in my moment of desperation. I don't even feel the sting of the bullet when it hits me in my shoulder, because all I can focus on is how the woman flails as the green slime crawls from her stomach to her chest, while also traveling down her legs. There's nothing she can do as it eats away at her. There's nothing anyone can do.

Tears well in my eyes, and I stumble back. I think I'm screaming, but I can't hear the sound of my voice. The world slows, blinding light erupting in my vision. The ground sneaks up on me as my back slams against it. Tiny black stars dance across my vision and the only way to get rid of them is to close my eyes.

A heavy weight crushes down on me, the hot pressure squeezing the air from my lungs. I flail, trying to free myself, but it's useless. No amount of struggling will save me. If I didn't know any better, I'd think I was on the brink of death.

A burning sensation erupts straight from my soul, and I jerk. The fire spreads from my chest to my stomach, singeing everything it courses over. The burning smell overtakes the putrid odor of demon. As foreign power burns through my demonic blood, it takes me a minute to realize that I'm smelling my own body. It's not my father's power though. It's heavenly.

After a long moment of agonizing pain, the world suddenly stops. My ears ring, my eyes blur, and my skin numbs. Then, I fall into utter darkness.

SOUL DEEP

I OPEN MY eyes to the sun shining brightly overhead. A figure hovers over me, silhouetted in the golden light, and I jerk upright, knocking Dylan back. Jumping to my feet, I spin around, expecting to see the horrible aftermath of using my demonic power on a human, but the office building is nowhere in sight. Neither is Zach. I can't even smell my Demon Watcher over Dylan's delectable scent.

Our dream garden blooms with life. Lavender roses blossom on deep green bushes. An angel statue trumpets water in a small fountain near a stone bench. Everything is vibrant and green and so full of life; it's unlike the dreams I had grown used to when my father knocked me out with his power. This reminds me of the times when I was still half-human.

I rub my palms into my eyes. "That did not go as I expected. Is the woman...?" I can't finish my sentence. I'm not even sure I want to know.

The sad look on Dylan's face speaks volumes. Of course I'm the one demon who has a conscience. The memory of the woman dying in the most grotesque way possible appears front and center in my mind and tears prickle in the corners of my eyes.

"Zach made sure she didn't suffer long," he says quietly as he takes my hands between his. "There was nothing more that he could do. Hell had already claimed her."

I press my lips together and stare as Dylan twines his fingers with mine. I'll never fully grasp the limitations of saving a soul. Some souls, like the pure souls manipulated by demons, can be intercepted before a demon procures them. But other times, the only way to save a soul is to let it go where it was headed. There are exceptions—me for one—but very few are privy to that kind of information—I'm definitely not on that list. I'm on the need-to-know-basis list. Let's just say it was an adjustment from feeling above everyone to knowing I'm at the very bottom of the angelic hierarchy, if I even make the cut. You'd think I'd get my own pedestal because I'm supposed to save the world. *Maybe if you actually did it.*

It takes Dylan's fingers grazing over my chin to pull me from my thoughts. I meet his chocolate eyes, my bottom lip trembling, and then he embraces me. I cry for a moment onto his bare shoulder, feeling stupid for the sudden lack of control over my emotions. It's embarrassing. I didn't even know the woman, and she shot me. I should be less forgiving.

"I'm sorry," I say, sniffling.

He rubs his hand in circles on my back. "You never have to apologize to me for having feelings. I'd be worried if you didn't."

"They just suck sometimes, you know."

He lets out a soft chuckle. "Look who you're talking to, love."

It doesn't make me feel better. It makes me feel like utter crap. "If you could shut them off, would you?"

"What kind of question is that? Should I be worried?"

I huff. "This isn't about me. Just answer my question."

"No." He doesn't even have to think about it.

"Why?"

"Come on, love. You don't want to go down this road. And in all honesty, neither do I. I've accepted things as they are. It might not be exactly how I had imagined, but what we have surpasses any romantic relationship. What we have runs soul deep."

His words send my heart racing. "Dylan."

He taps my nose. "Don't pity me."

"I—"

Before I can finish my sentence, the world shakes under our feet and bright light streaks through the dream. Dylan fades in and out of view before disappearing altogether. Ice flows through my veins. Everything hazes in brilliant light. It's so bright that it fades everything into pristine white nothingness.

"Wake up, princess." Zach's voice rips me from the white world, and I bolt upright.

As my senses awaken, reality hits me like an out-of-control bus, and I choke again on the demonic stench wafting from the open door of the office building. I try to push to my feet, my palms scraping against the rough asphalt, but dizziness sends me back to the ground with a thud.

"Whoa, now. Don't you think you've been hurt enough already?" Zach's hazel eyes crinkle in the corners while he waves his hand a few inches from my chest and torso.

I dart my gaze to the massive burn holes running down my clothes. Almost my entire stomach shows under the frayed fabric of both mine and Dylan's shirts, and I grimace at the puckered black hole right above my belly button. I try to inspect the other two bullet holes, but my neck screams with the movement. I'm sure if an ordinary human were to stumble across me, I'd scare them to death—that's how bad I look.

I wrap my arms across my chest to cover my lacy black bra. I kind of wish I didn't let Cadence talk me into buying such sexy bras, but she wouldn't hear otherwise. Zach smirks but his eyes never waver from my face. He's so pure that my state of being half unclothed doesn't even register in his mind. Like the time he walked into my room while I was half naked and proceeded to start a conversation like I wasn't standing in my underwear. It took me yelling and chucking an energy ball at him to realize why I was freaking out. And then he laughed.

I swallow a short breath of the stinking air. "I need your shirt."

"You're still not used to the smell?"

I flick his forehead. I knew I was going to have to spell it out. I wave at my bra through my holey shirt. "Hello! I'm not going on a rescue mission with my chest on display."

"You're making me do it," Dylan quips, speaking for the first time.

"Yeah, it's only fair," Zach says, holding a straight face.

Dylan laughs.

Heat crawls in my face. "Zach, your naivety is showing."

He glances between me and Dylan for a second before he pulls his ridiculous shirt over his head and hands it over to me without another word. My senses suffocate in the jasmine aroma that clings to the fabric, but I don't complain. It's a billion times better than the demon stink.

When I look over at Zach, I can't stop the grin from crossing my face. I've managed to get two angels shirtless in under an hour. And to think I didn't have any good luck. This has to be a new record. Cadence is going to die when I tell her about this. While I'm not going to do anything crazy like run my fingers across Zach's incredible abs, I can appreciate a godly creation.

"You're enjoying this way too much, princess," he mutters, pushing to his feet. He offers his hand to me to help lift me to mine.

I laugh. "Blame the demon blood."

"Sure, that's it. Now, if you don't mind, we have business to attend to."

I swoop my hand toward the door. "How about you lead the way this time?"

Zach doesn't wait another moment and strides forward to enter the building. Instead of following us, Dylan strolls to the end of the building and disappears around the corner, probably looking for other exits. I follow Zach's lead. When I enter the building, the demon stench nearly blows me away again. My knees weaken, threatening to send me to the disgusting floor.

"Keep your eyes on my back, Cami." Zach means business. "I don't want you to see the tainted woman's body." How sweet. He's trying to save me from the damage I've done. I deserve to see such horrors to remind me of what I'm capable of, but instead I listen to him.

"Don't mind if I do," I say, staring at the muscles rippling under his smooth skin.

As we make our way down a long, dark hallway, I close the distance between us. A trickle of light shines from the circular skylight to guide us deeper into the building. There are seven doors, three on each side and one at the very end of the hallway. I hold my breath for a second to see if I can hear any noise.

"Do you hear that?" Zach asks just as I hear a faint whimper.

"I think so," I whisper, the hairs on my body standing on end. It's been a while since something has creeped me out. I've grown tolerant of basically everything demon-related, but after seeing a soulless one, I'm nervous. Beyond nervous. I'm on the verge of panicking.

Instead of summoning power, I slide the dagger I rarely ever touch from its sheath strapped to my leg. Zach stops in front of the first door and presses his hands against it as though he can somehow determine what we're about to face on the other side. After a long pause, he cracks open the door, and I jerk my hand out and lock my fingers around his elbow.

The lingering scent of cinnamon and clove hangs in the stale air of a pitch-black, windowless room. Malicevile's scent is unmistakable. He's clearly been hanging around this place. He might even own it. He owns a lot of property all over the world—and not everything is up to his lavish taste.

"My father was definitely here." I lick my dry lips, pushing away my anxiety. Malicevile shouldn't be able to still stir these kinds of emotions in me. I'm so not looking forward to the moment I have to face him again, especially after he realizes how much I've betrayed him.

He might've been unbearable, but not everything about him was always bad. Still, whatever messed up, complicated relationship we share isn't enough. Not when I can't fall in line like the perfect demon daughter. All the awful things he put me through outweigh the good. It's like comparing the weight of a feather to the weight of the entire world. I just hate that I have to remind myself.

"Smell anything else?" Zach asks.

I inhale a small breath. "No. This room is empty."

Reaching into the room to touch the inside wall, Zach flicks on the light to prove I'm right. I gape at a trashed room that looks like it was used as a make-shift prison. Garbage litters the floor, remnants of fast food containers, paper cups, and scraps of rotting, untouched food. I step forward, the charred carpet crunching under my boots, and take in the nasty pile of blankets that sit inside a cage similar to the one from last night.

Zach squeezes my arm as he comes up next to me, a look of pain sweeping across his normally stoic expression he holds for moments like these. His brows lower over his hazel eyes, and he rocks on his heels once before spinning and pulling me out of the room with him. We can't save people who aren't here.

"I'm afraid we might be too late, princess," he mutters as he moves to another door. Flinging it open, he peeks in without turning on the light. This room has a window with a view of the side parking lot, and it's just the same as the first one.

I stride forward to the last door in the hallway, the one I thought I heard the small whimper echo from. "That woman wasn't here to protect the property."

With a deep breath, I hook my fingers on the door handle but don't open it right away. I wait a moment for Zach to come up behind me like a protective shadow. His cool breath tickles my hair as he quietly breathes right over my shoulder, his bare chest nearly touching me. I consider elbowing him to get him to give me some space, but he probably wouldn't move back. He has no boundaries when it comes to me. He takes his job as my guardian seriously.

"Go on," he says, bumping my shoulder to nudge me forward.

Clenching my dagger in one hand, I unlatch the door before I kick it open. The room emits a mixture of scents that overpowers me and I stumble back into Zach. He steadies me by sliding his arms over my chest to hug me against his sturdy form.

Something moves within the room, and a moment later, a huge rat comes squealing our way. If I didn't know any better, I'd think it was demonic and on a quest to tear off my leg with its yellow teeth. Zach picks me off my feet, and the rat runs into the hallway. I kick my legs, clipping him in the shin before he sets me down again.

"That rat wouldn't have hurt me," I say, annoyance lining my words.

"Better safe than sorry. People aren't the only ones who can tell when evil lurks about."

I roll my eyes. "I'm not ev—" I snap my mouth shut when my gaze falls upon a cage like the other ones. It's stationed in the back of the disgusting room. "Is that..." A mound of something hides underneath a blood-stained blanket.

"I'm afraid so." Zach pushes past me. "Stay there."

Of course my legs don't listen. I take an automatic step forward to follow him even though my brain screams for me to turn around. Zach unfurls his freaky black wings on his back, expanding them the length of the room. It makes him ten times more intimidating.

"Alive or dead?" I whisper.

Zach closes the distance to the cage, reaches in, and tugs the blanket.

Before he can answer, fire explodes behind me, knocking me off my feet. Suddenly, my whole world is set ablaze.

CRUEL FATE

ANOTHER WAVE OF orange fire cascades through the air, sending black smoke billowing through the room. Scrambling to my feet, I summon my father's demonic power and launch it blindly into the hall. I'm greeted with the low hum of an agitated voice before another blast of fire threatens to burn right through my clothes.

I hold out my hands protectively and absorb the rolling fire, sucking it deep into my soul. A shudder leaves me breathless, the familiarity of the power washing over me. It's a welcoming heat that I've so dearly missed.

"Evan," I say, my voice lost to the whooshing sound created by the flapping of Zach's wings as he snuffs out the fire I couldn't absorb.

A figure appears at the end of the dark hallway, lit only by the soft light of a fireball. Evan winds his arm back before chucking it directly at me again. Zach gathers his own power, setting the room aglow in heavenly light. It's rare for him to use it, and it stings my eyes a little, but he's not going to let my demi-demon boyfriend threaten us.

I catch Evan's fire in my hands and shift it back and forth between my palms.

"Cami? What are you doing here?" Evan asks, finally realizing that I'm not some stranger hell-bent on destroying him. I reacted with power only to protect myself.

I glide forward, stopping in the doorway. "I could ask the same question."

"Did you kill Cassie?" he asks, taking a few steps closer.

"It was an accident. She unloaded her gun on me."

"Are you okay?" He sounds like he cares. I'm not sure if he really does. After closing the rest of the distance, he reaches out and takes my hands, snuffing out the fire we were both holding between our fingers.

"I'll survive," I murmur. I saw him only yesterday, but it already feels like an eternity has passed us by. His patchouli and amber scent overpowers all the other aromas in the room, including Zach's ever-present jasmine. I can't stop myself from leaning forward to rest my head on his shoulder.

He brushes his lips against my temple. "Good."

Behind me, Zach clears his throat, drawing my attention away from Evan. It was way too easy to lose myself in his arms when there are a billion questions I should be asking him—like what this place is, who were in the cages, and where did they go.

"Princess, if you don't mind, we have a pressing matter to deal with."

I swivel in Evan's arms and spin to face my Demon Watcher. Zach is hovering in front of the cage with the body in it. It's not until then that I see a boy sitting up with the gross blanket around his shoulders. He's a live demi-demon, still in possession of his soul. But for how long? I have no idea.

Evan's hot fingers bite into my shoulder. "This is none of your business. You two need to leave now."

His sudden coldness puts out the fire he stirred within me. This isn't the boy I'm in love with who's talking now. This is my father's minion. And it breaks my heart to see how quickly he can change.

"Please, Evan. I don't want to see you get hurt," I whisper, reaching up to slide my hand over his.

"You mean more than you have done to me?"

Ouch. The soft moment we've shared is lost now among the trash that blows around the room in the current created by Zach's wings. There's nothing I can say to make Evan see reason, not when I threaten to intervene in the affairs of my father. It seems such a cruel fate that we find ourselves in this position, like the universe puts us together just to rip us apart over and over again.

"You know it's not on purpose." My bottom lip puckers out when I force myself to hold his unforgiving gaze. "I love you."

"You keep saying that like it's going to make a difference."

A girl can hope. "Please, don't do this right now."

"Then leave, Cami. You know what'll happen to me if you mess up things for your father. He doesn't need me like he did when he thought you were alive. He's already going to give me Hell for Cassie's death." A tiny bit of desperation underlines his words. It's one of the things that had worried me when I joined the angelic army. Without me to protect him, Evan must stand alone to face Malicevile's wrath. And I'm sure it's worse than ever.

I peer over my shoulder at Zach. "He's right."

Zach grimaces. "Are you suggesting we leave this poor soul in the hands of demons?"

Am I? For Evan's sake I just might be, but the thought weighs heavy on my mind. I don't think I could live with knowing that I purposely sacrificed an innocent demi-demon in hopes that Evan doesn't see the opposite end of my father's power. But I can't just abandon Evan either.

Zach doesn't wait for me to answer. He strolls over to me and grabs the back of my shirt, pulling me away from Evan. I don't get far, because Evan snatches my hand and jerks me away, something strange darkening his eyes. He stands protectively in front of me, like he thinks Zach might do something to hurt me.

"Touch her like that again, and you'll regret it," Evan snaps, threatening Zach with a ball of fire. "She might be blinded by your angelic light, but I see right through you." Whoa. Evan is all over the place, and it's tearing my poor heart apart. How can he be so distant and cold one second and then protective the next? Either way, my heart is ramming against my ribcage.

"Cami uses my light to see, thank you very much. And if you'd please let my charge go, I'd appreciate it. I don't think Cami wants to see us fight on her behalf." Zach meets my confused gaze. "Right?"

Against my better judgment, I suck in my bottom lip without answering as quickly as I should. That small moment of hesitation—the moment where the demon within me was thrilled just thinking about such a sight—was enough to give Evan a reason to launch a fireball directly at my Demon Watcher.

Zach flaps his wings, sending the fire off course while knocking both of us back into the hallway. Evan wraps his arms around me and presses me to him, absorbing the force of the collision to the floor himself. I lie on top of him, breathing heavily. He carefully rolls me off him before jumping to his feet to race back to the room.

"Evan, stop!" I yell, launching to my own feet to chase after him.

Fire and heavenly light explode in the room. Zach and Evan attack each other, neither of them even looking at me as they set their sights on one another, dancing around the room, throwing power from a distance.

And it's terrifying. I don't want either of them to get hurt, but I don't want to pick a side. The air hums with energy as the powers of Heaven and Hell battle it out with me in the center. Story of my life.

A small screech sounds from across the room as some of Evan's fire crawls along the wall and toward the cage with the demi-demon inside. His light green eyes meet mine, and I dash across the room, concentrating on absorbing the powers that are coming at me from both sides.

When my hands touch the small bars of the cage, the demi-demon cowers away. There's no mistaking what I am, and he's probably confused by the fact that a demon is walking around in the daylight.

"Don't hurt me," he says, hugging the blanket tighter around him.

I jiggle the lock a few times to see if I can bust it open. "I'll try not to." I know it's not what he meant, but it's better if I just swallow the annoyance stirring in me at his assumption.

A fireball slams into my back, knocking the breath from me, and I slump against the cage. I'm not the best multi-tasker when it comes to splitting my attention between absorbing power, breaking locks, and making sure Evan and Zach don't kill each other.

"Unholy Hell," I mutter as I straighten my shoulders. Evan isn't playing games. Peering over my shoulder, I grimace as I watch Evan try to corner Zach. Zach's evading him, but I know that he'll really start to fight at any moment instead of just being on the defense. "Come on, stupid lock."

Summoning the power I've collected from Evan, I heat the lock until it glows bright red. After an excruciatingly long minute, it finally gives way before falling to the carpet, smoldering the short fibers.

The moment the cage door swings open, another fireball rams into my back, nearly knocking me into the boy. It's enough to get me to jerk my neck to glance behind me. Evan glares while Zach blasts his heavenly light at the wall behind him. That fireball wasn't accidental. It was directed at me.

Hopping to my feet, I summon electricity into my palms and face Evan. This isn't the first time he has intentionally used his power against me, but this time is different. He wasn't obeying my father's orders. He hit me with a fireball of his own freewill.

I snap.

Zach doesn't even have a chance to intervene before I fly across the room and slam into Evan's chest, knocking him into the wall. I press my palms into his heaving chest and zap him with enough power to make his eyes widen and him slide to the floor. My demonic power awakens to its fullest, and I feel the small pinch of my horns as they cut through my skin.

Evan winces beneath me, dropping his hands above his head. His aqua eyes search my face, and neither of us lashes out. I grind my teeth, sucking in deep breaths to calm my nerves the best I can. I have not showed my true body in weeks, and here I am, unleashing Hell's fury on the boy I love.

"Princess," Zach says from behind me. "It's time to go."

I don't move though. I can't. All I can do is glower into Evan's eyes as I straddle his waist. He could knock me off if he wanted to, but he doesn't. A million thoughts cloud his eyes, and I'd give anything to absorb a mind reading ability. Because in this moment, I can't tell if Evan is disgusted or pleased by me—maybe a little of both.

"Get the demi-demon out of here," I say to Zach while digging my nails into Evan's shoulders.

"We'll go together," my Demon Watcher says.

I shake my head. "Just go. I'll be right behind you."

After a moment of hesitation, Zach scoops the demi-demon into his arms and strolls right past us. His jasmine scent follows him out, and I'm left with the warm goodness of everything that is Evan.

I lick my lips, trying my best to control myself. All the words I try to say stay lodged in my throat. I want to scream at him for using his power against me, for attacking my guardian, for being here in the first place, but what would be the point? It's not going to change anything.

Evan shifts his hands from mine where I pin them, and I let him. He reaches up and gently caresses his finger along the dainty crown of horns jetting from my forehead. I shiver under his touch, wishing he'd keep his hands to himself though my body begs for him to explore even more of me.

"This is why you don't belong with them, Cami. They're using you because you let them. What do you think will happen when you no longer serve a purpose? Do you think they're just going to let you loose on the world? How long do you think Heaven's going to accept a demon in their midst?"

His words sink to my very core, because it's not like I haven't thought about this before. I've seen the way the angels look at me with distrust. I've felt the pain and anguish caused by their sacred forms.

My lips tremble, but I don't respond. I'm not even sure what to say.

Evan brushes his finger under my eye and swipes away a hot tear that I wish I could've blinked away. I don't like how he's making me feel like I've made a terrible decision, that maybe he might be right in the end.

He leans up on his elbows and closes the space between us, brushing his lips against mine. "You don't have to go back with him. You can stay right here with me. I'll protect you."

My heart hurts with every single beat that passes as I find my voice to answer. "I can't," I whisper.

"You can." Evan kisses me again, sliding his arms around my waist, pulling me down onto him. My hips press into his, desire and need coursing through my mind, pushing away all my good reason. Letting him get so close, letting him into my carefully guarded mind was a huge mistake, but I don't regret it.

Evan's hands slide under my burned shirt and trail up my back, leaving behind tingling warmth. His lips move from mine, and he brushes them along my jawline to my neck. My mind whirls with a dozen memories—of all the good times we've had together. It makes me cling to him, kiss him harder. Before I know what I'm doing, my fingers hook to the hem of his shirt and I tug it over his head not even caring that the place still smolders around us. I didn't know how much I missed his touch until this very moment when it feels like I could survive the rest of eternity on his kisses alone.

"Tell me you'll stay," he whispers against my lips before cutting off my answer by sucking my bottom lip between his. My body reacts, heat coursing over my skin. His tongue brushes against mine and I taste the sweetness of his mouth.

I want to tell him I'll stay, that I'll turn my back on the fate of the world just to have even another minute in his arms, but I don't get the chance. A loud explosion erupts from behind. The tinted window shatters, and sunlight brightens the room.

The sun burns against my true body and I go from hot to smoldering. I scream, forcing myself to take on my human façade just in time to see the silhouette of wings stretch in elongated shadows across the floor.

Evan holds me against him, shielding me from the glorious light. His fingers lock so tightly onto me that I'm not sure he'll let me go even if I ask him to.

"She's staying with me." Evan's voice booms through the air. He's trying to talk on my behalf, making a decision I haven't yet decided on. A breeze manages to clear my senses so I realize what's happening.

"Is that true, princess? Is this what you want?" When my eyes finally adjust to the light, Zach's face comes into view.

"Yes," Evan says for me.

I crinkle my nose. "I—"

"Cami," Evan says softly.

I lean up and kiss him again before I pull myself away. The hurt that flashes through his eyes will surely be my undoing. Leaving him is a thousand times worse than letting him go. But I know deep down I have to. Even if Evan is right about the angelic army, about how they'll throw me away when I'm useless, at least I can say that I did something that was my decision. I ended up at Malicevile's side because I thought I was out of options. I thought any other sort of life was impossible. But I've found options. And I'm willing to pay the price. Even if I end up spent in the end.

"I want to stay with you, Evan. I do. But this isn't where I belong." I don't look at him as I say the words.

"Of course it is. You're a demon, Cami." His words are hard enough to break my strength.

Tears prickle in my eyes. "But I'm more than that."

Evan tries to close the distance between us, but I summon hot electricity in my fingers. "I didn't mean it like that. Of course I know you're more than that. You're everything to me."

I close my eyes, taking another step back. "Then you'll let me go."

Shaking his head, he says, "I can't, Cami. I can't!"

He rushes forward, fighting through the small shock of

electricity I toss at him. He doesn't make it within a foot of me, though. A gust of wind whips forward, knocking Evan away before firm hands lock around my hips and yank me out the window.

Zach sets me on my feet just outside the window, and I meet Dylan's worried eyes. He holds the demi-demon tightly in his arms. I can't tell what's on his mind, but I'm sure he knows how broken I feel. I wish he'd had a chance to warn me that Evan was going to show up, but he probably got out of the way before Evan had a chance to see him. I wouldn't expect Evan to refrain from trying to kill Dylan. Not for anyone, especially not for me.

"We can't leave him like this," I say. "My father will murder him if he doesn't have an explanation." Evan can't even whisper my name—no one outside a small group of people can. Even the demi-demon in Dylan's arms won't remember me.

Zach presses his lips into a thin line. "I'm sure he can handle him—"

I throw my hands up. "Zach! If you don't do something then I'm facing my father at sundown, and I'm pretty sure I'm not going to win."

"Fine, but the next time you let someone seduce you like—"

My forehead burns as my true body peeks through. It's enough to make Zach snap his mouth shut. He won't ever make me feel badly about loving Evan. He's lucky I don't send the rest of my father's power into that chest of his.

Without another word, he holds his hands in front of him and strides back to the window. A fireball flies past him, but he doesn't let it stop him. He ignites the office in his heavenly glow, keeping Evan down long enough to fly into the room and press his hand over Evan's forehead. As Evan slumps over and passes out, I turn away.

"Happy?" Zach asks when he climbs over the windowsill.

I shake my head, tears spilling onto my cheeks. "No."

He sighs, wrapping me in a cool hug. "I'm sorry it has to be this way, princess. How about I take you home, and we eat some ice cream? That's what you and Cadence like to do, right?"

I laugh through my tears. "I think I'm going to need a few gallons of it."

CROSSING THE LINE

RAINBOW LIGHT CASCADES across my soft carpet while I inhale and exhale at least a hundred deep breaths. Sleep is nowhere to be found, which isn't unusual considering demons don't usually sleep. But without the daylight realm to regenerate my body and mind, I've turned toward meditation and occasionally a little mind manipulation from Zach to force sleep onto me.

Unfortunately for me, meditation isn't working today, and I'm not in the mood to call Zach and ask him to come back from Seraphim Rock because I need him. I could use a break from him anyway, and I'm sure he desperately needs one away from me as well, especially after this morning.

After a moment of not relaxing, I slam my hands against my carpet a few times. The sun will set in an hour, and come nightfall, I'll be expected to be back at it, hunting my own kin to not only try to find out information but also to cut any competition that might try to take over where my father leaves off when—if—I manage to send him to Hell.

Dylan plops down next to me and rests a cool hand on top of mine. "You're going to start a fire if you don't relax."

"That's what I'm trying to do," I snap. I don't mean to take my frustration out on him, but I have a lot of it, and it's going to fall on whoever is brave enough to get within five feet of me. Unfortunately for Dylan, he can't resist.

"Then maybe you need to burn off some of that energy."

I swing my gaze to Dylan, a smile quirking my lips. "And how do you suggest I do that?"

"I can think of a few things." He flashes his dimples at me.

With a swing of my hand, I whack him across the arm.

He laughs. "I was going to suggest that we could spar, but I see that your mind is thinking about something else. Whatever you want, love."

My cheeks warm, a blush crawling up from my neck. "I can't burn off that much energy when I'll have you on the floor in a matter of seconds." Fire rushes to my ear. "I mean—"

Dylan tilts his head back and lets out a loud laugh. "You make it too easy to tease you."

"Don't get me started," I say with a playful punch.

He holds out his hand to me. "Come on. I was serious. I think it'll do you good."

"I'll hurt you."

"I'll heal."

Pursing my lips, I finally relent to his grin and take his hand. "Fine, but I'm teaming you up with Cadence. Maybe she'll teach you a thing or two."

"Hey, I might surprise you."

Dylan slides his arm over my shoulders and guides me from my bedroom and through the short hallway that leads to the living room where we find Cadence sharpening her daggers. She greets us with one of her beautiful smiles before setting down her favorite dagger that has a glittering, jewel-encrusted hilt.

"Dylan wants to spar," I say, watching Cadence pull her dark purple hair up into a high ponytail. She frowns for a split second, scrunching her brows. "And I need you to partner with him against me."

"You're making me team up with Angel Boy?" she asks, standing, placing her hands on her hips. "That's even more un-fair than having to spar with you alone."

I laugh. "I'll limit my powers."

"No green slime," Dylan says.

I cringe. "Wasn't planning on it."

"No electricity either," Cadence says.

Dylan rubs his head. "Or fire."

I raise my palm out. "Fine, but that's it."

Cadence scoops her weapons from the table and slides

them into their appropriate sheaths—one on her hip, one on each leg, and one hidden on her back under her jacket.

She doesn't offer one to Dylan. He doesn't ask.

I narrow my eyes. "You possess heavenly light now?"

"I guess you'll have to wait and see."

Uh-oh.

A few minutes later, I run half a dozen quick laps around the small gym connected to our living quarters. The church was donated to the angelic army by the alliance and was converted into a house for me since I refused to live among the angels on their little island. The island doesn't always settle nicely with my demonic blood when Zach forces me to visit. The distance from the mainland also played a factor in my argument to find somewhere else to live since hitching a ride by air isn't exactly my favorite thing to do. I much prefer driving myself around.

I grin as Cadence flips Dylan onto his back. She rushes to teach him a few moves and tries to pin him again, but he pushes himself up with his wings and knocks her back. She somersaults before springing to her feet.

Dylan charges Cadence, and I open my mouth and blow a long breath, sending a gust of wind to knock him off course. Cadence sidesteps and swings her arm out, clocking him in the chest. He stumbles, and she helps him by tripping him, sending him sprawling to the floor.

He presses his hands against the mat to push to his feet and meets my smile with narrowed eyes. "Don't think I'm going to hold back on you, love."

My smile brightens even more as I laugh. "Show me what you got, Angel Boy."

I don't know what I was expecting, but I definitely wasn't expecting Dylan to immediately charge at me, ethereal wings pushing him faster than I can even run. I kick into action and charge toward him, releasing another gust of wind that only slows him down a little.

Before he reaches me, I levitate a few feet off the floor only to have Cadence throw one of her knives at me. As I dodge the sparkling metal, Dylan rams his shoulder into my stomach. We fly through the air, his wings propelling us forward.

The air zooms past me, and I know if I don't do something, I'm going to leave a huge Cami-shaped imprint on the far wall. I swing my arm back to pop him in the jaw, but he catches my hand in his, holding it to his chest with a smile. Without electricity or even the disgusting green slime, I'm basically out of options.

Closing my eyes, I do the only thing I can think of. I stretch up and plant my lips against his. It was a sneaky, unfair move, but I'm a sneaky, unfair demon, and the last thing I want is to collide with a wall.

Dylan reacts, his muscles tightening while his wings slow, and it gives me the opportunity I need. Using levitation, I propel forward, putting all my weight to one side. Dylan doesn't even notice that I spin him in the air. A second later, we hit the wall, his wings disappearing as a shockwave knocks him on top of me, and we bounce and skid across the mat.

His heavy weight falls on me. He groans, resting his forehead on the mat just next to my head. I don't give him a chance to rest long before I link my fingers to the back of his shirt and flip him off me.

He doesn't move from the floor. Staring at the ceiling, his chocolate eyes blink a few times before finally meeting mine.

Cadence comes up next to me. "I think you broke him." She laughs as she nudges him with her boot. "What a dirty move. I like it."

"I am a demon after all," I say, crossing my arms, still tasting Dylan's lips. I wish it wasn't as good as it was, because now the joke's on me. This was the line I wasn't supposed to cross. Dylan was safely tucked away on the other side of the boundary I set between us. Now it looks like it was me who decided to straddle it.

Dylan finally managed to flash a smile through the pain of leaving a nice angelic indent in the wall. "If you always fight like that—"

"Don't get any funny ideas. I'd have much preferred to shock you, but there was no way I was the one getting smashed."

He leans up on his elbows. "It's way more fun to fight with you than your guardian."

I blush. "You spar with Zach?"

"Having a giant target on my back kind of changes my perspective on things. A lot has changed since I was residing at the Hunter's Academy, love. You know that."

He's right about that. He also doesn't have the luxury of twenty-four hour protection anymore, and he's sometimes forced to travel at night. I don't blame him for wanting to protect himself with more than what he's already been taught.

I offer my hand and help Dylan to his feet. He doesn't let go of my hand immediately, and I don't pull away until one of the double doors that leads outside swings open. Zach waltzes in, his eyes flicking over the three of us before he peers at the damage to the wall.

"You're supposed to be resting, not sparring, princess," he says, closing the distance between us in a few long strides. "And what have I told you about fighting with a human?" He glances at Cadence who glares.

I huff a breath. "I didn't fight with Cadence. She was Dylan's back up. And it was a fair fight."

"The wall would suggest otherwise."

I roll my eyes. "Don't you have better things to do than put in your two cents over what I do with my friends in my spare time?"

"I don't when I have to worry about your physical condition." He reaches out and yanks up the hem of my shirt, trying to get a look at my still tender bullet holes. He only gets it up to my belly button before I snatch his arm, twist it, and throw him to the ground with a loud thud.

I hug myself. "They're fine."

He stares at me from the floor "Then why are they bleeding?"

I peer down. *Oh, crap.*

Deep crimson, almost black blood soaks through the soft material of my tank top. I thought the heavenly light had staunched the bleeding completely, but I must've opened them up sometime during the fight with Dylan.

And of course now that I see them, they're starting to hurt.

"I'm fine," I repeat.

"Let me see them."

I shake my head. "I said I'm fine."

"Princess." He can argue, beg, and plead all he wants, but I'm too stubborn to admit that he's right, and I'm not in the best condition to face any demons tonight.

"Zachy-poo."

We glare at each other while Cadence and Dylan quietly stand nearby and watch the showdown. Zach might be an angel—a dang fierce one—but I'm Malicevile's daughter and am fierce in my own right. I sometimes like to take the opportunity to remind him that I'm not some sheep. Like he even needs the reminder, though.

His jaw clenches, a sudden light shifting in his hazel eyes. It's enough to make me tense and take an automatic step back. I don't know what he's thinking, but whatever it is, I know it's not going to make me happy.

I don't take the chance to find out.

Spinning on my feet, I dash away, pounding my boots against the mats. I head for the double doors, which is the best way to escape. Cool wind whips through my curly hair as I push them open and vault down the stone steps without touching my feet to them. This portion of the church faces a sprawling lawn that ends at a block wall that has been recently built to divide us from the neighborhood that keeps growing behind us.

I half-levitate, half-run over the squishy grass in the direction of the wall instead of the street that leads to the valley. The sun hangs low in the sky, threatening to set to unleash the demons back into the world to prey on humanity.

A shadow cuts across the grass, and I don't even have to look up to know that Zach will come after me from above.

"Seriously, princess. You're going to hurt yourself even worse if you don't stop."

"I don't want to be coddled," I say. "I'll stop running if you just accept that I'm okay."

"Don't make me do this," he says. Wind gusts through my hair as he swoops down.

I don't have a chance to ask him what when he lands in front of me, making me slam into his hard chest. It's just like hitting a wall, and I bounce back and somersault a few times over the grass.

My shirt rolls up with me, doing Zach a favor, and he audibly sucks in a breath.

I glance down and wish I hadn't. I might be a demon, and I might heal, but with a wound like the one in my stomach, it could be days and with a lot of pain without the sunlight prison realm. The other ones aren't any better. It's like my demon blood has fought with the residue left behind by the heavenly light, leaving my stomach a warzone. I'd hate to imagine what it would look like had the bullets been blessed. I might be able to touch sacred things, but they can still hurt me if they come in contact with my blood. I'm not immune to the holy, but I can tolerate it as long as I remain in complete control.

"This is your fault," I say, my stomach churning the more I look at the grotesque wound. Black veins spread out from the hole, trying to overtake my entire stomach. "If that heavenly light would've left me alone, I'd have healed properly."

"How was I supposed to know your body would react like this? It's not like we have a choice if you want to stay out of the prison realm."

Ugh. I guess I have to treat myself like I'm not invincible.

"This blows."

"Tell me about it, because now I think we're going to have to go."

I lean my head back into the grass. "No. Just give me a day. If I'm not healed by then, I'll reconsider."

"Sorry, princess. Not an option." And like that, Zach bends down, covers my forehead with his hand, and shuts off my world.

TROUBLE

THE SWEET NUMBNESS from the light prison realm washes over me in its warm goodness. I almost forgot what it was like to feel nothing at all—no pain, no heartache, no messy emotions—an indescribable emptiness that both satisfies me but reminds me of why I like to feel things in the first place. Because here, I feel one-hundred percent, unforgiving demon. Heaven's grace barely touches me.

A firm hand covers my mouth, startling me, and I bite into Zach's fragrant palm. He releases a low growl in his throat but doesn't remove his hand. And I can hear why. Voices echo from somewhere in the distance, and one of those voices cuts through the numbness to ignite hot fear deep in my Heaven-bound soul.

"We're probably safe, but be quiet just to be certain. I'm not blowing our cover because you can't control your mouth," Zach whispers into my ear so lowly that I almost don't pick up his words.

I bob my head, pulling his hand from my lips. Without speaking, I stand next to him and crane my neck forward like it'll somehow enhance my hearing. Deep within the trees of a gnarled forest my father stands next to a man I can only assume is Raphael. All I see is the back of a blond-haired man in a black suit. And my father, well, he hasn't changed a bit. His hair, slicked back with hair gel, gleams in the dusty sun about to dip into the horizon as the mortal sun sets on the earth realm. We had maybe an hour until dusk back on earth, but here, we have even less. Time speeds by on this plane.

"Another murder...hunters...angelic..." Taking a step closer, I strain to make out the conversation. I expect Zach to pull me back, but he doesn't. He follows my lead. "It's time we set a trap. We can't lose any more—"

Malicevile jerks his attention in our direction, startling me. I scramble back, tripping over a tree root, and land hard on my backside. Blinding electricity shoots over our heads and Zach covers me with his body, pressing heavily into me. His black wings unfurl and wrap around us like a shield. Footsteps crack against the dry ground; someone is rushing through the forest.

A demon hollers, but it's neither my father nor Raphael. From under Zach's arm, I watch a woman strut through the daylight prison realm, her pointy heels digging into the ground with each purposeful step as if on a mission. She strolls right by us without a second glance, and Malicevile shoots another energy orb through the trees and clips her shoulder, only making her waver a little bit on her feet.

I release a quiet breath. "I thought he saw us," I whisper.

Zach's chin digs into the nook of my neck. "You doubted my skills as your protector? I'm offended, princess."

"Considering my father's the most powerful demon on earth, and you expect that I'm the only one who can kill him..."

"That means nothing when it comes to keeping you safe."

I suppose he's right. I don't admit it, though. Instead, I say, "I guess you could be worse."

He chuckles, his jasmine fragrance blocking out the mixture of cinnamon, clove, nutmeg, sugar, and...incense? The woman's scent is unfamiliar, which means I've never met her before. The group of demons emanates a collection of scents deserving of a spice rack.

The voices disappear along with the scents, and Zach pushes himself up and stares at my face for an uncomfortably long minute. His hazel eyes sparkle in the hazy light, and I can't help but admire how attractive he looks—not in the I-want-to-press-my-lips-against-his hotness, but in the undeniable hotness that all heavenly—and some hellish—beings possess. It's more of an admiration.

A second later, his hotness fades when he boops my nose with his index finger, and then laughs. "You squirm a lot."

"Well, you make my skin crawl when you look at me like that."

"Hey, I can look at that soul of yours all I want. You gave it to me."

I release a low groan and smack my palm against his chest. "Doesn't make it any less creepy." I'm not actually creeped out, but I hate when he does stuff like this without warning. Vulnerability goes against my demonic blood, and the fact that Zach has an all-access pass to the most precious part of me makes my blood scream and not in a good way.

"It'd only be creepy if I mentioned how pretty it was."

I snort. "My soul isn't pretty."

He chuckles again. "You're right. Just glimpsing that filthy thing puts my purity on the line."

I shove him off me, my cheeks burning hotter than Hell. "You're a jerk."

"And you're fun to mess with."

He ruffles my curls before he gets to his feet, and I kick him in the shin. With an annoying smile on his lips, he hops back so I can't do it again.

Holding his hands up, he offers his surrender. "There's one more thing to check before we can leave."

The sun is almost completely gone from the sky, and we'll be back on earth in a matter of seconds.

I climb to my own feet, dusting off my jeans. "I can handle that myself."

He frowns. "Stop being difficult."

With narrowed eyes, I yank my shirt up to my bra to reveal my almost smooth stomach. Only a few small pink marks remain where the bullets had ravaged my skin.

"Happy?"

He nods as he hooks his fingers around my elbow to pull me to him. "Yup, now hold on, princess."

"We can't just wait until the sun sets?"

"Nope. You won't like where we'll reappear. I used your blood to portal us here, and it found your father out of instinct. We're pretty far from home."

Well, that explains a lot. I knew Malicevile just didn't happen to stumble upon my location in the real world. It sucks that my own blood betrayed me and tried to deliver me directly to my father. I'm not sure how I feel about that.

I slide my arms around Zach's cool shoulders. He lifts me into his arms a second later, expanding his wings out on his back. "It's so nice when you don't protest."

I roll my eyes without comment.

He places his hand on my forehead. "Sweet dreams, princess."

<hr>

"Feeling better?" Dylan asks, placing his hand on my shoulder as I stare at the gigantic lavender roses blooming before me.

I crinkle my nose, a little annoyed that I'm asleep by Zach's hand. I know we're already back in the earth realm since it takes seconds to cross, and I've already counted to sixty a few dozen times. *He did say we were a long way from home.* That's beside the point. He's taking advantage of the situation so he can fly in peace.

"Sort of." I turn my gaze away from the roses to look at Dylan. "I saw my father today." I don't know why I mention it, but Dylan's always been easy to talk to.

"And?"

"I don't know. It's just weird knowing that I'm expected to kill him."

"He's—"

I hold up my hand. "I know he's evil and totally deserves it. It's just—"

"There's more to him," Dylan finishes for me.

"Am I crazy?" *Please, say I'm crazy.*

"I don't know. I can't see what you see, love. And I know you better than to think that your thoughts are unwarranted. You're his daughter, after all. I don't know what it's like to have that sort of parental bond."

I frown. "But I shouldn't even have this bond."

He shrugs. "You were once human, Cami. Don't fault yourself."

I sigh. "Don't tell Zach about this, okay? I'm sure he's already going crazy enough because of Evan." My heart races as I think his name.

Dylan embraces me, pulling me against him. "You have to give us all a little credit. Zach's not a demon. He's more in tune to you than you realize."

"Is that why he likes to annoy the Hell out of me?"

Dylan laughs. "Says the little demon who likes to shock her guardian for the fun of it."

"Only when he deserves it," I argue.

The glorious sun hangs overhead, reminding me of what Dylan's wings look like when they light up the night. He squeezes me tighter without another word, and I just enjoy what his presence feels like next to my soul. His quiet comfort soothes the anxiety tumbling through me—anxiety that will come back in full force the second I open my eyes since I'll no longer have the prison realm to numb me.

"You ready to wake up?" Dylan asks after a moment. His fingers brush through my hair as he plays with the curls that cascade down my back in soft ringlets. Not only did the daylight prison realm heal my wounds, it took care of all the dirt and grime from the earth realm, leaving me looking the best I have in weeks.

I'm tempted to say no, that I'd much prefer to hang out in my sweet dreams than face the night ahead of me, but the world starts to shake without giving me a real choice. I close my eyes, still hugging Dylan, and when I open them, I meet his chocolate gaze, but we're no longer in the garden. He cradles me against him on the window seat in my room. My small lamp glows from my nightstand, and my bed remains made.

"What time is it?" I hate feeling so disoriented from traveling between planes unaware. Before I was anchored to the earth plane by heavenly light, crossing between earth and the daylight realm was a painless transition as one world faded into the other. But now, the night is pitch-black through my stained-glass window, and I know I've missed twilight.

"Almost midnight."

I shoot from Dylan's arms and hop to my feet. I can't believe so much time has passed already. It's unlike Zach to let me take such a long nap at night when the fate of the world is on the line, which means something's up.

Ignoring the fact that Dylan watches me, I strip out of my wrinkled clothes, change into fresh jeans and a shirt from my closet, and then step into my boots. I slide into my leather jacket that hangs on the back of my desk chair, and then stride to the door. It's not until I wrap my hand around the knob that Dylan crosses the room and locks his fingers on my shoulder.

"You should stay here with me for a few more minutes," Dylan says, stopping me from leaving.

I glower. "Did Zach put you up to this?"

"He thinks you need another night off."

"Do not. Now let go of me."

He holds his hands up and lets me go, but he stays right behind me. I jog into the living room and catch Cadence sliding her knives into their sheaths. Zach stands in the open door, his angelic sidekicks, Remi and Dani, hanging out on the porch. I spot Alana talking on her cell phone as she paces in a circle on the grass.

Everyone stops what they're doing to look up at me.

Zach flicks his gaze to Dylan for a split second before focusing all his attention on me. "You should be resting, princess.

You've had a long day."

I place my hands on my hips. "I've had plenty of rest—thanks to you. That was sneaky using Dylan as a distraction."

"Not a very good one apparently," Zach quips. He looks at Dylan. "You couldn't give us five more minutes?"

"And face a demon's wrath?" Dylan says with a smirk, flashing his dimples.

I summon electricity in my hands. "Oh, I'll show both of you my wrath."

It takes Alana cutting between Remi and Dani and staring at me with undeniable fear to make me hesitate. The two angels tug her back like I'd actually do something to harm my former guardian. It makes me angrier than it should, but I can't help it.

Zach steps closer, spreading his wings wide, creating an angelic wall in the middle of the room separating me from them. "Cami is just joking. She doesn't intend to unleash her wrath on anyone," he says over his shoulder.

His words are enough to make me absorb the power back into my soul. The fact that he felt the need to say them brings back the memory of my conversation with Evan this morning and how I'll be cast out the moment I'm not useful.

I rub my hand over my arm, half hugging myself. "Wow." It's hard putting my storming thoughts into words. "This feels a little familiar and not in a good way. And the last time it felt like this, I was strapped to a chair facing a bunch of people who thought I didn't deserve my life like I'm some kind of monster."

"Princess," Zach says, stepping forward. Dylan rests his

hands on my shoulders behind me. But I don't want to be in the middle on this angel sandwich. I want to get out of here. "No one here thinks you're a monster, and I really do think you should rest. We're only going out to investigate the little trap your father has mentioned to see if there was any way around it. I'd feel much more comfortable if you stayed here."

My forehead crinkles. "First, you're full of crap. I can smell fear, and even Remi is a little uneasy with my presence tonight. Second, you can't expect me to sit here and do nothing as my father tries to lure you guys out, even if you know it's a trap. You can't underestimate him, and I'm the only one immune to his power. I should be going."

"I can't take the risk. What if Evan is there?"

I shrug. "So what."

"You know how he—"

"How he what?" I dare him to say anything in front of a room full of people.

His long pause means he's not going to accept my dare. "The answer is no and that's final. This isn't some hunt to destroy a demon. This isn't even a rescue mission. We're just going to observe to see if we can intervene. If we can, great. If not, we'll at least be more informed than before we started." Zach's wings disappear as he closes the distance completely. He grasps my shoulders. "I know that you hate sitting around, and I know you want nothing more than to save the day, but your safety is my first priority and if I have to knock you out again, tie you up, and lock you in your room to do my job, then I will. Do you understand?"

Nope. Not happening. "Yes, I understand."

The second Zach turns his back on me, I shoot Cadence a look that makes her smile. But before I even have a chance to step forward to dodge past Zach, he spins and raises his hand to press it against my forehead. I duck, ramming into his stomach, and together we slide across the floor.

"This isn't fair," I say, flipping onto Zach before straddling him to lock his hands above his head. "I can help and you know it."

"You know she's right," Dylan says from above me.

"Thank you! At least someone has some faith in my boiling demonic heart." I smile at Dylan before I catch sight of the others staring at me as I argue with my Demon Watcher. It makes me self-conscious that I'm still holding him down, but I'm not going to risk him knocking me out until he agrees.

"I'll even tag along and keep her out of trouble," Dylan adds.

"You will, will you?" Both Zach and I ask in unison, like the suggestion to keep me out of trouble would be nothing short of a miracle. I'll admit it. I'm lots of trouble. I can't help it.

Dylan hooks his fingers under my arms and pulls me off of Zach. "Yeah."

Zach leans up on his elbows and sighs. "You two okay with this?" he asks his angel sidekicks.

I glare at them, daring them to tell him no.

Neither of them says anything. Neither does Alana or Cadence.

"Fine," Zach says, jumping to his feet. "But I swear, princess, if we come across your little boyfriend and you let him try to seduce you back to Hell again, I'll blast him into oblivion myself."

"Deal." I only agree because Zach wouldn't dare, and I wouldn't even let him try.

NO TURNING BACK

ZACH IS FULL of surprises because he let Dylan carry me in his arms instead of holding onto me himself for safekeeping. He probably didn't ask Remi or Dani because he knew I'd protest. Plus, I much prefer they handle Cadence and Alana. They can protect them while I watch Angel Boy's back while Zach leads the way.

Dylan keeps a dozen feet of distance between us and the angels as we fly through low clouds. Mist sprinkles over my skin, sending steam into the air, and I mess with the black hair curling around Dylan's ear. I brush some strands away and his jaw tightens, but he doesn't say anything. I continue to do it because I'm bored from the hour of being in the air and because I know I'm driving him crazy.

"You're going to lose your hand," Dylan says, craning his neck away.

I laugh. "It's a good thing I have two."

When I reach for his hair again, he snaps his teeth at me.

I laugh again, my voice echoing on the wind, and Zach peers at us over his shoulder. If looks could smite me, I'd be freefalling to the ground just about now. It's not my fault I deflect my nervousness with angelic distractions and teasing.

"God, he's so intense tonight," I whisper, turning my face toward Dylan to keep my eyes from watering on the wind.

"I'm surprised you're not."

"I'm not thinking about it."

"Well, you should. I know how you like to act before you think. You need to prepare yourself for everything Malicevile has to throw at us. Obviously, it's going to be something horrifying if he expects the angelic army to show up."

I hadn't thought about that. "Great."

"What?"

"Now I'm starting to worry."

"Good. Don't you remember how a good dose of fear will keep you safe?" But fear doesn't only keep me safe. It makes me volatile and reckless, too. Because I have a habit of turning fear into anger.

"Maybe you should turn around. Zach might've been right." Admitting as much leaves a bitterness in my mouth, one

I can't seem to swallow.

"If that's what you wa—"

A loud howl rips through the wind, cutting off Dylan's words. Peering down, I search the dark world below. Bright, flame-covered figures dart through the trees surrounding a winding road that leads up a hillside. Hellhounds streak through the night, and as I stare at their intense fiery forms, they leave spots in my vision. If hellhounds are nearby—and that looks like my father's entire pack—Malicevile can't be far behind.

But the hellhounds aren't the only things down below. With a bright blast of blue electricity that streams across the land, a figure attempts to slow down a hellhound. I don't even have to have a good look to know who the power belongs to. Jacie Hallowitz was the second demi-demon I had ever met and a close friend of David's, Evan's partner. His death affected her as much as it did Alana, and she tried to destroy me after my transformation. I can't help the anger I feel as I look down on her, but I know even though we ended up as enemies, we're not now. She doesn't deserve such a fate.

"The beasts are going to tear her apart," Remi mentions, dropping a few feet lower with Alana in his arms.

"Zach, if you take Cadence, I can grab her from above," Dani says, speeding up to surpass Zach. "I wouldn't even have to land." She is the fastest of the three of them.

Spinning, Dani tosses Cadence to Zach. The look that crosses my best friend's face is priceless. She doesn't even have a chance to squeal because Zach holds her against his galaxy-inspired T-shirt.

Dani descends a few feet when something catches my attention. Even from up here, I can smell the faint smell of cinnamon.

"Wait!" I call. "This is what my father expects you to do."

Dani flaps her golden wings and ascends to fly next to Dylan. "I can get to her. Don't worry."

But worry doesn't even describe the dread swirling through me. "There has to be another way. We have to get her from the ground level. Malicevile knows you guys attack from above."

An agitated yell sounds through the air as one of the hellhounds collides with Jacie, knocking her off her feet. She rolls with the beast before kicking it off and zapping it with her power.

I watch the pack, consisting of a dozen hellhounds, circle around Jacie. They surround her from all sides, not giving her much room to escape. Even I'd be in trouble if I were in that situation. I could stop one or two at the most, but an entire pack? Jacie's about to get burned while being eaten alive.

"Oh, God," Alana says from her place in Remi's arms. "There has to be something. She can't die like that."

"If you fly low enough, I can get a clear shot with my dagger," Cadence says, surprising me. "I'm an excellent thrower. It's what I would want if that were me."

A mercy killing.

My heart hangs heavy in my chest as a million thoughts

rush through my mind. I hate how powerless I feel in this moment, but it doesn't compare to the guilt and rage sneaking from my soul, shading my vision in shadows. I should be used to my father winning. I should even be used to his sadistic tendencies. But it doesn't make this any easier.

If only there was something I could do that wouldn't put my own life in jeopardy. That wouldn't risk all the effort we put into making Malicevile think I sacrificed myself for him. While I might be powerless in this moment, I'm the one in control.

"Okay," Zach says, responding to Cadence after a moment of consideration. "Dani, you fly her down. Don't get any closer than you have to." He tosses Cadence back to the other angel. "You have one shot, Cadence."

Alana lets out a small cry before composing herself.

Cool fingers brush the icy tears from my cheeks. Dylan has been just as quiet as I have been as the others discuss Jacie's fate.

A scream from below rips through the air as a hellhound latches onto Jacie's jacket, pulling her off her feet. She manages to zap it with power, but it only encourages another hellhound to grab her leg. The scent of burning flesh slaps me in the senses, and my stomach churns, but it's not the hellhounds' flesh that's burning.

Just as Dani starts to dive, Jacie throws her arms up and yells, "I give up! I'll do it!"

A low whistle sounds through the air as Malicevile calls off his hellhounds. My chest heaves, and I gasp in deep breaths in relief. I shiver against Dylan, cold sweat dripping down my temples. I don't think my heart can take much more of my father's evil antics. Jacie might not get eaten alive, but this is far from over. Malicevile would never make things so easy.

He's probably even more determined than ever since the angels haven't graced him with their godliness. This was supposed to be a trap of some sort after all—payback for the demons I've sent to Hell over the last few weeks. Not to mention the demi-demon we saved. I bet that set him off the moment Evan gave him the news.

My chest tightens with the thought, and the pain only intensifies as I watch Malicevile stroll through the trees toward Jacie. And he's not alone. Evan remains at his side like the good little minion he is, and behind them walks four other demons—Raphael, the unfamiliar woman from the light realm, and two mid-level demons who I recognize from our brief meeting while I was playing the good demon daughter, but can't remember much about.

The wind roars in my ears, making it impossible to pick up on the conversation since Jacie is no longer yelling. She remains on her knees, keeping her hands at her side. The demons approach her, but she holds her head high. She was never one to cower in the face of evil. If anything, I expect her to spit in it.

I close my eyes, afraid of what my father has planned next. It can't be so easy. He doesn't show mercy—not on someone like Jacie, who doesn't really have anything to offer him.

"Oh, watchers! Do you see?" Malicevile's voice echoes through the night as he peers into the night sky. "This is the future. The people you've trained against us will be running to us. They'll be begging to join us, and there's nothing you can do about it."

My father steps forward in front of Jacie and glowers down at her. The action is enough to freeze my fiery blood. I remember all too well what it feels like to be trapped in the weight of his demonic stare, feeling so hopeless. Feeling so alone.

"Watchers!" Malicevile yells again. "You're all nothing but cowards! I know you're up there somewhere. I can *smell* you. Show yourselves, and we might be able to work out a deal."

I dig my fingers into Dylan's arms. "He's lying."

Zach nods his head at me.

"Come on," Cadence says, whispering above the silence that has fallen between us. "Get me close. I can do this. I can save her."

"No," Zach says. "You'll never make it. There are too many of them, and Malicevile will know you're coming. That demi-demon's lost to us. I'm sorry."

Alana sniffles from Remi's arms, and he holds her tighter against him. It's a shocking sight to see on a usually emotionless angel. Or maybe he's just that way with me because of who I am. I can't blame the guy, though. He's been watching and fighting demons for who knows how long. Still hurts my feelings.

"Watchers! This is your last chance." My father's voice rings in my ears. "Make the deal or this little demi-demon will make it for herself." He turns to look at Jacie again. "See? Nobody cares about you. Nobody thinks you're worth saving after all. And to think, you spent all those years helping *them,* and they're going to just watch you fall."

My muscles tense as I curl and uncurl my fingers. How dare he make her feel like he made me feel, how the alliance made me feel. I can't stand the thought that Jacie might actually believe him.

"So, here's the deal, little half-breed. You will trade me your soul for the chance to serve greatness." Malicevile says the words so loudly, I'm sure he wants the entire universe to hear, to shake under his power. But I've done enough shaking and fearing and watching him destroy everything in my life. I've felt him break me, rebuild me, and chip away the pieces he didn't find desirable. I can't let him do that to Jacie. I can't stand by and watch him. He's wrong. I'm not a coward.

"I accept your deal." Jacie's voice stirs something dark inside me. The deal with my father binds her to him. I can feel it with everything demonic inside me.

"Good. Now, it's time you take a little trip home. Let's find out how powerful you really are."

Oh, no. Is he? As Malicevile holds out a dagger to Jacie, I can't bear to look. He's going to attempt to transform her, and she'll never make it. This is it.

"Cami," Dylan whispers. "Your power."

It's not until he says something that I realize electricity is rolling between my palms, singeing the fabric of Dylan's shirt. I accidentally shock him before snuffing it out, and his jaw clenches. My true body threatens to peek through my skin, revealing me for what I truly am. Something I'll never escape.

"Let's head out," Zach says. "It's better if we don't watch."

He gives me a sad look before flapping his wings and ascending higher into the sky. Remi and Dani follow suit, but I grip Dylan's face in my hands to stop him. He looks me dead in the eyes, fear lining his brows. Leaning forward, I brush my lips against his. I can't help it. It's not in a romantic way or in a way that'll lead to something more. This simple kiss is my way of showing him how much he means to me.

It's the only way I know how to say goodbye without uttering the words that'll tear me apart.

Because I can't let my father have Jacie. I can't let him think he's winning a moment longer. I don't care if Jacie has wronged me. I don't care if the angels think she's hopeless. I don't even care that I'm going to face Hell's rogue army. All I know is that I can't give up. I have to try.

"Cami, don't do this," Dylan whispers into my lips.

My breath quivers as I pull away. "I'm sorry."

"Love, I can't let you." With a flick of his wings, he jets us higher. But I don't let him get us far. Pressing my hands to his chest, I push a jolt of electricity into him, one just strong enough to get him to loosen his hold on me. I arch my back, pushing away from him with a force that sends him reeling.

"Cami!" His voice disappears on the wind as I summon every ounce of courage within me. There's no turning back now. I let myself fall.

SAVED

THE WORLD ZOOMS by as I freefall for what feels like eternity. My eyes blur with tears, and my stomach rises into my throat. The ground draws closer and closer to me, threatening to consume me. If I don't slow down soon, the impact will surely knock my soul from my body.

Squeezing my eyes shut, I try to summon my levitation, but I'm still too high up. I have to be closer to the ground, and even then, I'm sure it's going to hurt like Hell forcing myself to stop at this speed.

My heart races in my chest as I drop from the sky like a fallen angel, except I won't be losing my wings. I release a long, deep breath, pushing a gust of wind from my lungs. It's strong enough to send the demons scattering. They don't even have a chance to see me coming.

The wind slows my fall just enough that I find my levitation, slamming against the invisible barrier hard enough to knock another breath of wind from my lungs. In that small moment where the world suddenly stops, I take the chance to search around. Jacie lies on her stomach, her face in the dry grass.

I don't have a chance to get to her, though. A powerful blast of light erupts from behind me, setting the whole world aglow in angelic light. A heavy weight smashes into me, and black wings encircle me, shielding me from my enemies.

We hit the ground, rolling a few times before hitting a tree. The trunk splits with a deafening crack, and Malicevile's bright electricity sets the branches ablaze. I peek through Zach's black feathers as my father pushes to his feet and dusts himself off. He doesn't have a chance to get far, because another blast of heavenly light soars through the air and hits him in the back as one of Zach's sidekicks attacks from above.

"Princess," Zach whispers into my hair. "Are you trying to get us killed?"

Raphael joins in the fight, sending a dazzling red orb zooming through the air toward the trees. More heavenly light shines radiantly around us. The demons' skin sizzles, but it barely slows them down.

"I know you're here, watcher. Show yourself." My father

sends another blast of power our way. Zach shields me before I have a chance to try to absorb it and tenses when the electricity shocks him in the side. Even now, even when we're trapped, he still protects me from my father. He's willing to die to keep me hidden. And it pisses me off—not at Zach, but at Malicevile for putting us in this position in the first place.

Inhaling a deep breath, I hold it for a moment until Malicevile gets a step closer. He stumbles but catches himself with his levitation. He's going to close the distance, and there's nothing we can do about it.

"Malicevile!" My heart nearly explodes at the sound of Dylan's voice ringing through the air. "How does it feel that you underestimated me? How does it feel that I got to Cami?"

Oh, God. Dylan's going to get himself killed.

"Don't speak her name!" My father roars, shooting an energy orb into the air. It crackles and sparkles as it catches on one of the treetops.

Zach doesn't waste the opportunity. He tugs me to my feet, pulling me back. But from this spot, the trees are too thick, and there's no way he can launch us into the air.

"I always knew Cami was too good for this world. I just wish she hadn't wasted her life on you." Dylan's apple scent wafts around me, and I nearly scream out his name as my father attempts to blast him again.

"Face me, nephilim! I'm not going to murder you. I'm going to rip those wings from your back and make you suffer. You'll wish you were in Hell, but I wouldn't dare let you near

Camilla."

Dylan only lets out a forced laugh.

The air around us buzzes with so much power as the angels try to keep the demons at bay, but the demons fight back with everything they have. It won't be long before Remi and Dani will have to back off before they risk getting hurt. Our opportunity to leave is turning nearly impossible. But I'm not leaving without Jacie.

Pulling away from Zach, I rush forward toward the demi-demon. She lies motionless on the ground, a pool of blood seeping from her body. Cool fingers grip my arm, stopping me in place. Malicevile turns his gaze from the sky in our direction, but he looks right past us. A moment later, he strolls toward Jacie and nudges her body with his shiny designer shoe.

"We'll find out at sunrise." I was so focused on Jacie's body that I didn't even notice Evan come to my father's side. "Cami disappeared with the sun."

Malicevile kicks Jacie again and again until he flips her body over. Tears blur my vision as I peer into her empty eyes. I'm too late. Jacie's dead. All of this was for nothing, and now I'll surely die along with my friends by the hands of my father exactly how I've always imagined. Because I won't be joining him. I can't. My soul belongs to Heaven, and there's no way Malicevile will allow me to live like this.

Malicevile clears his throat. "No point in waiting. Her soul never left. It is mine for the taking. I assume a demi-demon cannot be demon-bound." Which means that definitely leaves

Evan out of the running for the next transformation.

Malicevile kneels down next to Jacie despite the commotion continuing on between the angels and demons. It's like he doesn't even care that people are fighting around him.

I suck in a breath when he lowers his hand over Jacie's chest. Her soul shimmers into view as my father starts to extract it to add to his collection. I know exactly what it's like. I've done it for him at least a dozen times.

I don't even have a chance to think before I'm flying forward away from Zach. Running as fast as I can, I bolt through the trees toward the clearing. Jacie might be dead, but her soul isn't lost yet. My father might have bargained for it, but his blood runs through my veins. I can steal it right out from under him this very moment before he claims it.

Zach latches his fingers to my shoulder, but he doesn't stop me like I expect. He keeps us invisible and pushes me forward, flapping his startling black wings on his back. With his free hand, he throws a stream of heavenly light at my father, blinding him. Evan knocks Malicevile over and shields him

My fingers caress Jacie's soul. It hums in my hands, and I pull it away and take it into me. I stretch out my arms so Zach can pull me into the air. Malicevile blindly launches power into the air, and the sky explodes in a shower of sparks. I absorb it with everything in me, protecting Zach while he ascends toward the sky holding me only by the back of my jacket.

When I look down, Malicevile is screaming at the other demons, tossing his power at anyone who gets too close. But it's not him that draws my attention. Evan peers up at me from his spot next to Jacie's body. And then he shakes his head. It's in this moment that I see the hope slip from him, because with the death of Jacie, he sees his own death. He finally realizes that he'll never get a chance at forever.

My heart aches as Zach navigates us through the air. When we're far enough away, he tugs me up higher until he wraps me in his arms, cradling me securely against his taut chest.

"What you did back there—"

I release a low sob as my shoulders shake. My adrenaline fades with every breath, and then all I can do is peer into Jacie's golden soul. It shifts and moves between my fingers. This is the longest I've ever held a soul, and her life slowly flashes through my eyes.

"I'm sorry," I whisper. I'm not talking to Zach, though.

"Cami." Zach's voice wraps around me like he's talking to a small, frightened child. "You were very brave tonight. I'm proud of you."

Tears trickle down my face at his words. "I was too late. I can't believe I was too late."

"No, you weren't. You saved her. You didn't give up." He holds me closer. "I've always had faith in you, Cami. I've known you were special since the moment I was assigned to you. But now, seeing you hold that beautiful soul... You've given me so much hope. I want you to see it, too."

Memories of Jacie's life trickle through my mind, pulling my attention away from Zach. She was a fierce fighter from a young age. She believed that even one person could make a difference in the world. Images of her and her husband cross my mind, and I weep with sorrow, feeling the heartache she felt the moment she knew she'd never see him again. Images of other hunters flash through my mind, some familiar, some not. David appears before me and then Alana. And Evan, too. Lastly, my own image greets me, and I don't look like the scary demon I am. Jacie's soul projects me exactly as I was the first time I met her. It feels like a lifetime ago, but in the end, she didn't see me as a monster. She saw me as me.

"Oh, love. I knew you could do it." Dylan's voice brings my mind back to the present as he flies before me, carrying Alana in his arms.

I laugh as I cry. "I could kill you, Dylan. I can't believe you did that."

"I'd do anything for you, Cami. You know that."

My gaze falls on the other two angels and Cadence. Remi's shoulder is blackened, and his arm hangs limply at his side. It's why Dylan's holding Alana. Dani isn't much better, but it's her leg that had taken most of the demonic power. The sight of them sends fire coursing through me. I want to turn around and make my father feel their pain.

Zach gently knocks his chin to the top of my head. "No more fighting tonight, princess. I know what you're thinking, but we'll all live and heal. Your father can wait for another night."

"I'm not sure that I can."

He releases a breath. "I know. And that's why I want you to close your eyes."

I frown. "No. You're not going to knock me out. I won't let you."

"Trust me, princess."

"I do. It's just—"

"Trust me." Reaching his hand up, he gently covers my eyes, and the world melts away.

<hr>

"I honestly thought I'd never see you again."

My mouth drops open as I spin to face the familiar voice. "Jacie? I don't understand. What are you doing here?"

"You saved me, Cami." Tears sparkle in her coffee brown eyes. "Even after everything, you saved me."

She wraps her arms around me, and I bury my face in her mahogany hair. A shiver rushes through me at how real she feels. "I shouldn't have had to. I'm so sorry. My father, he—"

She pulls away and shakes her head. "Don't you dare apologize for that demon."

"I just—" I take in a deep breath. "I swear I'm going to send him to Hell. Even if it's the last thing I'll ever do in my eternity, and even if I have to drag him there myself, he won't get away with this." But I'm afraid I'm all talk and no power.

She smiles. "Look at you. And to think that Alana ever thought she had to protect you. David was always right. He knew you'd do just fine."

Hearing his name cuts deeply into my soul.

She touches my cheek. "Hey, no. Don't cry. David would hate himself right about now for doubting you in the end. He was only human, after all."

I squeeze my eyes shut for a second to compose myself. "I wish you were alive."

She nods. "Me too. But I'm okay, Cami. This isn't the end."

"I feel like you should tell me everything you want me to pass along. It's the least I can do."

She shrugs. "There's nothing they don't already know." She hugs me against her. "But I want you to stay positive, okay? I want you to know that everything will work itself out in the end. You're not in this alone."

The scent of apple and rain pulls my attention away from Jacie. Dylan shimmers into view next to us. He smiles with sad eyes as he looks between me and Jacie, and then she throws her arms around him.

"Is this it?" she asks him.

My heart falters. "Wait. I'm not ready."

Jacie laughs. "But I am."

I hug her again. "I'm afraid I won't ever see you again." There's no following where she's going for me. Immortality rests heavy in my heart for the first time in months. It's different thinking about it, but facing it in this moment is another story.

"You don't have to see me to know that I'm here, okay?"

I sniffle back a sob. My words get lost in my throat, so I

just nod my head.

Jacie takes Dylan's outstretched hand. "Goodbye, Cami. Don't forget what I said. You'll never be alone."

And with those words, Jacie shimmers from view as her soul leaves me forever.

Dylan pulls me into a hug. "It's time to wake up, love."

But I don't want to. I want to stay in this dream for the rest of time.

LOVE RUINS THE WORLD

"SHE'LL WAKE UP when she's ready." Zach's voice cuts through the darkness.

I'm not sure how much time has passed, but until this second, it's like I wasn't existing at all. Comforting numbness cradled my soul when my dream world collapsed, taking Dylan with it. The transition usually takes only seconds, but something feels different this time.

"Are you sure she's okay?" It's Dylan. "You didn't see her when you ushered Jacie's soul."

"No, but I felt her. Cami just needs time. That was the first soul she's ever taken for herself, and a pure one at that."

"I think I should check on her." Cool fingers twine with mine.

"She's fine. Look at her soul."

"It's not her soul I'm worried about."

"Dylan, I know Cami means a lot to you, and I know how it pains you to see her like this, but you have to give her space. How is she ever supposed to do her job if she's constantly worrying about how everyone feels or even how she feels? It's bad enough that I have to deal with the demi-demon, but now I'm starting to be concerned about you, too." I hold as still as possible even though Zach's words get under my skin. He has no business worrying about my relationships with other people.

"You have nothing to worry about. Cami's made her decision quite clear."

"That's not what I meant. What you did the other night, facing Malicevile, was stupid. I had everything under control, and you put yourself in danger."

"It's not like my life is crucial in saving the world." My heart races hearing Dylan's admittance. He might not be crucial in saving the world, but he's crucial in my world.

"Oh, but that's where you're wrong. Cami would've blown everything had anything happened to you. You honestly think she'd stand by while her father tortured you? Broke you? She does crazy things for the sake of strangers. I couldn't imagine what she'd do for someone she loves."

After a long moment of silence, Dylan says, "Maybe you're right. Maybe I should go."

His hand slips from mine, and I jerk upright and yank his arm until he sits back on the edge of my bed where I can wrap my arms around him and bury my face in his shirt.

"How about you stop imagining what I will or will not do in the face of a terrible situation and just tell me that you're afraid I'll ruin everything." I swing my gaze to Zach and narrow my eyes. "Don't you think I need to care about people to have something worth fighting for? Because the world alone means nothing to me. It's the people in it I care about."

"Point taken, princess." I expect Zach to argue more, to tell me how weak that kind of mindset makes me, but he doesn't. Sometimes, he's full of surprises.

"And you." I jab my finger at Dylan's chest. "You should know better than to suggest you leave for my sake. That never works out, and you know it. Leaving doesn't make me safe or stronger—it doesn't make you some good guy. So, don't you even think about disappearing unless it's what you need to do for yourself. I can respect that you don't want all my baggage, or to fight in this war. But don't use my wellbeing as an excuse. It would just piss me off, and pissing off a demon is something you don't want to do."

"You're cute when you're angry," Dylan says, smiling at me.

"Don't even start."

"Yeah, please don't," Zach says, getting to his feet.

I laugh, pulling away from Dylan. Zach motions for me to get to my feet before surprising me with a hug.

"Aww, my guardian is such a sap sometimes," I quip. "I thought you'd enjoy a nice break from me."

"Four days isn't a break, it's more like a vacation. And I did enjoy myself, thanks." Zach releases me and pokes my nose.

I bat his hand away. "Are you kidding me? Four days? What did I miss? Is the earth covered in fire and brimstone? Does my father have his new army? Is everyone okay?"

"Relax, princess. We survived while you got your beauty sleep, but if you're feeling up to it, I'd like for you to run an errand with me."

"What kind of errand?"

"You'll see."

<hr>

My heart slides into my stomach the moment Zach pulls his old, yellow Toyota Tercel to the curb of a busy street an hour north of our house. I insisted he drive since we have almost a whole day of light and after freefalling in my insane attempt to save Jacie, I'm not exactly in the mood for angel transportation.

But I wish I wasn't here in this spot at all.

Across the street sits a sleek, red Mustang convertible with the top down, and not just any old Mustang. It's *my* Mustang. My first and only car courtesy of my father, and I kind of want to hop out and steal it.

"Let me out," I say, shoving the door. Zach's car isn't just old, but it's also beat up and missing not only the window crank but the door handle as well. "I only need a minute, and we can replace this piece of junk."

He glowers. I'm pretty sure I've just offended him. Whatever. This car is going to die and leave us stranded somewhere—not like he cares. "I didn't bring you here to reclaim your possessions, and talk about my car like that again, and you can walk." *I knew it.*

"Sheesh, sorry. But I'm still stealing my car."

"No, you're no—"

A loud thud, followed by black smoke, erupts from Zach's door. I nearly jump from my skin as the car shakes again when something slams against it. More smoke clouds the air as flames lick the old paint on the Tercel, eating their way across the hood.

Zach slams his hands on the wheel once before flinging off his seatbelt. He doesn't even get his hand on the door handle before two palms slam against the window, blocking our only exit. If there's one thing I hate, it's being trapped—in a burning car, no less.

Anger washes over me so hot and fast that I don't even have time to think. I shove my shoulder into my door with enough demonic strength to break the latch and bend the frame. Flying from my seat, I rush around the hood of the car to face the jerk brave enough to mess with me.

I freeze in my tracks, hands clenched before me with power swirling in my palms. Evan meets me with an easy smile, though fire lights his intense blue eyes. The last time I saw him, which feels like only hours ago, he was looking more hopeless than ever. But that boy doesn't stand before me. This is the confident, slightly devilish boy I've grown used to. But it doesn't stop me from waltzing forward and shoving him back as hard as I can.

As my palms connect to his hard chest he barely wavers on his feet. I'd have an easier time knocking down a brick wall. When I attempt to shove him again, he wraps his fingers around my wrists and tugs me to him. My hands stay locked between us, but I could easily escape if I wanted to. Swiftly turning me with him, he presses my back against the driver's side door where Zach remains.

"Are you stalking me, babe?" He only calls me that when he's in one of his playful moods.

I suck in my bottom lip for a second before I say, "I had no idea you were here."

He hums under his breath like he doesn't believe me. "Then what are you doing here? Do you live nearby?"

"Wouldn't you love to know," I say, twisting the front of his shirt between my fingers.

"I bet I could convince you to tell me," he whispers, leaning forward to brush his lips along the skin just below my ear. I shiver under his warm breath. I can't let him try to seduce me again. He knows how to manipulate me better than anyone, playing with my love for him.

"That sort of information comes with a price." Slowly untwining my hands from his shirt, I gently slide them to his shoulders until I lock him in place against me. His heartbeat thrums against mine and his body heat washes over me. It's such a different sensation than I'm used to. Angels and humans run a lot cooler than me. Evan, he's just as hot. I can't help but fantasize about what it'd be like to press his skin against mine.

"Name it, and I'll pay," Evan whispers, closing the space between us until his mouth is an inch from mine.

I don't let him kiss me though. I can't afford to lose myself to him, knowing that he's playing a game with me. A fun game, but a game no less. It also helps that when I turn my face away, I spot Zach staring at me from behind Evan. He must've climbed out of the car from the passenger's side.

All he does is cross his arms and watch me for a moment before he mouths for me to be careful. He suddenly launches into the air, the gust of wind created by his wings strong enough to push more of Evan's weight against me.

"And I thought your shadow would never leave your side," he says, peering into the sky though Zach has already disappeared from sight.

Furrowing my eyebrows, I think the same thing. Zach said we were running errands, but it looks like he has something else in store, and he forgot to mention it to me. But why leave me with Evan? Especially after the last time.

"You make him uncomfortable," I say, instead of relaying my thoughts out loud. It's a better explanation than nothing. If I know anything about Zach, nothing he does is coincidental.

"Good." He brings his hands up to my face and stares into my eyes. "Now about that price."

"About that." I place my hands over his and tug them from

my face before he kisses me. "Why don't we get out of here?"

He tilts his head to the side. "You're serious?"

"I guess we can stay here if you're concerned that my guardian might get worried...or if you're afraid."

He slides the keys to my Mustang from his pocket. With a quick jerk of my hand, I steal them away from him. He only laughs as we cross the street, and he opens the car door for me before I slide onto the cool leather seat.

Evan hops into the passenger's side and squeezes my knee with his fingers when the engine roars to life. I stare at him in my peripheral vision, a dozen memories stirring within me as I recall all the times we've sat together in this car. His patchouli scent caresses me, and I stomp the throttle and jolt from the curb, letting the wind steal it away to keep a clear mind.

"God, I've missed this," I say, navigating around slower cars, speeding well over the speed limit. I don't have a destination, so I just drive.

"The car?" Evan leans forward in the seat.

I shrug. "All of it. You and me. If only my father wasn't such a psycho."

"They've really brainwashed you, Cami. Your father might be ruthless, but he doesn't do things just for the fun of it. He does what's necessary. You act like he treated you so terribly, but he gave you everything you could've ever wanted. He trained you and protected you. He was setting you up for a great eternity without having to be under someone else's rule. He wanted you as an equal. You weren't just some possession to him. You were his daughter, Cami. His family. He cared about you."

"He cared about what I could do for him. He cared about controlling me and turning me into him. He didn't care about me. If he did, he would've given me your soul."

"You know why he didn't."

"Can I ask you something? And be honest."

"Anything."

"I've known a lot of demon-bound people, Evan. And you, you aren't like most of them. They're desperate about their situation. They fight with themselves about doing a demon's bidding. But you, you act like you enjoy being with Mal. If you weren't bound to him, would you stick around?"

He's quiet for an extremely long moment. His answer should've been easy. It should've been an automatic no. But here he is, weighing the question in his mind. And it has nothing to do with him being bound to my father.

"I don't want to answer," he finally says after another long moment of silence.

"Because you would stay." My forehead crinkles at even the thought. I had no idea that his answer would be to remain by Malicevile's side. I had always just assumed Evan would return to the side of good. He grew up hunting. It was all he had ever known.

"You wouldn't understand."

I stomp the throttle harder, pushing the Mustang to move faster like it'll somehow take me away from Evan though he still remains by my side.

"How could I? You would stay with him even if I wasn't there. I'm starting to think that I made up our relationship in my head, that you never loved or cared about me. God, I'm such an idiot. You've had so much more time under Malicevile's influence, I guess we never stood a chance. And to think I was willing to risk the balance of the world for you."

"Cami," Evan says.

I shake my head. "Don't say my name like you love me. You're manipulating me and using me. You just want to bury yourself deep in my soul so you can just tear it apart."

"Stop putting words in my mouth. This has nothing to do with how much I love you."

"Then what does it have to do with?"

"Me. I've learned a lot being by Malicevile's side, and he's right about a lot of things. I can't just return to people who think I'm beneath them. You know we never fit in with the humans, and we sure as Hell don't fit in with angels."

Tears burn my eyes as I swerve between lanes, hitting the small bumps in the lane dividers. Evan grips the door panel when I jerk the wheel to cross the double line into oncoming traffic to speed past two slow cars blocking my way.

Evan reaches over and grabs the wheel, turning it so we drive back to the right side of the road before we collide with a semi. I'd have waited for the last second to punish him, to make him feel what I'm feeling. Like he's trying to kill me with my broken heart.

"You're not who I thought you were," I say, wiping my hand across my cheeks.

"I haven't changed, Cami. Now, please. Pull over before you get me killed. You might be immortal, but I'm not." He spits out the last words like it's all my fault.

"Well, I wish I weren't!" Jerking the wheel, I cross the lanes and turn onto a side street that takes us off the main road. I drive a few blocks until we reach a dead-end that overlooks a valley with the ocean in the distance. I cut off the engine and turn in my seat to face him. "You have no idea what it's like knowing that everyone around you is going to die, and they're going somewhere you can't follow."

"Then why don't you just help me transform? Why are you being so stubborn? I don't get it, Cami. You don't have to lose me."

I close my eyes because I can't look into his any longer. "You know I'd give anything for that to happen. But the odds are stacked so high against you that you'll end up in Hell, and I can't even go there if I wanted to. I'd rather spend the next few dozen years fighting and arguing about this than lose you now."

"That's why we test it on someone else first," he says. His warm breath tickles my lips, but I still don't open my eyes. "Just tell me, Cami. I traded my soul for you to live. Can't you at least give me the chance to try?"

My bottom lip trembles as he softly kisses me. He's trying so hard to break me down. But what's the point? Even if I told him how, it wouldn't work. And even if by some miracle it did, we'd still be on opposing sides. He'd still be with my father, taking the spot I gave up. He'd put me in the same position I'm in with my father. He'd force me into cutting his heart out, leaving me with nothing but his fire burning through my veins.

"Please," he whispers.

The scent of jasmine hits me as my Mustang suddenly bounces, and Zach lands in the backseat. I frown, turning my gaze to his mud-covered boots on the pristine leather. I might not get to keep my car, but it bothers me nonetheless. *Where has he even been?*

Fire erupts in Evan's palms, but I take his hands and absorb his power.

"Have a nice chat?" Zach asks, glancing between us.

Neither of us responds to his question.

"I happen to have caught the end of your conversation, and I'm pretty proud of you, princess."

"For what? Telling my boyfriend that it's impossible to turn him into a demon? It wasn't hard because you know better than anyone that Heaven's not going to—"

"To stop you if your little boyfriend gives me something I want." Zach expands his black wings on his back.

"What?" I ask. He has to be joking. Or lying.

"Yeah."

"You know he won't do anything without talking to my father first."

Zach smiles. "I know."

The motives behind his little errand sink in. Zach was using me to get to Evan. He purposely brought me to him to torment him. To remind him that he could never be like me—at least not without help. He must have a lot of confidence in my father's inability to recreate my transformation on someone else. So much so that he's willing to risk giving away my biggest secret.

And I don't know how I feel about it.

"I'm listening," Evan says without acknowledging me.

"Tell your master that I'll give him the answers he wants if he voids the contract you share over your soul."

My heart speeds up, thudding against my ribcage so hard that I'm afraid it'll blast my chest wide open. I thought this kind of deal was out of the question. Out of everything Zach could've asked for—like for an exchange for one of the demi-demons—he wants to get Evan's soul back. The thought leaves me reeling, because it will not only put Dylan at risk, it'll put all angels at risk. And for what? Evan won't come back with us. It'll be a wasted deal.

"Zach," I say, my voice shaking. "This isn't a deal you want to make. Evan—he's—"

"I'll take this to Malicevile. I'm sure we can figure out a deal."

I shake my head. "No."

Zach ignores my protests. Instead, he offers his hand to Evan, and they shake on it. A second later, my guardian slides his hands under my arms and launches us both into the air.

"You're making a huge mistake," I say when he lifts me into his arms to cradle me against him.

"This has to be done. I can't risk you not fulfilling your destiny because of him."

"He's not going to leave Malicevile's side."

Zach's face remains expressionless. "I'm well aware of that, Cami, and I'm sorry he turned out to be such a disappointment, but I honestly don't care where his loyalty lies or what side he fights for. What I care about is that nothing, and I mean nothing, stands in your way."

I glower, my head burning as my dainty horns reveal themselves in the sunlight. "You should've told me, Zach. You should've asked me if I was okay with this first."

"I thought you'd have gone for it."

"Why? Malicevile owning Evan's soul was the only excuse I had to justify his actions. Now that I'm not going to have his soul and he's chosen to stay, I have nothing!"

"Don't you think it's better that you found out now?"

"No!"

"Why?"

"Because now I'm starting to think Evan is right. You're using me! You don't even care about me."

"Don't say that. Of course I care about you, Cami."

"Then you wouldn't have put me in this position. You wouldn't have made me feel like my love for people will ruin the world."

"Cami."

I smack his chest. "Just stop! I can't talk to you right now."

He opens his mouth, but then snaps it shut with one look at my smoldering forehead. I'm so angry that I don't care if the sun tries to take me into the light prison. I don't even care if I'd have to go alone. Because in this moment, I feel Hell coursing through me, and all it wants is for me to fight my guardian for my soul back.

And if I let it, I'm sure Hell will win.

ANGELIC AFFAIRS

NOTHING BUT A dark hallway greets me when I leave the quiet of my bedroom. It's taken me hours to cool off and get myself under control, and now that it's night, I'm dying to get out of the confines of these holy walls.

Music hums from behind Cadence's door, and I knock a few times before she swings it open to greet me. Alana sits on the bed behind her, messing with a few weapons she has scattered across the black comforter.

"I'm going out. Want to come? I could use some bait." Cadence crinkles her nose at the fact that I referred to her as bait, but she knows the drill. It's not the first time she's lured out a demon for me. They have a thing for feisty hunters, and Cadence fits the role perfectly.

"Where's Zach?"

I shrug. "Probably peering at you from over my shoulder like the creep he is, but that doesn't matter. He's not welcome to show his annoying self. I'll blast him if he does."

"Can I join you two?" Alana asks, sliding a dagger into the sheath at her side.

I flick my gaze to her. "Did I hear you right? You want to go on a hunt with *me?*"

She sighs. "Well, if you're going to make a big deal out of it."

"A huge one."

She throws her boot at me, making me laugh. She smiles, and something in my heart stirs—happiness? Relief? It's been so long since I've felt it that I don't even know what it really is, only that it makes my smile widen and makes me feel good for a change.

Alana's smile fades as she crosses the room to me. She stands in front of me for a long moment before she slings her arms around me and pulls me into a hug. I bury my face into her shoulder, catching a hint of her mango shampoo, and I hug her back even tighter. It's been so long since she's hugged me that I forgot how familiar and comforting she was to me.

I pull away with tears in my eyes. "What was that for?"

"For being you."

"A demon?"

She slowly shakes her head. "No, for being Cami. I know we've had our ups and downs—"

"And sideways and circles and explosions..." Not to mention all out trying to murder each other. I don't mention it though. I'm sure she hasn't forgotten.

Her lips disappear as she presses them together for a second. "Those, too. But I've come to realize that I was severely mistaken. Losing David—that was hard. But losing you—pushing you away—I hate myself for it. I know we can't get back what we've lost, and I can't do anything to change the past, but I just want you to know that if it comes down to you against the world, I'm siding with you."

I stand in shock. I can't help it. This was the last thing I expected. I swallow the lump thickening in my throat. "Even if I sometimes do the wrong thing?" Evan comes to mind and how I'll do anything to not let the deal go through.

She doesn't even have to think about it. "Even then, because I know that whatever you do, you felt it was for the right reason. And in this world, sometimes doing the wrong thing for the right reason is the only way to get through."

A tear trickles onto my cheek. I've been holding in my conversation with Zach all day, so it's about to spill over and drown us all. I've wanted so badly to talk about it, but I'm ashamed. Because now I don't want to go through with the one thing I've been desperate to accomplish for so long. How can I pass up what might be the only chance to free Evan's soul? To unbind him from my father? Because I know in the end, he might end up in Hell no matter what. His soul is so tainted that I don't even know if he can be saved. If he'd even want to be.

"This is so messed up," I mutter.

Alana frowns. "Is this about killing Malicevile? I know it'll seal Evan's fate but—"

I hold up my hand. "It's not what this is about. Zach—he—" I take a deep breath. "He's bargaining for Evan's soul."

Alana's face lights up, a huge smile crossing her face. I don't think I've seen her this happy since—ever. Her smile alone makes me feel like I deserve to be a demon. Because I know with my next words, I'm going to devastate her.

"But I think it's a bad decision," I finally spit out.

Her smile falters. "Cami, this is Evan we're talking about. Why would you think this could ever be a bad decision?"

"Because he's changed, Alana."

Cadence moves from her place for the first time. I had almost forgotten she was in the room. "You're worried he'll stay with your father," she says. Unlike Alana, Cadence had the chance to be with Evan when I was a demon. She had a chance to see the effect my father had on him.

I suck in my bottom lip and squeeze my eyes closed for a second. "He's planning to stay. He told me so. This sort of deal will end badly. It'll put the angelic army at risk, too."

Cadence nudges my arm. "Why would Zach—"

"Because he doesn't care about Evan. He doesn't care about you two or even me. He's here to destroy Malicevile, and I'm the only way he knows how. He—"

"Princess." Zach appears in the corner of the room. I knew he was here, hiding in his creepy way to eavesdrop.

I blast him with an energy orb, scorching the front of his unusually plain T-shirt. "Leave me alone. I'm still angry with you." When he doesn't move, I blast him again. "Next time I'll make it hurt."

"Cami, please. Have a little faith that things will work out as they should, will you?"

"As they should? What does that even mean?"

"Please, I'm doing the best I can. I want your father dead and you don't want Evan to lose his soul. It's more than we can hope for."

I wring my hands together, thinking about his words. Yet they still don't feel right. "I don't want Evan to go to Hell either. Not to mention that you don't know my father like I do. Dealing with him is not only dangerous, it's deadly. I think you're taking an unnecessary risk."

"Because I have faith."

I inhale a deep breath through my nose. "Well, I'm sorry. I don't. Not in this at least."

"Cami."

My heart races as I try to summon the courage to say the next words. "This is enough. I don't think I can have you as my guardian anymore. I want someone else. Someone with less interest in my life."

"You don't know what you're saying, princess."

I motion for Alana and Cadence to head to the door before

I turn my back on Zach. "I do. Call someone now, because I'm going out, and if I even think you're shadowing me, I'll hand you over to the demons myself."

⁘

Cadence parks in the packed parking lot of a familiar night club bustling with demonic activity.

The Morningstar is a favored hangout for demons and their minions, and the last place Zach ever wanted to take me. But Zach's not in charge anymore. I am. If he expects me to kill my father, I'm going to do the one thing I know will give me a better advantage—target as many upper-level demons as possible in hopes that I can acquire their power. If I do this, maybe it'll help me when things go wrong—because they will.

Cadence cuts the engine and shifts in the seat to look at me. "Are you out of your mind? This isn't carefully hunting a demon. This is suicide, Cami."

Alana leans between the seats. "What is this place?"

"One of my father's favorite hang outs," I answer. "And if you don't want to join me, that's fine. I understand. You can go somewhere safe and pick me up in an hour."

"I'll go," Alana says. "No demon would ever suspect a hunter to show up. Could be fun."

"Until they corner you and make you trade your life for your soul," Cadence says. It's not often that she doesn't want to participate, and it somewhat surprises me. "Once we get in, we'll never make it out."

Alana's quiet for a long moment. "You know, they can't

barter for our souls if they're already in someone else's possession." She smirks at me.

Opening and closing my mouth, I stare in horror at Alana's insinuation. She doesn't mean making a deal with me, does she? That's crazy talk and might be crossing a line. I've never been a deal maker, especially for souls.

"That's actually not a bad idea," Cadence says. "Why haven't you ever mentioned this sooner, Alana?"

"Because she didn't trust me before," I say, interrupting. "And you shouldn't trust me now. I'm a demon, guys. Yeah, I'm mostly good, but your souls? No way."

"Cami, make the deal," Alana says.

"No."

Cadence reaches out and grips my arm. "She's right. Do it. Put a time limitation or something if you're scared. Hurry. A demon's coming."

What? We haven't even made it through the door. *Crap.* This was not how I wanted to start my hunting night. I should be sneaking up and cutting hearts out from behind, not confronting someone face-to-face. What if I'm recognized?

A tap sounds on the window, startling me. I don't look over my shoulder, though. Instead, I say, "Fine. I'll trade each of you a dollar to possess your souls for an hour."

"Deal," they say in unison.

A loud bang sounds on the window, and I slowly swivel in my seat to glance at a woman wearing a glittering halter dress with a tight hemline, enough jewelry to start a boutique, and the prettiest jewel-encrusted strappy heels I've seen. She's stunning in the most terrifying way possible. She scratches her sharp nail against the glass.

Her violet eyes, with diamond-shaped pupils like my father's, stare directly at Cadence.

A cool hand pinches my shoulder, and I jerk to look at the backseat where Remi now quietly sits next to Alana. *Ugh.* Of course he's here and shielding only me.

Remi's silent, brooding personality makes it way too easy to forget that he's replaced Zach, at least for the night. I hate his particularly creepy shielding act, because unlike Zach, he uses it against me all the time, quietly protecting me from view while also staying out of my sight in true, noninvasive angel fashion.

Cadence hits the button to roll down her window. "Can I help you?" Luckily, Cadence doesn't scare or intimidate easily.

The demon brushes her sleek strawberry blond hair over her shoulder, revealing sparkling diamond earrings. "I'm a promoter for The Morningstar and want to invite you into our VIP room. Free drinks for you and your friend." She motions to Alana in the backseat without even questioning why Cadence is looking like a sexy chauffer.

"Say yes," I whisper.

"That sounds like fun," Cadence says, while unbuckling her seatbelt.

"Cami, this is a terrible idea," Remi says, speaking. I almost forgot how deep his voice is because he never says a word. He's the silent, keep-his-distance type.

"Of course it's a terrible idea," I tell him. "And that's why it's perfect. You don't think I'm actually going to allow Cadence and Alana to go inside, do you?"

He grumbles. "Zach's not going to like this."

I roll my eyes. "Good."

Before I have a chance to argue with him more, the demonic woman saunters around the hood to open the door for Cadence. Alana climbs from the backseat with Remi right on her heels. I throw myself into the driver's seat and scramble out, somersaulting to the ground just before the woman slams the door closed. The last thing I need is for her to see the door magically open and realize something isn't right because I'm hidden from her view or get stuck in here while my friends end up inside without me.

The woman smiles between Alana and Cadence, and I pick up her peppery scent as we walk straight into the breeze. It's about half a block to the nightclub entrance, and a few other demons lurk in the parking lot. I have about half a block to sneak up and obliterate this woman's heart, but now that I have a clear view of the area, I'm not so sure it won't attract attention. I can't take on half a dozen demons at once and protect my friends, but I guess I'll have to try. Six demons are way better than the dozen that wait inside The Morningstar.

"If I grab them now, I think we can get out of here before we draw too much attention," Remi says.

When I'm about to agree, a harmonious voice calls out, "Cadence! What a surprise. And you brought a friend."

My. Damn. Luck. Standing on the sidewalk, looking hot as usual, is none other than Raphael. I knew he had frequented this club before, but the last thing I had expected was for him to be standing out front out of the spotlight or to recognize my best friend.

If Remi wasn't the swearing type, I'm sure he's about to be one soon.

Raphael closes the distance, giving one look to the demonic woman that makes her back away. I consider following her to take her out, because I didn't come all this way to leave empty handed.

"I hope you're prepared to kill, Cami," Remi says, eyeing me in his peripheral vision.

"Raphael? You want me to kill Raphael?" Questioning a demon's death wasn't something I'd ever thought I'd do, but now that I look upon Faith's father, a demi-demon I've grown close to, I'm not so sure I could go through with it. Faith loves him, and he's not exactly the worst demon I've ever met—all things considered.

"It is your job," he reminds me.

Nope. My only job is to prepare to kill my father, not Faith's. I'm sure Raphael has a wicked mean streak, heck, I've seen it, but this is different.

"And your job is to protect me, not tell me what to do."

I'm pretty sure Remi's about to quit, but he doesn't get the chance because Raphael reaches out and touches Cadence's chin, staring deep into her eyes like he's trying to charm her with his demonic abilities.

Leaning close, he says, "It seems I was mistaken about you. I thought you were pure of soul, but it looks like someone else beat me to the claim. Now, which pathetic demon have you aligned yourself with? Surely not Olivia. She has nothing to offer unless you're willing to trade your soul for a night of fun. I wouldn't even ask for your soul for that. Fun comes for free from me."

I blink a few times in surprise. The last thing I expected was for Raphael to hit on my friends. Maybe he never tried anything before because I had claimed Cadence as my human when she asked me for help when I lived with Malicevile. I know he liked Cadence and even offered to trade me something for her, but still. I want to slap that alluring smile from his face. The sudden blush from Cadence's, too.

"Stop looking into his eyes," I whisper into Cadence's ear.

She stiffens before me, averting her attention to a couple who walks along the sidewalk hand-in-hand. "And why does my soul interest you, Raphael?" She slides her hand over the sleeve of his suit jacket, causing him to smile wider—a smile dazzling enough to even enchant me.

"Look at yourself, doll. We could have a good time."

We both giggle. I can't help it, and obviously neither can Cadence. This is going just great. I'm a demon for crying out loud, and I know he's trying to charm his way into Cadence's soul. Thank God I'm the one possessing it, but it's not going to last long.

"Cadence, remember why we're here," Alana says, speaking up for the first time.

Raphael turns his attention away from Cadence. He tilts his head, narrowing his eyes, and then asks, "Why is that? All demonic affairs come through me, and I don't like when someone tries to sneak something past me."

Alana clears her throat. "It's not a demonic affair."

"Then what is it?"

No. Please, don't say what I think you're going to say.

"An angelic one."

Unholy Hell.

SHUT OFF

RAPHAEL TILTS HIS head toward the sky and releases a loud laugh, nearly sending my soul from my body. Nausea rolls through me, and things go from bad to worse as Alana takes matters into her own hands. Without even having to ask, I know Zach put my old guardian up to this. Alana wants Evan back as much as I do, but she didn't see him. She doesn't know what we're about to lose.

I reach out and grab her shoulder. "What do you think you're doing?" I hiss into her ear.

"I'm sorry," she mutters.

"What was that?" Raphael asks.

Alana doesn't respond. Instead, she reaches for her dagger on her hip. The moment her fingers touch the hilt, a red orb bursts in Raphael's hands. It's enough to make Alana take an automatic step back into me.

"Who do you think you are, *human*?" Raphael asks.

Cadence steps between them and holds her hands up. "Wait. We're not here for a fight, Raphael."

"Not with you at least," I mutter.

Raphael narrows his eyes. "You have ten seconds to explain yourselves before I kill you both and give whatever demon holds your souls an early gift."

Sucking in a quick breath, I start to summon my power, but two strong hands yank me back. Jasmine assaults my senses, and I jerk my elbow back and smack Zach right in his collarbone. He doesn't let me go though. Instead, he locks his arms around me in a hold so tight that I can't break free.

"You jerk! You're not supposed to be here." I snarl, feeling my true body peek through. More often than not, Zach's the reason I lose control of my temper.

"Did you honestly think you could fire me? Princess, we're forever and always. An angel doesn't break its vow. Plus, Remi doesn't like you much."

I thrash in his arms. "Let me go!"

"No, not yet."

"We're here to discuss the release of Evan's soul in exchange for the information regarding the transformation of demons," Alana says, speaking up, drawing my attention away from my infuriating guardian.

"Oh, that," Raphael says, his voice cutting through my rage. I freeze, my fiery blood cooling, as I turn my attention to Alana and Cadence. "What I want to know is why would the angelic army want to barter that sort of information for one measly soul?"

The scent of cinnamon and clove trickles into my senses. "I was wondering the same thing," Malicevile says, his charming voice sounding through the air.

My father steps out from the shadows of the building where I notice a side door. Zach squeezes me against him, and my gaze flickers to Remi, who stands within reach of Alana and Cadence.

"Because it's what Cami would've wanted," Alana answers, facing Malicevile head on.

A smile creeps across Malicevile's face when he spots my old hunter guardian. "Little hunter. What a pleasant surprise. I've been waiting to fulfill one of my daughter's last requests. You broke her heart, you know, and for that I thank you. She might've never come to my side had you not. Which is why your death shall be swift and painless." Electricity erupts in Malicevile's fingers. My heart seizes, and I step on Zach's foot as hard as I can before ramming my head into his chin. I'm through waiting to see how this plays out.

"I guess you don't want to know how to transform demi-demons after all. Touch me, and you'll never find out." Alana holds her head high. I'm proud of her in this moment, how she still manages to look evil in the eye without flinching.

"Good girl," Zach whispers from behind me to Alana. We're still visible to her and Cadence. "Keep him talking. Keep him interested. Ask him to see Evan."

"I know you're curious," Alana adds, listening to Zach.

The electricity disappears from Malicevile's fingers. "Silly hunter. I'll humor you because you might be useful one day, but I know it's not you who holds the answers." He searches over the empty parking lot. "And I know you're not alone. Show yourself, watcher. If you don't, the hunters are dead."

"Ask to see Evan first," Zach says to Alana.

"We need to see Evan first," she says.

Malicevile sends a blast of power near her feet, causing her to jump back. I stroll a few feet forward but stop short when my father turns his gaze directly to me. His vibrant green eyes shine in the low lighting of the streetlamps, and his lips curl into a wicked smile. But he's not looking at me.

Footsteps sound behind me as the scent of patchouli drifts closer. Zach yanks me to the side just before Evan walks directly where I was standing. This is one of the few times Zach hides me from him. With a tight jaw, Evan stops at Malicevile's side without giving Cadence or Alana a second glance.

Malicevile slides his arm over Evan's shoulders and squeezes him. "It seems these people want me to return your soul to you. They think it's what my dear Camilla would want."

Evan glowers at Alana. "They have no idea what Cami would've wanted."

Thank you. Of course I know he knows what I really want, but it's nice to have someone stand up for me when Zach makes it impossible to do so myself.

"You make a good point, Evan," Malicevile says. "What is it you think Camilla would have wanted?"

"For you not to have made the deal with him in the first place," I answer.

"I think she would've wanted me to remain where I belong."

"That's not true," I say like everyone can hear me.

"Do you still want to make the deal now, watcher?" Malicevile asks into the air.

Zach sighs next to me. He takes my hand in his, forcing me to look at him. "I'm about to do something I might regret, so if things go south, I want you to get out of here, princess. Remi will see to it that you're safe."

"What are you going to do?"

"What I came here to do."

My forehead crinkles. "I don't understand. How did you know?"

Malicevile steps in our direction. "Watcher? Show yourself."

Zach ignores my father. "I know you, Cami. When you said you were going hunting, what better place to come than the one place I asked you not to?"

Tears burn in my eyes. "You used Alana. You played her emotions."

He shakes his head. "Alana asked to help on her own."

"Then why have me here? You know I'm against this."

"I wanted you to see for yourself. I wanted you to know that Evan's soul would be returned to him."

"And how do you know my father is even going to do it?"

"Hello, watcher. I never thought I'd see you again." Malicevile reaches out and grabs Zach by his shoulder before he has a chance to answer my question. He revealed himself on purpose so he wouldn't have to answer me.

Zach's wings unfurl on his back, blocking my view as he faces my father head on. Both Alana and Cadence back away from Raphael, and he lets them go. Remi reaches out his hands to them, and a moment later, Raphael blasts a red orb where they were standing. Remi concealed them from view, just like Zach still does for me.

"And how brave of you to show yourself after everything we've been through," Malicevile says. He's more familiar with Zach than I was aware of. I can sense they have history. Most angels are familiar with upper-level demons. My father never spelled it out for me, though I know he wasn't always a creature of Hell, but it's been a long time since he's been near Heaven. Their acquaintance leaves me with tons of questions. "Nice wings. I have a pair just like them."

A muscle in Zach's neck bulges as he glowers at my father, knocking his hand away from his shoulder. The angel and demon look about to start a war that I'll have to step in the middle of before they destroy the entire world.

"I don't have all night, so let's work out a deal. I want you to void Evan's contract over his soul with you in exchange for the information regarding demi-demon transformations," Zach says.

My father taps a finger to his chin. "And how do I know you're going to tell me everything I need? How do you even know?"

"Cami confided in someone before her death. And, if I don't, Evan's soul can remain in your possession."

Malicevile's eyes darken at the thought of my death, well, the one I had faked. It's the secret that drives Evan mad since he can't speak the truth thanks to Zach's angelic power. It's the same power Zach used on me so I couldn't tell Malicevile about him before I knew he was an angel.

"The nephilim. Of course she would tell him," Malicevile quips, using his knowledge of my relationship to Dylan to confirm his own suspicions.

"Your daughter was full of surprises. Now, do we have a deal?"

Malicevile shakes his head. "No, keeping Evan's soul isn't good enough for me. If you lie to me, I want your wings."

"No," I whisper. "Zach, I'm serious. Don't do this."

"Deal," Zach says, reaching his hand out to shake Malicevile's.

My breathing quickens as power ripples under my skin. My father will see to it that Zach doesn't hold up his end of the bargain one way or another. And then what? An angel willing to trade their wings to a demon would force them to fall. Zach would be sent to Hell. And then what would I do? This is why I wanted him to stay out of my business. I refuse to be responsible for Zach's fall from grace.

Malicevile grins as he pulls out a small envelope from his pocket. Without having to look at it, I know it contains Evan's contract. It feels weird, knowing something so small contains someone's entire eternity. It makes the small deals with my father, ones based on verbal agreements alone, feel like nothing.

Malicevile tears up the contract before handing it to Evan. "Your soul is now your own."

I hold my breath, expecting the world to stop spinning. I expect the sky to open up to send down sparkles and glitter and confetti—something to celebrate such an important event. I expect Evan to erupt in light. I expect him to smile, to cry, to do anything. Instead, he scatters the pieces of his contract across the dirty cement before crossing his arms. He's totally shut off from the world.

My heart hurts with every beat as I feel it shatter into a million pieces. How cruel of Zach to insist I see how this all plays out. I would have believed him had he just told me it was done. But now, I have to watch as Evan chooses my father once again, and this time without the influence of his tainted soul.

"I'm sorry," Cadence whispers from behind me.

I wipe my hand across my cheek and glance at Remi holding onto both Cadence's and Alana's hands. I meet his gaze. "Get them out of here. It's not safe."

"I'm not to leave you, Cami," he says.

"Do it. Now." I reveal my true body with my words, and Remi pulls my two friends against him before launching into the air. I know he won't go far, but at least no one else has to watch as my life falls apart before my eyes—all my hope for having Evan by my side crushed like the glass bottles littering the concrete.

"...Hell-bound without demonic contract," Zach says. I've been so focused on everything else that I've missed part of the conversation. "Because as you know, demon-bound souls remain on this plane unless ushered to Hell. The soul must go on its own."

I consider throwing power at Zach to shut him up, but then it would breach his contract. I hate how I have to listen helplessly as Zach gives away my biggest secret in exchange for a soul that we don't even get to keep.

"That much I figured out," Malicevile says. "Hell-bound, killed near dawn, have the will to live. Tell me something I don't know."

Zach clears his throat. "Gladly. I bet you didn't know how close Cami was to her nephilim watcher when she was a demi-demon."

"Oh, I'm quite aware she fancied him."

"Cami allowed Dylan into her soul, and Dylan vowed to always protect it. They had made an agreement that if anything were to ever happen to Cami, he'd save her from Hell."

Malicevile's jaw twitches at this information. I don't think

I've ever seen him look surprised before. "You mean that a nephilim risked his soul to travel to Hell to intervene? That would've meant that Cami would've ended up in—"

Zach shakes his head. "No, because Cami decided she wasn't ready to die. She ripped her soul free from Dylan, and because her soul had already touched Hell, it triggered the transformation. She lost her human life, but her demonic blood—your demonic blood—took over. It's how she ended up in the light realm."

Malicevile's eyes darken at Zach's revelation. "So I have all but one thing I need to build my demonic army." In a quick motion, Malicevile jerks his hand out and wraps it around Zach's shirt. "An angel."

A scream rips from my throat when Raphael grabs onto Zach's wings, sending smoke into the air as he touches something godly.

"Well, look at that," Raphael says, turning to Evan. "I think we just found one."

SACRIFICE

PANIC SEIZES MY chest as Malicevile and Raphael attack Zach, lighting the night with red and white power that heats the air with an intensity that settles deep into my bones. The edges of my vision turn crimson red, and I gather all my strength to face the man who threatens to ruin not only my world, but the entire world.

Another scream rips from my mouth, sending a gust of wind at the demons. Raphael sends a lava bomb in my direction. I absorb it into my soul, rushing forward to close the distance.

Malicevile slashes his sharp nails over Zach's wings and

Zach yells out, the black feathers of his wings scattering across the concrete. Zach attacks back, blasting heavenly light through the air. My father grins. His face smokes from the power, but it does nothing to stop him; he punches Zach in the jaw so hard that I hear bones crack.

Zach falls to his knees, taking another bout of power from my father. Malicevile doesn't plan to kill Zach or ground him. He wants to force Zach into submission so he can be the angel he needs to transform demi-demons. And I can't let him even try.

As I rush forward, Remi's hands lock onto the back of my shirt and he pulls me back. I knew he wouldn't be far away, but I can't let him intervene. I don't care what Zach wanted. He might think he's strong enough to withstand my father—and he might be—but if I can do something, I will.

"Let me go!" I scream. "I can't let them do this!"

Remi doesn't listen. He tugs me higher into the air, and I do the only thing I can think of. I release a burst of power into the angel, shocking him enough to loosen his grip. Thrashing, I break free from his hold and fall a dozen feet to the ground. It all happens so fast that I don't have time to concentrate on levitating. My body hits the ground hard, but I don't let it stop me.

I throw another energy orb at Remi as he swoops down to pick me up again, and a shower of sparkles cascade through the air and to the ground. Pain washes over me, making it hard to breathe. I roll to my knees and press my palms into the gritty ground to get back to my feet.

Rushing forward, I dart toward Malicevile and Raphael as they slash their nails across Zach's luminous skin.

"This is for my daughter," Malicevile says, kneeing Zach in the chin, knocking him onto his back before blasting him with another orb of energy.

My blood burns so hotly that I swear my veins glow. I can't watch my father torture and hurt the angel who swore to protect me, all in vengeance for my supposed demise. Because he thinks Zach's responsible for my death.

"Stop!" I scream, summoning power into my hands. The green slime swirls in the perfect ball. I need something other than Malicevile's power to make him stop.

Raising my hands over my head, I chuck the power directly at Malicevile. His suit jacket smokes and he doesn't even know what hit him. I summon Malicevile's power next and shoot a blinding white stream of lightning at Raphael, sending him flying back a few feet.

Before I have a chance to attack Malicevile again, a heavy body collides with mine. I skid across the rough ground, screaming as the asphalt scrapes the skin from my back. Patchouli and amber cloud my senses, and I freeze. Evan hovers over me, his crystalline eyes locking me in a stare I can't seem to break. Zach and Remi might be too hurt to hide me from the demons for much longer.

My breath catches in my throat, facing Evan. I was afraid of this moment, looking into his eyes, knowing that even now, he fights for my father.

Forcing myself to remain in control, I slam my hands into his chest and shove him off me in time to see Malicevile grab Zach by his feet to drag him. Evan reaches out and snatches my wrist, holding me in place.

"Let me go before I hurt you," I snap.

"Sorry, Cami," Evan says, pulling me to him. "Your feather-brain guardian is going to seal my eternity with you." Whatever mind control Zach has done on Evan has worn off. He shouldn't have been able to say my name. The shield must be weakening or already broken.

I jerk in his arms. "Don't do this, Evan. I swear I'll never forgive you."

"We'll see," he says. "Eternity is a long time, and I have a lot of patience."

"I warned you!" I summon hot electricity into my palms and push it into Evan, sending him reeling. Any other time, I would have figured out some other way to get him to see reason and release me, but I don't have time.

"Cami!" Evan yells. His voice echoes through the air as I race toward Malicevile.

Pushing forward, I narrow my eyes on my father. I'd like to ram my knife through him right about now. There's no way I'm letting him get away with this, even if it jeopardizes everything. The angels can try their hardest to shield me from the demons, but they're already failing since Evan saw me. All I need to do is touch my father. All I need to do is show him that I'm not dead.

A brilliant, heavenly light erupts through the air as Remi speeds to earth. I expect him to head toward me, but instead he flies at my father, blasting him with light. He's doing everything in his power to stop me from intervening, even if it means getting himself hurt, or worse, in the process.

Raphael sends a lava bomb at the angel, and it collides with Remi's chest, sending him spiraling through the air and over the building.

This might be my only chance. I can't hide from Malicevile forever, and there's no way in Heaven or Hell that I'm letting him take my guardian from me. He already took Evan.

"Dad!" I yell, my voice echoing through the night. "Dad, stop!"

As the sound of my voice reaches him, my father freezes in place. Without Remi, my protective shield is completely down, revealing me to the world.

Without hesitating, I half-levitate, half-run toward my father and ram my shoulder into his chest, knocking him off his feet. We tumble to the ground with me on top of him. He takes the blunt force of our fall. Locking my fingers to the front of his shirt, I shake him for a moment, and he stares at me with an unfamiliar look frozen on his face.

"Camilla?" he asks, like he's not sure if I'm real or not. "You're alive."

I don't respond to him. Instead, I turn my attention to Zach, who now sits up. Raphael stands nearby, looking between me and Malicevile, Zach long forgotten.

My bottom lip quivers. I never thought facing Malicevile like this would leave me feeling more confused than ever. It's too easy to fall for his familiarity.

"I don't believe it," Malicevile says, reaching up to push my brown curls behind my ears. "You have no idea how relieved I am to see you." He leans up and embraces me, breathing his hot, cinnamon breath against my shoulder.

This was not the response I was expecting. I thought for sure Malicevile would be breathing fire if he ever saw me again. I thought he'd immediately try to rip my heart out. But now, as he leans back to gaze at me again, he looks like he's seeing the best thing in his existence. Like I'm the most important thing in the world to him.

I lick my lips and pull myself together. "I can't say the same thing about you." It takes all my willpower to build a protective wall around myself to stop from falling into old habits. This demon is not my ally.

A flicker of darkness crosses his face, but he doesn't respond. What looks like a million thoughts cross his mind, his diamond pupils expanding and retracting. I wish he'd say something so I'd know what was going through his head. Discovering that his daughter is alive has to leave him with so many questions.

After another long, quiet moment, he says, "They got to you."

I purse my lips. "Nobody got to me, Dad."

"I've underestimated you, Camilla. You went through so

much trouble to get your boyfriend's soul back that I regret not giving it to you in the first place. How could you get yourself into this mess? Your soul—it's—"

"Heaven-bound," I say for him. With a flick of my hand, I point at Zach. "Meet my guardian."

Malicevile glowers. "He won't be for long. You've accomplished what you wanted to do, so now it's time to come home."

I force away the trickle of fear that ices my back. "You're not going to lay another finger on him. That angel belongs to me, and you can't have him."

His jaw tightens. "Don't be silly, my dear."

I dig my nails into his chest, ripping the fabric of his shirt. "I mean it. He's mine. Now, if you don't mind, we'll be leaving."

Malicevile leers at me, curling his lips up to show his teeth. His eyes flash red as he peers long and hard into my eyes. This is the side of my father I remember. "You think I'm going to let you leave? I just got you back. You are *my* daughter. You belong to *me*. I don't care if you gave your soul to some lowly angel or if you think you'll somehow redeem yourself by falling back into Heaven's grace, but all of that can be changed."

His arm flies up, and he locks his fingers into my hair, flipping me up and over him. I smash onto the ground and the air whooshes from my lungs. Malicevile doesn't allow me to stay down long. He yanks me to my feet by my hair, my scalp screaming with pain, before he tosses me onto his shoulder.

He's delusional if he thinks I'm just going to let him carry me away like some misbehaving toddler.

"Grab the angel, will you, Raphael?" Malicevile asks from over his shoulder.

The moment Raphael touches Zach, I break. Bright, heavenly power explodes from my fingers, blasting Raphael into the side of a Hummer. His body dents the door as he slides down, his face blistering from the holy power that fights the demonic power in my soul.

Grabbing the back of Malicevile's jacket, I force him to arch his back a few inches backward. It's enough to flip my legs up to escape. The sudden motion causes my father to stumble. I tuck my head toward my chest as I fly to the ground, barely stopping from smashing my skull when I levitate a mere inch from the asphalt. Swinging my arm out, I lock my fingers around Malicevile's ankles and yank, pulling his legs right out from under him.

Wind whips around me, swirling the scent of jasmine through the air. Zach's back on his feet, his wings expanded wide. He blasts Raphael again with heavenly light, stopping the demon from closing in on him.

Fire lights the darkness behind him when Evan comes to his senses after the shock I caused him. He has a clear shot at Zach.

"Watch out!" I yell, shooting a blast of sizzling power at Evan. He ducks, glowering at me. Malicevile attempts to grab me again, wrapping a strong arm around my waist. We're outnumbered, and my father's too powerful. Hope slowly drains from me, and I meet Malicevile's green eyes when he spins me around.

"Camilla, I don't want to fight you."

"Then let us go."

Zach yells behind me, and I peer over my shoulder. Raphael and Evan manage to restrain him. My chest heaves, a cry ripping from me. Zach's forced to his knees before the demons. His hazel eyes meet mine, courage and strength still lining his eyes, completely opposite from the utter despair that I'm sure shines from mine.

"Not happening," Malicevile says. "I don't care if you hate me for the rest of time. There's no way I'm allowing you to fall back into the angelic army's hands. I refuse to let you fight against me. That is not your place. Your place is by my side whether or not you remain willingly or if I have to chain you to me."

Shaking my head, I let my hair whip my face. "I'd rather die." With a flick of my hand, I yank my dagger from the hip holster hidden under my jacket. I point the dagger to my father first before flipping it to point the blade at my own heart.

Blood trickles as I press the metal into my skin.

"Camilla, no!" Malicevile yells.

"Then let Zach go!" Shadows edge my vision, pain burning through my heart as I press a little harder. "Is he really worth my real death to you? Because I'm not afraid to die. I've been prepared for it since the moment you came setting my world ablaze."

Malicevile studies my face for a second before turning to Raphael. "Release him."

Zach stumbles away, taking the chance to launch into the air. He doesn't leave me, though. He circles overhead, swirling the fragrant air of demons around me.

"Drop the dagger, Camilla."

I don't. All I do is raise one of my hands into the air.

In a quick motion, Zach swoops down and grabs me by the wrist, pulling me into the air. But when Malicevile blasts energy at him, Zach's grip falters. I crash to the ground, my dagger clattering away under a car.

The demons surround me. Even if Zach could get to me, there's no way they'd allow him a second chance to make it out alive.

"Cami." Evan's voice wraps me in warmth, calming the wild fear that swirls through my soul. "We're not your enemies. It's time to come home."

I tilt my head to the sky, meeting Zach's eyes. His brows furrow; he's probably running a million plans through his mind, none of them coming out in our favor. My father doesn't give second chances, and I'm all out of fight.

Slowly, he nods his head. He wants me to go.

I just hope he knows what he's doing.

Releasing a long breath, I wrap my arms around myself. I watch Zach disappear into the night sky, leaving me in the hands of the man I'm supposed to kill, the man I know I'll have to kill. I just hope I'm strong enough. Because in this moment, I realize to succeed, I'll also have to kill the boy I love. He's the one who will stand in my way. But deep in my heart, I know I can't do it.

Warm hands slide under me and pull me from the ground. "Stop acting like this is the end of the world," Malicevile says, cradling me against him.

But it is the end of the world.

And I've lost.

NOT AN OPTION

"I APOLOGIZE FOR not having a room prepared for you, Camilla. Obviously, I thought I was never going to see you again." Malicevile guides me into a huge suite with a king-sized bed resting against a midnight blue wall. A few shelves line other gray walls, containing framed photos with pictures of both me and my dead sister Melanie with Malicevile. He even has one of Evan and me from the first week that I was a demon. Who knew a demon could be sentimental. *He gets that from you.*

"You're insane if you think I'm sharing a bedroom with you," I say. Apparently Malicevile had been busy buying yet another piece of property. The house, which is much smaller than all his other estates, only has three bedrooms, but he turned one into an office. He chose this location because it was near Raphael's, and they have a lot of business to take care of.

"Don't be ridiculous. I'm moving into my office for now. Not like I use this room for sleeping."

Ew. "I don't want to know any more."

He chuckles. "You know I like being a father."

Double ew. "Shut up. I haven't even been gone long."

A knock sounds on the door frame, and a pretty woman in a pencil skirt and blouse holds up a few dry cleaning bags in her hand. Her sandy hair hangs in perfect waves around her shoulders, and when she meets my father's gaze with her turquoise eyes, she beams a smile. "Mr. Hellshire, I've picked up what you have asked for."

A grin crawls up Malicevile's face as he crosses the room and takes the bags from the woman. His hand lingers on hers just for a moment, and she sucks her bottom lip between her teeth.

"Hey, lady. You might want to be careful. My dad is a demon, and he'll steal your soul." I cross my arms over my chest and smirk when the woman blinks the surprise from her eyes. She's definitely only hired help, or else she'd know better than to get all googly-eyed for my father.

Malicevile forces a laugh. "I'm sorry, Cherie. My daughter has forgotten her manners."

Cherie offers a warm smile. "I had no idea you had a daughter. You look too young to be a father of a teenager."

I snort. "Those are the demon genes." I face Cherie. "You should really consider finding a new job. The last assistant my father had died when he lost his temper. Remember poor Rebecca? She was so innocent."

I might've been partly responsible for Rebecca's demise, because she got stuck in the crossfire in a fight between my father and me after the first time I had visited his house. I had no idea until after I transformed into a demon about her death. By that point, I didn't even care. Since then, it's basically always been Evan doing Malicevile's bidding. I guess he's moved up and his position of errand boy was replaced by Cherie since my fake death.

Malicevile heaves an annoyed sigh. "Will you please excuse us, Cherie? Camilla's had a long night and could really use some rest. You can go ahead and take the rest of the night off, and I'll see you tomorrow evening when I get home."

Cherie glances at me before nodding at my father without a word.

"What? You won't be home for lunch, Dad? I hear it's going to be a sunny day. I plan on heading to the beach."

"Camilla."

"Oh, that's right. The sun is for the godly. Like *me*."

Cherie quietly excuses herself when Malicevile glowers in my direction. He closes the distance and locks his firm fingers around my wrists, shaking me once. "Impossible. You are a demon."

I guess I went too far. I should've kept that vital information to myself. It could've been my ticket out of here, and there would've been nothing Malicevile could do about it. Actually, there might not be anything Malicevile can do about it.

"I guess you'll find out in—" I glance at the clock. "A little over an hour."

His jaw twitches as he studies my face to see if I'm purposely just trying to get under his skin. I meet his green eyes dead-on, holding a serious expression.

"So you better enjoy my company now, because the only way I'm staying here is if you chain me to the floor, and even then, good luck to you. My guardian is excellent at his job."

Malicevile surprises me by closing his eyes for a second before he moves to sit on the end of the bed. He runs his hands up his forehead, sliding them over the top of his gelled hair before he links his fingers together on the back of his head.

I shift awkwardly on my feet when he doesn't say anything to me for a good five minutes. The drawn out silence is worse than all the times he yelled and blasted me with his power, because of how unpredictable he is in this moment.

"You remind me a lot of your sister," he says, his voice nearly a whisper. "She always had such strong convictions about her purpose in life. She constantly fought me about everything. She wanted so badly to change the world, to leave her own mark. But she was careless. She thought because her soul was good, that people would just accept her and trust her—she thought she could trust others, too. But what she couldn't see was that people were using her. She was naïve to think that just because she wasn't Hell-bound, that people wouldn't care that she was half demon. It's what got her killed."

"The alliance is practically dead, Dad. You're responsible for their destruction. You know they're no match for demons of our caliber, not since you've kidnapped their best fighters."

"I'm not talking about the alliance, Camilla. You can't honestly think that your little guardian believes you're truly good. You're blind if you don't realize that they're using you. They're losing power and have become desperate. They're relying on the fact that you were once human. They're preying on your humanity."

If only he knew what Zach wants me to do. It's the last thing I'll ever mention, because I'm dead if he thinks for one minute I might cut his heart out when he least expects it.

A thought hits me hard. This whole revelation might actually be a blessing. Because now I'm back in Malicevile's midst. We had planned to surprise attack my father when I was powerful enough, but I can still surprise him now.

"You don't think I know that?" I ask after a moment. "Of course they're using me. I'm their best weapon. But, look what I get in return. I can walk in the sun. Blessed barriers don't have an effect on me. I don't have to worry about other demons trying to hurt me to get to you."

"And how long do you think this is going to go on? You're a demon. Hell runs in your blood. One day, you'll slip up. It might be an accident, but they won't care. They'll rip all they've given away and tear your heart out. And don't think you'd actually end up where you think you belong."

A shiver runs over my back at his words. "I have faith that something like that won't ever happen."

"Faith won't keep you alive. It'll only give you peace when all is lost."

He's wrong. Faith gives me the strength to keep fighting despite all being lost.

I shuffle to the bed and sit down next to him. He slides his arm over my shoulders and hugs me against him. This is one of those moments that plants a seed of doubt in my mind, but then I remember how he attacked Zach. How he ripped feathers from his wings and scratched his arms. It's enough to remind me that Malicevile might be my father, and he might act like a man, but under his charming façade lies a demon who wants to rule the world.

"So, what now? Are you going to lock me away? Treat me like some prisoner?"

"Is that what I need to do to get you to stay? Because I'll put up a million locks if that's what it'll take to keep you from them. You can fight me all you want, Camilla, but you mean too much to me just to let you slip through my fingers again."

I sigh. He'll know something is up if I don't protest. I'm not one to go down without kicking and screaming. Summoning my icky slime power, I mold it into a sphere in my hands. Malicevile watches my new power as I hold it in front of me. "Got this one a couple days ago. Pretty cool, right?"

He narrows his eyes. "It was you who stole my demi-demon."

I ignore him, tossing my power up and down. "I hear it hurts like—"

I drop the power directly on his lap and Malicevile throws out his hands protectively. His fingers smolder when he catches it and tosses it to the floor, the power searing a hole into the wood.

My father roars while he shakes his hands out, pelting the room with tiny slime balls. "Camilla! I thought we were past this kind of behavior!"

"And I thought we were past trying to control me!" I yell right back.

I summon more power into my hands, but I don't make it far before Malicevile tackles me to the floor and shoves my face into the wood. The sleek floor feels cold against my cheek, and I relax as my father's heavy hands shove into my back.

Power blasts through me, sending static through my curly hair. I didn't expect anything less from Malicevile. This is exactly what I wanted. Because I can't sleep on my own, and with the sun close to rising, I'm sure he's going to make it hard to escape. And I need to get a message to Zach. I need him to know I'm okay. I need him to know that I have a plan.

"Stop!" I scream. "Please."

My pleas only make Malicevile push power harder into me. "You leave me no choice, Camilla."

A second later, shadows haze my vision, and I succumb to darkness.

"Your guardian is an idiot." Dylan is pacing in a circle a few feet away when I open my eyes.

His ethereal, golden wings expand out on his back, shading me from the sun overhead. I rest in the warm grass, leaning back on my elbows without moving. Wind created by his wings plays with my hair, sending his rainy apple scent over me in a delicious wave.

"I don't know what he expected to accomplish," I say.

Spinning around to face me, Dylan strolls the few steps between us and plops down on the grass next to me. "When Remi brought Cadence and Alana home without you, I just knew Zach had messed up."

"Alana helped him," I say. I understand why she did it, but it doesn't hurt any less. It's like no one cares about my feelings. "Zach's lucky he didn't get himself killed."

"He knew you wouldn't allow it."

Zach always swore that he had faith in me, and it's not until this moment that I believe it. After everything, he trusted me enough not to automatically go with my father. He trusted that I'd figure out how to get him away unscathed.

"You think? I nearly stabbed myself in the heart to save him."

Dylan releases an angry growl while he shoves his fingers into the grass to rip pieces up. "Oh, love. I swear, anyone who ever doubts your loyalty and goodness deserves a trip to Hell."

His words bring a smile to my lips. "I'm no saint, Angel

Boy. Ask my father. He thinks I'll mess up badly enough for Heaven to turn its back on me."

He groans. "So, Remi was right. Malicevile has you."

My brows crinkle together. "Zach didn't even have the decency to tell you?"

"Zach never came home."

Fear laces around my heart, tying itself into a knot I can feel with every beat. "I don't understand. He saw that there was no way to get me from my father so he left me."

Dylan reaches out his hand and links his fingers with mine. "He'd have never abandoned you, Cami. His sole purpose in existence is to watch you regardless of where you are. You know this. It's not the first time he's planted himself by your side in Malicevile's presence. He just didn't reveal himself."

I guess they're called Demon Watchers for a reason. A sinking feeling settles in my stomach the more I think about Dylan's words. Zach has always kept me on a need-to-know basis. I can't help but think that maybe, just maybe, this might have been his plan all along. He knew I'd have never in a million years agreed to return to Malicevile. I hadn't even planned on seeing him until the final moment before I cut his heart out and sent him to Hell. But why change the game now? Why give up such a powerful secret, risk ruining everything, and put me back where this all started? I can't see the end-game here, and I don't like it.

I glare at my hands. "He's punishing me."

"Now why would you say that?"

"I fired him."

Dylan chuckles. "It doesn't work like that, love."

"Obviously. But why would he do this? I did what he asked of me, and I was happy. Now I'm away from my friends, away from you, and I'm pretty sure I'm going to wake up in a cage."

He leans into me, resting his head on my shoulder. "You'll have to ask him yourself."

"What if I never see you again?" My heart hurts at the thought.

He squeezes my hand in his before kissing my temple. "Don't talk like that. When has distance ever stopped us before? You know I'd travel anywhere to find you."

The world around us starts to shake as reality threatens to pull me back. I shift to face Dylan before I embrace him and breathe in another breath of his scent. "I'm not ready to leave. Let me stay."

He blinks in and out of existence. "Stay safe, Cami."

"Dylan, please."

But he's already gone.

Bolting upright, I thrash around, exploding with bursts of power. Sparks rain down on me and burn small holes into the comforter that covers only half of me. I blink a dozen times, my eyes adjusting to the pale sunlight that shines in through the window.

I'm surprised that I'm not in some cage or closet—somewhere I can't escape. I'm in Malicevile's room.

But I'm not alone.

"You better freaking give me at least five good reasons why I shouldn't blast you all the way back to Heaven." The sweet scent of jasmine permeates the air, covering the lingering scent of cinnamon and clove from the room.

"One, I have great style. Two, you enjoy seeing me shirtless. Three, you'd be lonely without my company. Four, I'm witty. And five, I'll make sure your soul remains safe. Oh, and good morning, princess. It's nice to see you, too." Zach stretches his legs on the bed next to me, but he's not crowding my space with a pillow between us.

His chestnut hair stands up in all directions, and he needs to shave, but other than that, all remnants from last night have disappeared. Including his dirty outfit. It's not until this second that I realize he's wearing something of Evan's. I should know. I bought the button-up because it matched his eyes.

Electricity sizzles in my palms. "You better try harder."

He smirks. "You didn't go through all the dramatics of threatening self-sacrifice just to kill me yourself."

I glower. He makes a good point, but it does nothing to ease the anger, annoyance, and fear twisting through my muscles. "Oh, but I sure want to. I can't believe you, you jerk. You went and took a nice hunt and turned it into my worst nightmare. I was so not ready to return to my father's side."

"You never would've been."

"But why? You could've warned me."

"You'd have never agreed."

"Damn right!" My voice rises through the room.

He reaches out and presses his hand over my mouth. "Calm down, princess. This isn't the end of the world." *But it is!*

People need to really stop saying that. He doesn't remove his hand from my mouth right away so I lick his palm. The gesture startles him since I'd usually attempt to hurt him, and he yanks his hand away and wipes it off on his jeans. You'd think my saliva was made of acid with the face he makes.

"It might as well be the end of the world," I snap. I hunker down and pull the blankets up and over my head.

"What are you doing?"

"Pretending I'm not trapped in a room with you."

"Who said you're trapped?"

I fly out of bed and cross the room. As I reach out to touch the knob, Zach latches his fingers to my shoulders and spins me around. His hazel eyes meet mine for a moment before he wraps me in a hug, covering me with his scary black wings.

"Before you do that, we need to get one thing straight," he says.

"What?"

"We're not leaving here until one of two things happen."

"What's that supposed to mean? You know you can get us out of here whenever."

"Not now. Our mission has been slightly altered. Now that Malicevile knows how the transformation works, we're going to make sure he's never successful. Plus, it'll be easier to hunt when we're amid demons. No one will stop you, daughter of the most powerful demon on earth."

"You really have that much faith, Zach? What are the two things that will happen?"

"Of course I have faith. Look who I'm guarding. And as for the two things, only one is important. We'll leave when you send Malicevile to Hell."

"Okay, but I need to know my other option."

"It's not really an option."

"The other thing is if I die, right?"

He shrugs. "Like I said, that's not an option."

NOT LIKE THIS

UNCERTAINTY HANGS HEAVY in my mind as I think about the new course my life has taken. First, my guardian has lost his mind. Second, Malicevile isn't the one imprisoning me here—it's Heaven. Third, things are about to get tricky. Fourth, I'm not sure my heart can handle the constant pull in different directions.

Even though I'm a demon, I'm still susceptible to demonic charm, and my father is the most charming person. Unless he walks around showing off his true body while killing mercilessly, it's hard to keep focus. He's not an all-around bad guy—and because of that, I'm petrified of the position I'm in. It's unfair, really.

Hours have passed since I woke up this morning, and yet no one has even bothered to check on me. The door is unlocked, I checked that myself, but the moment I had cracked it open, I closed it because I'd rather pretend there's no escape. I have no idea what games my father is playing, but I'm afraid to find out. Just because the bedroom door is unlocked doesn't mean I could safely exit. And because Zach told me of our new plan, it's not like I'm going to even try. So now, I'm entertaining myself by watching my guardian sweat as he does thousands of push-ups without his shirt. It was fun for the first fifty, but now I'm just bored, and it feels wrong flipping on the TV to lose myself in countless hours of shows I'll probably never get to finish watching.

A knock resonates on the door while I pace in figure eights around my room. Zach disappears the moment the door opens, and I turn my back and stare at the wall so I don't have to meet Evan's gaze. His scent wafts through the air, his boots thudding against the wood floors. Warm hands slide around my waist as he hugs me from behind, treating me like no time has passed between us at all. Like nothing has changed.

"Have a good nap, Sleeping Beauty?" he asks, spinning me in his arms. My hands press against his shower-damp, bare chest, and I can't stop my eyes from trailing down to his bone-hard abs he's worked daily to maintain. The corner of his lips curls into a smile, and he wraps his fingers around mine, bringing my hand to where my eyes linger.

He glides my fingers across his skin, and I shiver. Breathlessly, I say, "First you trap me and now you torture me."

He leans closer until our hands are pressed together between us. "You're not trapped here, and if you think this is torture...imagine what I'm going through."

"You? You chose to stay here. You chose Hell, Evan."

He smirks. "That's not what I mean. You torture me, Cami."

"Why?"

He leans even closer, his lips merely an inch away, threatening to brush against mine with his next words. It's enough to make me turn my head.

Evan rests his forehead on my temple, and I glance to the spot Zach last was. Would he leave me if he thought things were about to get hot? Because it sure feels like I'm getting pushed in that direction. I'm not even sure I want to resist. That's why this is torture. I want so badly to fall to my desires, let my demonic side loose, and act like Evan's the only one in the world. Like kissing him is the only way I'll ever survive.

"Because of this," Evan whispers. "You're holding back. I know you want me as much as I want you, but you're torturing us both by pretending to be some godly demon with morals. You know, kissing me won't corrupt you."

"You're the one who should be worried about corruption," I say, fire igniting just under my skin where his fingers trail at the hem of my shirt. "Just because you've regained possession of your soul doesn't mean I'm not going to try to take it."

He hums under his breath. "I'd like to see what you'd give me for it."

My heart. I don't say it, though. Hearing him turn down such an offer could leave me in ruins. Because my heart is worthless to him. If it wasn't, he wouldn't be playing with it now. He wouldn't be trying to cut it open to crawl inside to make me go against the one thing I want for him—which is to remain half human. To not transform into the one thing we used to both hate.

"I don't make deals." My words don't even sound out as I say them.

"Come on, Cami. I've missed you." If he heard me, he doesn't acknowledge it. He runs his fingers up my back, pulling part of my shirt with him so our stomachs touch. He's so incredibly hot, both physically and temperature-wise, that I suck in a breath while tingles wash over me, my body begging to find out where this could lead. "I can't stand you pulling me to you and then pushing me away. Please, can I kiss you?"

The fact that he's asking my permission to kiss me, asking me to let him in again, is enough to make me nod. Because really, what distraction could be better than losing myself in everything that is Evan?

Evan's lips brush against mine, his kiss ever-so-soft and warm that it feels more like a whispered plea. A test to see how I react.

And boy do I react. His lips uncork all my pent-up emotions, and I devour his kiss while he slides his arms around me to lift me from my feet to carry me to the bed. His hands tug at my shirt before my back hits the soft mattress, and then he's lying on top of me, kissing my jawline, down my neck and over my shoulder. His fingers slide under my bra, and he kisses me so deeply that my protest disappears from my mouth as the clasp lets free.

His hot body presses me deeper into the bed, his elbows on each side of me as he slides his tongue over mine, his mouth as sweet as I remember. I let out a small moan that he kisses away.

"You're beautiful," he whispers as he pulls away to admire me. "More beautiful than I remember."

A smile plasters across my face, and fire lights his eyes. Reaching my hands up, I pull him back against me, tracing my fingers around his firm shoulders to link them together on the back of his neck. He buries his face into the crook of my shoulder, his warm breath against my skin driving me insane.

"It's like my mind was clouded the last few months," he continues. "But now I'm seeing and feeling things like I should be."

"And how's that?" I ask, brushing my fingers through his hair.

"With every little piece of my soul, and you fill up every part of it."

I meet him with another kiss. "And I love you with every piece of mine."

He grins as he kisses me more fervently, trailing his hands to my waist. My body explodes with love and passion and desire as I remember what it's like to be with Evan completely—heart, soul, and body—and how much I want to be with him now. I don't even care that night is coming or that the world could erupt in fire and brimstone when my father's through with it. I don't even care that my nosey guardian is probably cursing to high Heaven for me to pull myself together before I let my demon win. But I am my demon, and I've won. If I'm stuck in this house, I'm going to at least enjoy the benefits that come with being with the boy that breaks me and completes me.

Evan shifts the blankets around us, and I gaze into his liquid blue eyes as he captures me in his intensity. Being near him, so vulnerable yet in control, pushes all my worries away. This moment couldn't be more perfect.

And then the scent of jasmine trickles through the air.

"Princess, what did I say about letting yourself get seduced by—"

Evan flies off me and throws a fireball at Zach before I even have a second to register what's going on. Wrapping the sheet around me, I hop from the bed with one hand raised, and I get between the two of them as Evan tries to attack my guardian again, sending a fireball at me instead. The sheet catches fire, leaving me no choice but to drop it to the floor to extinguish it.

"Zach, go wait in the hall!" I yell, pointing at the door. I turn to Evan. "And you, get dressed."

Evan swipes his hand down his face but doesn't budge until Zach crosses the room. When Zach steps into the hall, I turn my gaze back to Evan. His chest heaves with anger, and we stare at each other. This has to be the most uncomfortable situation ever.

"That guy's a pervert," Evan mutters.

I open my mouth to defend Zach, because really, he's not so much a pervert as he is my guardian. If this kind of stuff got to him, he'd end up as one of the fallen ones. He's innocent in a way that he doesn't think anything of it, but I know nothing I can say will make things right for Evan. He sees things through his humanity, his human half. Zach is way above all that. Plus, he interrupted before things went too far.

"Zach's just looking out for me," I say quietly.

"You don't need looking out for, Cami. Especially not now." He points to the door. "And that guy, he's trying to get between us. He's mad because you're here. But make no mistake, I'll kill him if he tries anything stupid. You don't belong with him. You belong with me."

If only he knew. I don't mention it, though. Instead, I close the distance between us and wrap my arms around his neck. I rest my head against his chest for a moment, just breathing in his scent until he relaxes under my touch.

"We'll get this all worked out, okay? You know I love you. You know I want to be with you. But it doesn't mean that I belong with you, Evan." I brush my lips against his hot skin as I say the words. I can't meet his gaze.

He holds me tighter. "You can't leave with him, Cami. You leave, and I will follow. Do you want to lead me back to the angelic army? It's what Malicevile wants."

I frown. "You'd never make it back with that kind of information. Zach will wipe your mind if you even tried."

"You'd really allow him to do that? You'll leave me to face your father's wrath? Because he will kill me, Cami. It's why you're not locked up. He made it clear that if I lost you or if you ran away, and I didn't stop you, he'd destroy me." His chin rests on my shoulder.

Of course my father would threaten something like that. "Then why do you stay?"

"You know why."

"Is it worth the risk?"

"It's my eternity. You'd fight for yours, wouldn't you? I just thought you'd fight with me, you know. After everything, after all the time I gave up. It hurts that you don't want the same thing for me."

I close my eyes to stop them from watering. This will be the argument to destroy everything we are—everything we have together. It's what could end us. "Of course I want to spend our eternity together—it's just—" I pause, inhaling a small breath. "Not like this. Not as demons. I hate what I am. I hate the evil that runs through my blood. I hate that the souls I could possess would be marked for Hell unless I give them to an angel. I hate that I have to do and feel everything with every part of my being all the time."

"Cami, you might hate what you are, but that doesn't mean I will. You don't get to decide what's right for me." He leans back, forcing me to look at him. "And I know this is supposed to be how things are."

I let my hair fall into my face. "You can't know that. You could die and end up in Hell just as easily."

"Who cares? I'm going to end up there anyway. Might as well take a chance."

There's no arguing with him. If he gets the opportunity, he's going to take it, and there won't be anything I can do about it except hope that he can beat the odds. But then what? He'll be just another demon to worry about. He will no longer be the demi-demon I fell in love with. But, I'm not the demi-demon who fell in love with him either.

A small tap on the door brings my mind to the present. Wasting time discussing this isn't going to make a difference. It's just going to take away from the precious time I have with Evan—the time I've yearned and dreamed about. Because, it'll all come to an end.

"Princess," Zach calls. "Can I come in now?"

Evan ignites another fireball in his hands. With a quick touch, I snuff the fire out before I move to hand him his clothes. I slip into my own clothes when he dresses, and then I pad across the room to open the door for Zach.

I give Evan a warning look. "Zach is my guardian and not a threat to you. Please, behave. I swear I won't try to run away."

Evan's cheek twitches as he clenches his jaw. "And if he tries to take you?"

Zach huffs. "If I wanted to take her, she'd already be gone."

"He's right, Evan," I say.

"Then why are you here?" Evan asks Zach.

"You might not believe me, but Cami means a lot to me, and I'd never trust her life with anyone else. I'm here to protect her from your world. To shield her when need be, to help her with her heavenly duties, and to keep her on track."

Evan steps closer to me and drapes his arms over my shoulders, holding me against him. Being Hell-bound makes him more jealous and possessive than he was when I first met him. He'd have never given Zach a second thought. I admit it, though. I like this side of him.

"The only protecting she needs is from you when you don't find her useful anymore," Evan says, his voice low.

"My job is a lifetime commitment and not based on Cami's usefulness. So, you better get used to me because Cami's immortal."

Aw, Zach's a little possessive, too. I smirk at my guardian. I can't help it. "Eternity is a long time to shadow me, Zachy-poo. You sure you're up to it?"

"Forever, princess. I'm your sidekick."

Evan huffs, clearly annoyed by our playfulness. "Don't get too attached, Cami. You know I'm going to tell your father. Zach has no business being involved in demonic affairs."

I don't let his words get to me, because I knew he'd never willingly keep my guardian a secret, not when my father would love to use Zach. My expectations have hit rock bottom the last few weeks. It keeps me from being disappointed.

I spin to face him. "I know. And that's why I'm going to apologize now."

"For what?"

Evan doesn't even have a chance to fight before I hold him while Zach covers his eyes with his hand. A moment later, Evan slides to the floor as Zach wipes away his existence from his memory.

Zach helps me move Evan to the bed, where I sit down on the edge and face my guardian. Through the window, I see the sun hanging low in the sky, casting a hazy glow over the room. It won't be long before my father returns to this world, fire blazing in his eyes.

"We have about ten minutes," I say. "What should I do when my father returns?"

Expanding his wings out on his back, Zach turns his gaze to where I'm looking at the sunset. "How do you feel about going on a hunt?"

I frown. "Malicevile will never allow it. He probably won't even let me leave this room."

He taps his chin and hums. "I'm sure you'll figure it out, princess."

With his words, he disappears from view, leaving me with Evan, who shifts on the bed before opening his eyes. He smiles when I look at him and opens his arms wide for me to fall into. Snuggling up next to him, I run my hand over his chest.

"Your father's going to be upset I didn't get everything done that I was supposed to," he muses, way happier than he was moments ago. Thank God for a little heavenly power to change the mood.

I silently thank Zach. "He'll get over it. Because you're mine now."

"I am, am I?"

I smile. "Always."

HEAVEN AGAINST HELL

"NO." MY FATHER turns his back on me and struts to the bedroom door.

With a flick of my hand, I blast a slime ball at the wall near his head. "I wasn't asking for your permission! If you expect me to remain here and by your side, it's going to be by my rules."

He spins and glowers. "So, you want to stay?"

I close the distance and place my hands on my hips while levitating a foot to meet his gaze. "Yes."

"Why?"

"Because I'm not leading you to the angelic army."

He taps my forehead. "My beautiful, intelligent daughter.

That doesn't matter. I have patience. The angels will come looking for you."

"So, until then, you're going to do as I say. Evan is mine and only mine."

"Did he give his soul to you?"

"He doesn't have to. And I'm not letting you destroy whatever good is left in him, got it?"

He rolls his eyes. "Anything else, my dear?"

I straighten my shoulders. "I'm going out with you wherever you go."

He lifts an amused eyebrow. "You'll be bored. Why don't you and your half-breed enjoy a quiet evening here? I know Cherie would love to help you turn this room into something more to your liking."

If anything, I'll scare Cherie off to make sure she doesn't end up dead. "Hanging out with you sounds...delightful, though."

"Camilla." He reaches into his pocket and pulls out his wallet before handing me a grand in cash. "Find something else to do because you're not coming with me."

"Whatever." I'll just follow him.

He leans over and kisses my forehead. "I honestly never thought I could miss this, but I did. I'm happy you're back in all your infuriating, stubborn glory. Now, I'll be back around midnight. We can enjoy a late dinner."

"I'm ordering pizza."

"Then save some for me."

When he opens the bedroom door, Evan waits on the other side with his arms crossed over his chest. Malicevile whispers something I can't hear in his ear, and Evan nods while glancing in my direction.

"Hey, you can't tell him what to do," I say.

My father only laughs as he strides down the hall, leaving us alone. I wait until I hear the garage door hum before I run back into the room and grab my leather jacket off the chaise lounge. Peering around for a second, I narrow my eyes at a framed display case hung on the wall with a few weird daggers in it. I knock it over, shattering it on the wood floor, and I scoop up a knife with a golden hilt. It looks old, like hundreds of years old. I prick my finger on the end of it and watch blood pool on my fingertip. It's still sharp. It should do.

Evan locks his fingers around my arm, stopping me in place. "Where do you think you're going?"

"Come on, I need to catch up to my father before he disappears," I say, forcing him to stroll along with me.

"We can't just enjoy more alone time?" he asks, hooking his fingers around my waist to play with the curve of my hips. "I know you want to."

I sigh. *I will not be seduced. I will not be seduced. I will not be seduced.* "That's tempting and all, but I've been here all day, and I want to get out. I want to have some fun."

"Your kind of fun looks a little scary," he comments, motioning at the dagger.

"Did getting your soul back turn you into a softie? 'Cause I can fix that." I lean up and nip his lip once, leaning back before he can kiss me.

He grins. "You're going to get me into trouble."

"I'll make sure to be the one who punishes you then." I stroll away, smiling at his excited expression, his blue eyes lighting with fire.

He matches my pace as I nearly run from the house to find my Mustang parked in the driveway. Evan tosses me the keys without me having to ask, and I get behind the wheel and start up the engine, feeling it vibrate under me.

I fly out of the driveway and floor it through the neighborhood. Malicevile's already out of sight, but I don't need to see him when I have an aerial view coming directly from my guardian. Evan doesn't have to know that, though. He can think I'm a badass at tracking.

"Princess," Zach whispers, dropping into my backseat. He's shielding himself from Evan, so only I can see and hear him. I'm surprised, though, because I know he'd like nothing more than to remind Evan that we're the ones in control. "Malicevile just pulled into an apartment complex about a mile from here." He quickly gives me directions before he stands and launches into the air from my backseat.

I spot Malicevile's Maserati parked in the middle of the small apartment parking lot, not even in a space. He blocks two cars in, his car still idling, and I pull around to the side street to park.

Evan exits before me, shaking his head when I rush to stop

him in his tracks. I'm not just going to pop in and surprise my father during a business meeting, but what I will do is wait for him to leave so I can find out whatever he's doing from the demon he's visiting. And I can tell it's a demon from here. The air is thick with the scent of incense, which is quite funny considering it makes the place smell like the converted church I live—lived—in.

Pulling Evan along with me, I stroll down a cracked cement walkway, passing overgrown bushes and a few opened windows protected only by flimsy screens. Whoever lives in this building must be used to living with the constant nagging fear caused by demons or else they'd be locked away tight.

Evan strolls to the corner of the building ahead of me, and I linger a few feet behind him. The noise of a television hums through one of the windows, and I peek in and see a couple making out on the couch. Now that's one way to ignore the fact that evil lives next door. They don't even glance up as I blatantly watch them. It's not until a cool hand rests on my shoulder that I figure out why.

"Let's make it fast, princess," Zach says from behind me.

He disappears when Evan peers over his shoulder at me. Strolling forward, I stop just at the edge of the building, holding onto Evan's muscular arm. I lean forward an inch to see if I can get a good view of what's going on.

Malicevile shakes a familiar woman's hand on the front porch of a middle apartment before turning his head to look in my direction. She's the one from the light prison realm. I scramble back out of view, knocking into Evan, who steadies me on my feet. With a smile, I stand up on my tiptoes and give him a soft kiss before I slide the gold-hilted dagger from my belt.

"No demon will take you seriously with that," Evan whispers, trying to snag the blade from me.

I gently press it against him, cutting a small hole in the front of his shirt. "That's the point. Unlike my father, I don't need to act like the most terrifying monster around to be one."

He smirks. "You're hot when you talk like this."

"Just wait until you see me in action." I summon a small burst of angelic light in my hand and soak the blade with it until I can sense that it'll do the job.

I press my index finger to Evan's mouth to cut off any more of his words. Being here, lurking in the shadows with him, stirs up a few memories from when we used to collect souls together. It was a game for the both of us, and I thrived off tormenting the damned. And really, being here, even with a Heaven-bound soul, is no different except that my victims have changed. And hunting demons is way more thrilling. They never cry during confrontation and always fight back. My demonic blood loves the thrill.

Footsteps sound through the night, and my father finally heads back to the parking lot, leaving the demonic woman behind. She closes the screen door to her apartment, but not the regular door. I link my fingers through Evan's hand and tug him along with me.

"You want to know about Pricilla?" Evan whispers as we rush toward the door.

I freeze in my tracks. "You know her?" Why wouldn't he? He's been by my father's side for months. Maybe following my father around wasn't the best approach, not when Evan could lead me to every demon he knows in the area—that is, if I can convince him to do so.

He nods. "Yeah. Her power's like mine, but ten times more powerful. She could knock you back a few feet and burn this place down in seconds if she wanted to."

Interesting. I've always admired Evan's power and have loved using it whenever I borrow it. It might be a nice addition to my growing collection. Way better than tornado breath and slime balls.

"That sounds awesome."

"Malicevile thinks that's what will happen when I transform. My power will increase."

I frown. Talking like it's a sure thing leaves a bad feeling in the pit of my stomach. Sucking in a breath, I force myself to smile without commenting. I nod and pull him forward with me.

I don't even have a chance to raise my hand to knock on the screen when the demon, Pricilla, appears before me. She flicks her gaze from mine to Evan's before she opens the door. Her slick straight hair is cut in an angled bob, brushing her sharp chin. She narrows her amber brown eyes while clenching her fingers into fists at her sides.

"What are you doing here, half breed, and who is this?" She crinkles her nose, giving me a once over.

I step in front of Evan, half blocking him. "I assume my father hasn't mentioned my return from the dead."

Her face softens for a moment. She takes an automatic step back as I take one closer. Her dark auburn hair shines with golden streaks in the harsh lighting from a torch lamp positioned in the corner of her small, though nice, apartment. It's classy with modern furniture and doesn't look like it belongs in this run-down building. The perfect lifestyle for an upper-level demon who doesn't meet my father's power but is working her way up in the world. She probably chose to assist my father for that very reason.

"How? Your father said—" She flicks her tongue over her lips, pausing. "Why would he lie? I attended your funeral."

Oh, that. I try to suppress the memory of my father holding what was more of a spectacle than a memorial in my honor. Zach let me go to see things for myself, and I'd never seen him so riled up. He actually acted like he cared, not like the guests who attended to honor me even cared—except for Faith. I still feel guilty that she had to go through that—and that she probably still doesn't know. Not if Malicevile hasn't told his minions. Raphael probably wouldn't tell her either. He actually might care about her heart and wouldn't want to get her hopes up. At least, that's what I think he'd do. I guess the only way to find out is to ask.

I don't respond right away. I can't. Because a moment later, the scent of cinnamon trickles through the air, and my father comes up behind me. So much for thinking he left.

He clears his throat. "Evan, take Camilla home immediately."

I swivel on my feet to face my father. He clutches a thick envelope in his hand. He must've gone to his car to retrieve it instead of actually leaving. I sure got ahead of myself. But that's not going to change why I'm here. I have a job, and my mind is already set.

Evan tugs on my arm, but I hold firmly in place. I know if I move, I'll lose my opportunity.

Sweat trickles on my forehead, and a tiny bit of fear sneaks up on me at the worst possible time. Demons can sense fear. *Crap. Crap. Crap.*

"Camilla," Malicevile says.

As he steps forward, I yank my arm from Evan and push him toward my father. It gives me the opportunity to enter the apartment and close and lock the door behind me. It won't stop my father, but it'll slow him down.

The room lights up as Pricilla ignites fire in her palms. The fire glows more intensely, the flames blue instead of the orange I'm used to. She doesn't back away from me but instead faces me head on.

"What are you doing?" she asks. "You're putting me in a terrible position. I don't want to hurt you."

"I'm sorry," I say. I don't know why I suddenly feel the need to apologize to a woman I don't even know.

Loud banging on the door forces me to step forward. Pricilla holds her fire out at me but doesn't launch the ball. She must not know that nothing she does to me can physically hurt me if I expect it, and I'm ready to absorb that tantalizing power of hers to keep it as my own.

"Princess, now!" Zach's voice rings in my ears as he appears by my side.

The demon's eyes widen in surprise, but she kicks into action a second later, shooting the fire at my guardian instead of me. Rushing forward, I plow into Pricilla, knocking her back and off her feet. She struggles beneath me, and I latch my fingers around one of her wrists, trying to hold her in place long enough so that I can send her to Hell.

With her free hand, she slaps me across my face, knocking me off her. Hunting demons of her caliber is a lot easier when I had Cadence by my side. And Zach, he's useless in this moment. He's not going to risk using powers that might leave behind traces of himself. Because then, Malicevile will know he's by my side. He'll figure out how to get Zach to show himself, and then I'll either have to kill my father immediately or die trying. Neither I'm ready to do at the moment.

And I think Zach knows this.

"Hurry, princess," Zach whispers. The front window shatters. I have only seconds to complete my mission before my father forces me to fail.

Pricilla climbs on top of me, pressing my face sideways into the musty carpet. She holds me down but doesn't attack me. All she does is restrain me. It's a different move from all other de-mons who find themselves in her position. Most would attempt to take me out. It might have to do with the fact that Malicevile is close.

"You're protected by a warrior. Heaven must really like you," Pricilla says as I struggle beneath her. "Does your father know?"

My silence answers her question.

"Camilla!" Malicevile roars from the shattered window while pushing glass out of his way to come in.

Zach disappears along with his jasmine scent, leaving me alone. If my father gets to me before I can overpower Pricilla, I'm doomed.

"I can't wait to see the look on his face when I tell him," she says.

A million scenarios race through my mind. I should've just waited and came back later. I was stupid to think that I could possibly succeed. And now, this woman is just waiting for my father to come in and win him over with her charm. Because she was smart enough not to try to kill me. *Oh, unholy Hell.*

I do the only thing I can think of. I scream.

A long, agonizing wail escapes my lips, startling the woman enough that I break my hand free, cutting the woman's leg with my dagger as I pull it up.

"Dad, help!" I yell when she snatches my wrist, digging her nails into my skin.

Electricity lights the air as Malicevile sends a small jolt of energy directly into Pricilla's back. She meets my gaze dead-on, and surprise widens her amber eyes when I thrust my dagger forward into her chest.

In one last effort to save herself, Pricilla ignites the blue fire in her hands. She shoves her palm to my chest all while bleeding out right onto my face. I absorb her power, shifting the dagger, twisting the blade in her chest.

My father hovers over me, blocking the light, and I slide the blade free. But Pricilla isn't dead yet. As my father reaches down to grip her shoulders, I punch my hand directly into her chest, scraping my fingers on the sharp edges of her shattered ribcage. Her heart pulses within my locked my fingers. Malicevile jerks the demon back, but it's too late for her. Her heart remains beating in my hand for a second longer before she explodes in a spray of dark crimson, almost black blood.

My vision tints as a rush of energy runs through me, burning me from the inside out. My soul screams, the new power latching to me, burrowing so deeply that I'm afraid the heat will sear my soul and burn what's left of the heavenly light that remains at constant battle with the darkness I allow to consume me.

With a thud, I hit the carpet. The room spins out of control. My stomach twists, the vile power creeping through me, and it takes everything in me to hold onto my consciousness. Malicevile stands over me, and I blink, watching his lips move, but I can't hear him. All I can hear is the roar of flames licking through me. If I didn't know any better, I'd think I was actually burning alive.

Bending down, Malicevile reaches out and tucks his fingers into my arms before lifting me to my feet. He holds me out in front of him, inspecting me. I think he's saying my name, but he's not yelling. He doesn't even look angry. His eyes crinkle in the corners, his lips twisting downward, and then he drops me. Smoke drifts from his fingers, his hands blistering, and he stands there frozen in shock. It wasn't my new demonic power that burned him. It was the heavenly light that emanates from my skin. My body is attacking itself. Heaven against Hell, and neither seems to be winning.

But there's nothing I can do. I'm not letting go of any of the power. I can't.

Another figure appears beside me, and Evan touches his fingers to my cheeks. Their worry seeps into me, causing me to panic.

I lick my lips, trying to find my voice, but nothing happens. Everything—the power, my soul, my humanity, my demon blood—it's all consuming.

The edges of my vision darken, and I swear I see Zach lingering behind my father. But he doesn't turn to see my angel. All he does is gaze down at me.

A moment later, Zach's eerie wings expand on his back, and the black feathers appear as dark as the void that steals my consciousness.

SAME BLOOD

"CAN'T YOU SEE she's in pain? You have to do something!" Dylan's voice rips me from the numbing darkness.

"She needs the heavenly light to stay anchored to this plane." Zach's voice remains even.

"But it's hurting her."

"And she'll pull through it. Give her credit. She's more powerful than anyone believes."

"Not if it makes her self-destruct."

My head spins as two of the guys closest to my heart argue over what's best for me without even asking my opinion. That seems to be how it always works. Everyone assuming what I should do, be, feel, not feel, love, hate, fight for, fight against—constantly pushing and pulling me, claiming to know what's best. But in the end, no one really knows the answers to any of this. No one knows me better than I know myself. And it's time that I remind them.

Sitting up on my elbows in the soft grass of my familiar dream garden, I blink away the dark blue stars dancing around my vision. Both Dylan and Zach turn their attention to me, but only Dylan moves forward to close the space between us before dropping down next to me to hold me in his angelic arms.

His dewy apple scent pushes away my splitting headache, and he holds me without speaking for a long moment. I snuggle against him, enjoying the coolness of his arms and the palpable love he has for me, something I can only feel when our souls are so close.

I can also feel Zach's soul, and his purity is unlike anything I've ever felt before. It's hard to explain, how his soul can feel so deeply for me in a love unlike Dylan's. A love I've never felt in this state. The only thing I can compare it to is the love I feel for my parents—not my demon dad—but my birth mom and the man who raised me as his daughter. But even then, Zach's love can't compare. It's selfless, irrevocable, unwavering. Loyal. Unchanging.

My gaze flickers to his, and he greets me with his easygoing smile. "No wonder the nephilim likes to visit you in your dreams. They're quite lovely."

I open my mouth to say that they haven't always been this

nice, but instead say, "What are you doing here? Shouldn't you be watching my body?"

He shrugs. "I am, and you're fine. Quite heavenly, actually. Your father is very displeased that he can't touch you at the moment without getting burned by your holiness."

I snicker, bumping my shoulder against Dylan's. He doesn't return my smile though. "I bet."

"I've never heard someone swear so much at Heaven."

"Okay, I need to see this. Wake me up."

"Not so fast," Dylan says, lacing his fingers through mine. "Your body is in a lot of pain. It's threatening your soul."

I frown. "What?" My soul hasn't been put at risk since I gave it to Zach. That's what he's for, to take care of it.

"Don't let him worry you for nothing, princess. Your soul is fine. I promise. I won't let anything happen to it." It's like Zach's read my mind. But something in Dylan's expression makes me worried. What could possibly happen to my soul with all the demonic power attaching to it?

Dylan glares at Zach. "Don't you think you've kept enough secrets from her? You might have her best interest at heart, and you might think you're doing Cami a favor, but you are not the one who should make these types of calls. It's her soul. She should know what's really happening."

Oh, God. When Dylan wants to include me in on a secret, it must mean it's serious. "Hell's trying to sway me again, right?"

Deadpan. Zach gives nothing away.

"It's worse?" I can't think of anything worse.

With a sigh, Zach says, "I don't know, honestly. It seems that the sudden influx of demonic power isn't boding so well with your Heaven-bound soul. And it's not helping that the angelic light wants to battle with it."

"Seriously? I think Heaven and Hell have chosen the wrong person to fight over. I'm really not that special. I'm not even confident in my choices half the time." I glance up at the sky before looking at the ground, like these places actually hide in the clouds and under my feet. "Did you get that? I'm not worth the struggle." I wonder if anyone besides my angels is listening.

Dylan squeezes my hand. "Stop doubting yourself, love."

"I just don't want to be a disappointment if I fail."

"You're not going to fail," Zach says.

"So what now? I can't fight for the world if I'm stuck here."

"I think you should expel Heaven's light," Dylan says.

Zach scowls. "Please, don't. You know how terrible the daylight realm is. It's such a waste of our time."

"Then what do you suggest, Zachy-poo?"

"Can you dispel one of the demonic powers? How about the weird breath one?"

"That's like asking me to cut out one of my organs."

He rubs his chin. "Not all of them are necessary."

I glower.

Twisting his lips to the side, he stares at me a moment before saying, "There has to be a way."

Thoughts swirl through my mind as I think about how Malicevile does it. And then it clicks. He gets his power from souls. Collecting them and keeping them has not only allowed him to possess his infinite, unstoppable power, but it also makes him stronger, faster, and nearly impossible to kill. I never asked how it worked, but I know it does work.

"Souls," I whisper. "It's how Malicevile does it. It's how Heaven and Hell do it, too. You know that. It's why the balance is off. Because demons are trapping souls in the earth plane."

Both angels look at me with curious expressions.

"You can have mine," Dylan says quietly. "If that's what it takes to help you. It's yours."

I shake my head. I could never ask him to do that. I could never damn him to save myself.

"I bet your boyfriend would give you his," Zach says.

I grimace. "He just got it back. I can't ask him. Plus, his is on the wrong team. I think I need a good soul."

"Well, I don't think that's going to be possible, princess, unless you take Dylan up on his offer."

"But then he'd lose his wings. My dad said that even nephilim can fall." Tears prickle in my eyes at the thought. "I won't do it. I'd rather suffer."

"Sometimes sacrifices must be made for the greater good, love. Please, accept my offer." Dylan leans into me, hugging me to him. "I know you'll treat it with care. I trust you."

But I don't trust me.

"We could ask Cadence."

I sigh. "No."

"Stop being stubborn, princess," Zach says. "As long as I'm your guardian, I'll make sure you don't accidentally usher a soul to Hell. You can return it as soon as your mission is complete."

He's starting to sound like the warrior the demonic woman called him. "Can't you just find me a soul that's unattached to a body or something? I'd feel better with a stranger."

"Angels don't keep souls lying around, princess."

His comment strikes a thought within me. Gasping, I wave my hand over my face while smiling. I don't know why I didn't think of it before, and it'll be a heck of a long shot, but I do know someone who leaves souls lying around: Malicevile. He also happens to have the one soul I could use. The soul I need.

My sister.

Dylan glances at Zach. "What's happening to her? Is she okay?"

I lightly smack his arm. I guess it's been a while since he's seen me glimpse an ounce of hope.

"I think she has an idea."

"Shut up, you two. I'm sitting right here. And I do have an idea. I know of a Heaven-bound soul in the possession of a demon that I can take." I beam a brilliant smile at Dylan. "Melanie's. My father said he could keep her soul since she was a part of him. He didn't want her to go to Heaven."

"He what?" Zach asks in shock. I just assumed he knew so I never thought to tell him.

"Yeah, he keeps her soul somewhere. I just don't know where. But if we can find her, I can take her. Souls in my father's possession act the same to me as if they were mine as long as I can touch them. We share the same blood and all."

"Okay, but how do you expect to steal a soul, especially your sister's soul, from your father?"

My spark of hope suddenly snuffs out. "I have no idea. I can't exactly get it if I'm unconscious."

Zach blows out a heavy sigh. "I guess the nephilim gets his wish. You're going to have to dispel Heaven's light so you can function when you're awake. And then, you have seven hours to find your sister's soul and take possession of it or plan to spend the day with Malicevile."

This night couldn't get any worse.

DON'T BELONG

I THRASH ON the bed, pain searing through me. Every breath I take hurts worse than the one before, and if I can't stop the pain soon, I'll black out again.

But how?

The thought was just in my mind before I opened my eyes, and now it's gone, like the pain suddenly stole all my thoughts away so I have to focus solely on my body as it fights with itself. Power against power, Heaven against Hell, my soul against my demon side.

Taking another deep breath, I scream.

Warm hands grip my shoulders, pressing me down. My

levitation kicks on, sending me into the air, before I'm pushed back down again. Through my blurry eyes, I glimpse a silhouette in the soft lamplight, but I'm so overwhelmed with agony, I can't concentrate on figuring out if it's Zach or someone else. If only I could smell something—but even that sense is gone, too.

"Cami! Cami! Please, tell me what happened. What did that demon do to you? I can't help you if I don't know what's wrong." It's Evan.

His deep voice wraps around me, and I cling to his every word. It stirs a memory within me, and it's enough to remind me of what I have to do.

Raising my hands up, I blast my heavenly light at the ceiling. The force of the power is great enough to knock Evan off his feet, sending him to the floor. Voices yell, furniture topples to the ground with a thud, and glass shatters. Chaos ensues as I dispel every ounce of the heavenly light as fast as I can.

My body lifts from the bed, and I rise toward the ceiling, my back arching, my skin glowing. It's bright enough that it burns my eyes, so I close them and concentrate on the redness of my eyelids.

"Cami, stop!" Evan yells.

But I can't.

I won't.

It's the only way to make the pain stop. It's the only way to get the power in my soul to stop fighting.

The faster the power leaves me, the more anxious and frightened I become. Every negative emotion comes swirling from the dark depths of my mind, threatening to leave me useless. Because even though my soul is Heaven-bound, everything else belongs to Hell, and the more demonic power I possess, the more unbalanced I become. It feels like the weeks after Malicevile shoved his power into me all over again when my soul hadn't decided whose team to play on. It feels like at any second, my soul will fissure and split all over again, allowing the most evil parts of Hell into my soul to sever my ties to Heaven.

As the last bit of icy power exits my body, I vault toward the ceiling. A wave of warmth rolls over me like I'm sinking into a hot tub, and then I hit the ceiling with a bang before losing my levitation to drop back to the bed.

When my back hits the soft blankets, my ears ring and my eyes water. A second later, all falls silent. No one moves or breathes. No one rushes to my side. If I didn't know any better, I'd think I had suddenly developed the power to stop time, or maybe I just lost my hearing.

"Cami?" a voice whispers in my ear, but I can't turn my head. Exhaustion blankets me, threatening to take me from the world. "Cami, can you hear me?"

I take a moment to swallow, my throat burning from the forced expulsion of air when I screamed, before I raise my hand up a few inches. Hot fingers lock onto mine, holding my hand tight, and then Evan bends over me to look into my eyes.

He's crying. One of his hot tears drips onto my face, and I blink. I can't remember a time I have ever seen him cry. Even before he had traded his soul to my father he was always so in control. But now, he just looks tired and broken.

"I thought Heaven was taking you," he whispers. "I thought I had lost you."

With my free hand, I reach up and rub the pad of my thumb under his eye, swiping away another tear. "I'm still here," I whisper.

He nods while bending down to rest his head on my chest. "I can't stand this. I can't handle knowing that one day we'll be apart forever."

"I know." Because it hurts me just as much. The odds are against us. "But I can't help you, Evan. I don't have that kind of power or authority."

Sliding his arms around me, he pulls me into his lap. "I don't want to talk about this now. The last thing I want is to argue. Please, just kiss me."

So I do.

Slowly, I brush my lips against his, feeling the softness and sweetness of his kiss as he reacts to my closeness. His patchouli and amber scent washes over me, pushing my thoughts away, and I sink deeper into him. His love swells over me, surrounding me with the good left within him. This isn't a kiss of seduction and desire. It's a kiss that reminds me that Evan loves me and how much I love him. How much I need him in my life. That no matter what side we're on or who is against us, he is my soul mate. I've felt the connection since the moment I laid my eyes on him. And my connection to him in this moment is stronger than ever.

After a long moment, Evan pulls away but keeps me firmly in his arms.

Someone clears his throat from the doorway, and I bring my gaze up to meet my father's green eyes. He doesn't smile or rush to my side. Instead, he holds his blistered face expressionless.

"What happened to your face?" I ask.

"You happened, Camilla. It seems Heaven decided to use its power against you. It was burning you up from your soul. And you thought they were on your side." He strolls forward and sits on the bed next to us. Gently, he glides his fingers over my arm but nothing happens. My angelic light is officially gone. "At least you managed to get rid of it."

I suck in my bottom lip for a moment at his comment. If I hadn't talked to Zach before this, I might have believed my father. Because it did feel like Heaven's light was rejecting me, but in reality, I was rejecting the light with all the extra Hell power. Power no one knew I was even capable of absorbing and keeping for myself forever.

"That doesn't make any sense," I say, even though I know I should keep my mouth shut. "I'd think they'd thank me for killing that demon."

"It was self-defense, Camilla. Had I known Pricilla would've tried to hurt you, I'd have reconsidered all the deals we made. But I suppose that doesn't matter now." He links his fingers together in his lap. "Raphael will be disappointed, though. He had taken a liking to her."

Who wouldn't have? She was gorgeous in her human façade. And she was technically nice because she wasn't trying to kill me. A hint of guilt creeps through my mind, but I push it away as quickly as it comes.

"I'll make sure to send him a card," I say, sarcasm lining my voice. It's the only way I know how to deal in this moment.

"You can tell him yourself if you'd like. He's waiting for me in the hallway."

I had thought I heard more than two voices. I point to my father's face. "Did I...to him?"

He nods. "He actually got the worst of it, my dear."

Whoops. "Yeah, I'll pass for now. Give him time to heal first."

Malicevile chuckles. "That's probably a good idea. Now, if you'll forgive me, I have another appointment I'm late for. This time, please stay here until I get back. I'd like to spend some time with you later before sunrise."

He might get a whole lot of bonding time with me if I don't figure out where my sister's soul is. He's made it too easy to forget that I'm supposed to be on a mission. "You can't make me stay," I say, automatically arguing. It's what I do best with him. I hadn't actually planned on following my father, but he'd get suspicious if I didn't say something otherwise.

"I can try, but I really don't want to. For once, can you stop being difficult?"

"Under one condition," I say.

"What, my dear?"

"I want to see my sister's soul."

His smooth face turns serious as he lowers his brows and bares his teeth at me. "Why?"

"Because she's my sister."

"You're lying."

"Make the deal."

"Absolutely not." Without another response, Malicevile stands from the bed and strides across the room. He doesn't even look at me as he slams the door. Then, I hear him lock it. Awesome.

The scent of jasmine tickles my senses. "Smooth going, princess. Did you really think that was going to work?"

I wrap my hands around Evan before he can jump to his feet to attack my guardian. In a quiet voice, I say, "Don't try anything crazy, Evan. Zach never leaves my side. If you didn't try to hurt him or tell my father every time he shows up, you would already know."

"This is his fault," Evan practically spits out.

"No, this is my fault." I close my eyes and summon the fire power I acquired from killing the woman tonight. It ignites blue in my fingers. "As it turns out, I get to keep the power of some of the upper-level demons I kill."

"Princess, don't give away all our secrets," Zach warns.

Evan reaches out and runs his hand over my new power. It jumps from my hand to his, and he cups the flame. He can't absorb it, so he snuffs it out a moment later. "Cami, do you know what this means?"

"That I'm awesome?"

He doesn't find my joke amusing. "No. It means that you're going to have an even bigger target on your back. It's bad enough that demons see you as a way to get to your father, but if anyone finds out, they're going to assume you're a threat and try to destroy you. Your father, he—"

"He can't know."

He nods. "The moment he thinks you're more powerful than him or pose a threat—"

I cut him off again by putting my finger to his mouth. "This is one of the reasons I'm on Heaven's side, Evan. There's so much you don't know. So much I can't tell you because of your Hell-bound soul. But having all this demonic power doesn't sit well with my own soul or heavenly light. That wasn't the angels turning on me. I had no choice but to get rid of it. I might be powerful, but my body can't handle so much good and evil alone."

He motions at Zach. "This is why you don't belong with them. I bet you'd be fine with only demonic power."

"I do, though. Without him, I'll get trapped in the prison realm. I need the angelic power. This is the only way I can live with myself. I can't go back to how things were. I don't want to. You know how I feel about everything. You should understand."

"But if it hurts you—" He sounds just like Dylan.

"That's why I need my sister's soul. Possessing a Heaven-bound soul will give me the strength I need to stay split between Heaven and Hell." I reach out and grab his hand. "I need your help finding it."

"He'll kill me."

"I would never allow it."

He huffs out a long breath. "Okay. If it means I get to spend the days with you, I'll do it."

"Heaven thanks you," Zach says from my other side.

Evan glares. "I'm not doing this for you or Heaven. This is for Cami."

Zach shrugs. "Whatever you say."

<hr>

Malicevile locking the bedroom door was more for show than anything, because it takes me all of thirty seconds to burn the knob right off the door before kicking it open. His cinnamon scent, along with the sugar sweetness of Raphael's, lingers in the hallway as I follow Evan toward my father's office.

As my fingers touch the locked door, I hear someone behind me, and I swivel to face Cherie in all her human cuteness. She dresses to impress, professional yet sexy, with the way her blouse hugs her curves, showing off a tiny bit of her cleavage.

She places a hand on her hip and frowns at me. "Mr. Hellshire told me you were grounded, Ms. Camilla. I don't want to have to call your dad and tell him you've left your bedroom."

Evan steps between us like Cherie is somehow a threat to me, or maybe he's worried about how I'll react toward her.

I peek at her from over Evan's shoulder. "Stand back,

Cherie. I don't want you to get hurt."

She takes an automatic step back when the blue fire erupts in my palm, and I press it into my father's locked door. I push the door open and peer around his tidy office. Along the built-in bookcases are a few shelves with cylindrical vials on them, but it's not nearly the amount of souls I've seen in my father's possession. And I highly doubt he'd leave Melanie's around with the others. Hers is special.

Sighing, I turn back to Evan and meet Cherie's utterly shocked expression. Her mouth hangs open in horror as she gapes at me, and if her chest wasn't heaving, I'd think that I might have killed her by surprise.

"I told you my father was a demon, which makes me one, too."

She opens her mouth to scream, and Evan rushes over to cut off her scream with his hand. I look at the space in front of me. "Zach?" I ask my invisible angel. "Can you do something about her?"

Cherie shrieks against Evan's hand when Zach appears behind her and covers her eyes with his hand before knocking her out. "Want me to encourage her to quit?" he asks, leaning her back against the wall.

I shake my head. "No, she can quit by her own freewill. If she leaves, then Malicevile will just find someone else or use Evan. And I don't feel like fighting with my dad about that yet. He's going to be pissed enough as it is."

"Sorry, Cherie," Zach whispers.

I move into the office to get a better look around. Just as I suspected, Melanie's soul isn't on the shelf with all the naughty souls my father decided to keep for himself instead of sending them to where they belong.

Running my fingers along the cool glass, I randomly snatch a soul and hand it to Zach. "In the mood to lighten Malicevile's collection?"

Zach tosses the soul back to me. "Maybe some other time, princess."

Shocking. I don't ask him why; instead, I set the soul back on the shelf where I found it. "Well, this is a bust."

"I didn't bring you in here for the soul, Cami." Evan heads for the desk and pulls a set of keys from the top drawer before tossing them to me. "I brought you here because we're going to need these."

The keys look antique—brass and iron—with different etchings along the tops. I've never seen them before. "What do these go to?"

"Your father's vault. You didn't think he'd leave all his souls somewhere unprotected, did you? He has them scattered in quite a few places, but I know exactly where your sister's is. He keeps it with some of the—" He snaps his mouth closed and turns his gaze toward Zach.

"With the what?"

He looks like he's going to bail on me at any second and leave me to face the sunlight prison realm.

When he doesn't answer, I stroll forward and meet his

gaze. "Tell me, Evan. This is important."

He sighs. "He keeps your sister's soul with a few of the demi-demons. But if I take you there, you have to promise to leave them be."

I flick my gaze to Zach. "I can't promise that."

"Then I'm not taking you."

"Seriously?"

"I love you, Cami, and as much as I want to help you, I'm not going to go against your father. Not only will he not help me with the transformation when the time comes, he'd kill me and send me to Hell."

"I hate to say that he's right, princess," Zach says. "But I think his sacrifice will be worthwhile."

Zach's words catch me off guard. "What? I already don't have a lot of time with him."

"We have more important things to worry about than your love life. Evan chose his side, but the others, they're being forced into making these decisions. It isn't right."

I throw my hands up. "Don't you dare lecture me on what is right and wrong, Zach."

His wings unfurl on his back as he runs his hand over his head. "I'm starting to think being here is a big mistake. You're losing sight of your purpose. Freeing Evan's soul was supposed to help you fulfill your duties, not make you turn against me."

"Is that what you think? That I'm not on your side now? You know I didn't want you to go through with that deal. You're the one responsible for this mess. Now, stop blaming me and my emotions for your shortcomings. You're the worst guardian ever, Zach, and I've had it! Stay out of my business." Harsh, I know. But he pissed me off.

My words stab him right in his pure little heart, and hurt sweeps across his face. The edges of my vision haze red, and even my deep, long breaths aren't enough to stop my true body from slicing through my skin. There's so much demonic power swirling through me that my Heaven-bound soul can't do anything except whisper quiet warnings to me that if I don't calm down, I'm going to lose it.

"If that's what you want, princess," he says after a minute.

I grip my knees, trying to control myself, but it's impossible with my anger. "Yes. It's exactly what I want."

With my words, Zach disappears before my eyes.

"You don't need that guy, Cami. It's you who's been doing him a favor," Evan says, rubbing his hand between my shoulders, easing away the tension in my muscles.

I finally manage to hide my true body. Ignoring his comment, I ask, "Can you please just take me to my sister's soul. I promise not to do anything about the demi-demons, all right?"

He nods after a moment. "Think it'll matter now? I'm pretty sure your watcher would be fine with locking you away in the daylight realm."

I grimace. "I guess we'll find out in a few hours."

"I hope I'm wrong."

God, so do I.

CAN'T LOSE HIM

"I WOULDN'T HAVE wasted so much time had I known this place was so far."

Evan pulls my Mustang through the wrought iron gate of a place I've never been to before. The Hellshire Estate, introduced by an iron sign on the gate, is more like a compound than a house. My father's other estates can't even compare.

The immaculate lawns are lit with solar lights peppered through all the lush plants and trees. A circular driveway wraps around the front of the house and leads to a separate garage, which looks like it could hold eight vehicles. A chandelier hangs from the covered driveway, lighting the glittering ground.

Double doors sit in a huge archway with opaque glass surrounding them with light shining from within. Ivy vines climb the walls, making the fortress look more like a massive hedge than a house. It looms three stories high and balconies jet out from some of the upstairs sliding doors.

Evan climbs from the car the second after he cuts off the engine. I don't move from my seat, studying the place. Coming to the front door was way too easy. There should be guards, hellhounds, traps, anything to keep us from entering the fortress.

Opening my door, Evan reaches out his hand and helps me to my feet. "You look scared."

I straighten out my leather jacket, touching the dagger on my hip. "I don't get scared." It's a flat out lie, and Evan knows it, but he doesn't call me out on it. "But, something doesn't feel right. Why hasn't my father brought me here before?"

Evan laces his fingers through mine and pulls me toward the door. "Keeping you out of his demonic affairs, I guess. You'll have to ask him. It's the first place he brought me when I traded him my soul. It's where he broke me and got me to turn off my humanity. Don't let the luxury of it fool you; this is your father's hellish kingdom. Where do you think he keeps those living who still have souls?"

My stomach tightens with knots. I was too concerned with my own life before that I never thought to ask. "That doesn't explain why we can walk right up to the door."

"I'm Malicevile's right hand and you're his daughter. We

have access everywhere."

"I thought Raphael was Malicevile's right hand demon?"

His eyebrows peak on his forehead. "Raphael and your father have a mutual agreement. They're strictly business partners. Your father would not risk allowing Raphael so close to what he has spent centuries building, not when Raphael is one of his biggest threats. Raphael would destroy your father given the opportunity."

He'd also be the one to try to take my father's place, which means he poses a threat to me as well. Especially now, more than ever, since he knows the key to transforming a demi-demon. I'm sure Faith will be forced into it even though she wants nothing to do with Hell.

"I see your point." As the words exit my mouth, a low growl rips through the night as a hellhound appears in view. Of course he'd have a pack of broken werewolves around to protect his property.

I snap my fingers a few times, encouraging the hellhound to come closer. Its deep growl reverberates in its throat as it slinks closer, cautiously. Holding my hand out, I let the beast smell my fingers before its black, frothy tongue slides out to lick my knuckles.

"Good boy," I say, scratching the wolf on the top of his head. "Now go on."

Instead of leaving, it remains by my side until we reach the front door, and Evan pushes it open. It's not locked.

Before I can enter, Evan pulls the back of my shirt in time

for me to watch a cloud of smoke erupt in the foyer. It slithers through the air like it's searching for something. In one quick breath, I blow the smoke away to clear the air.

A whimper sounds from the right, and Evan pulls me in. I meet the startled gaze of a young girl around my age.

"I wasn't expecting you here tonight, Evan. Warn a witch next time. I could've killed you." The girl steps from her spot, relaxing her shoulders.

"A witch?" I ask. I've only ever heard rumors about witches. Most creatures stay far away from both hunters and demons. The last thing I expected was to find one at my father's secret compound.

The girl moves closer, studying my face. She gets within inches of me without even hesitating like most people would. She smells like sandalwood and pine trees, similar to a demon, but not as potent. I study her right back, taking in her smooth skin, bright brown eyes that flash to black every so often, and her wavy black coffee-colored hair.

"You sound surprised," she says, almost a little too late after I asked, like she wasn't going to respond to me at all.

"Witches are almost extinct. I never expected to see one working for my father," I say.

Her eyes darken with my words. "You're supposed to be dead, Camilla. Malicevile's been having me seek out potential mates for weeks now. Do you know how much time and energy that takes?"

She actually sounds mad that I'm alive. "Um, sorry. And

gross. You're the one to match my father up with humans?"

"Yeah. I did an awesome job with you, didn't I?"

She looks like she's a teen. I don't mention it, though, because anger sneaks up on me. I think about how she's the one who damned my mom's fate. She preyed on a family who had no business dealing with demons. Of course, if she hadn't I wouldn't be alive...but still.

Electricity erupts in my fingers. "I should kill you for making my parents suffer."

Evan touches my shoulder, bringing my attention to him. "It's not going to change anything, Cami. Come on. We're running out of night." He turns to the witch. "It was nice to see you again, Elora."

As he pulls me away, Elora burns daggers with her eyes into my back. She has one of those weighted stares that you can feel, and she makes me feel all sorts of wrong. My muscles tighten, each step increasingly uncomfortable, until we turn down a hallway that leads to an elevator.

I hit the call button. "How on earth did a witch fall into demon servitude?"

He shrugs. "Don't know. Don't really care, honestly. Elora might look innocent, but she's ruthless. She kills before she questions things, and it's not even because of your father. She possesses her own soul. I heard she was cast out by her coven for using blood magic."

"You're an expert on witches now or something?" I ask. Because I barely learned anything about them—or many other creatures for that matter—from the Hunter's Academy.

He kisses my temple as the elevator door slides open. "Definitely not. It's just what I heard from your father."

Evan hits the B button, which I assume stands for basement, but when we descend and the door opens, the letter D would be more appropriate because the place looks like a dungeon. The icy air swirls around me, causing me to shiver when we step in an all-cement hallway. It's pitch-black until Evan summons his fire into his hand, lighting the wall next to us until he finds the light switch. I half expect to find unlit torches to carry, but power hums in the room as recessed lighting illuminates the dank corridor.

I suck in a small breath, immediately regretting it when my nostrils fill with a mixture of mildew, rot, and body odor. I have no idea where the stench comes from, only that something has to be causing it.

Pulling me forward, Evan guides me down the corridor a few feet until I realize where I'm picking up the stink. There are dozens of doors lining the hallway, all with grate covered windows to allow us to see into cement rooms.

A groan sounds out from the first, and I halt in my tracks to peer through the little cutout at a man who sits with his knees curled to his chest in the dark cell. The shock of seeing a person in such horrible living conditions tightens knots in my stomach. I've always known my demonic father was a monster, but for some reason, I never imagined he'd imprison people like this—the living who have bound their souls to him.

And it's disgusting.

"Oh, God," I whisper, though it's more of a prayer. Because it takes everything in me to let Evan pull me away. Bile rises in my throat, the air permeating with more disgusting scents, and I try my best not to look into the windows of each door. I'm afraid I'll lose it if I do.

"If it makes you feel any better, they aren't good people," Evan says. He squeezes my fingers while pulling me along.

We turn down another hallway, and I clench my jaw. This place is a maze. "It doesn't. Did he keep you in a cell like this?" I never asked Evan about the weeks after he'd been taken.

Evan quickens his pace, his eyes narrowing, and he refuses to meet mine. "It doesn't matter. Malicevile did what he did to show me how strong I am."

"You're so brainwashed." I don't mean to say the words out loud, but they slip out as I think about what my father has done—things Evan will never tell me—to the boy I love.

In one quick motion, Evan spins me and pushes me against the hard wall. His eyes burn with an intensity so hot that it sears into me, causing me to release a small gasp. His hands press the wall on both sides of my head, trapping me in place, but it's not like I'm going anywhere, not with how close his body is to mine.

He leans closer, his warm breath tickling my cheek as he says, "I could say the same about you. You so badly want to do all these things for people who couldn't possibly love you like I do. You've always been so concerned with others, fighting whatever you thought the good fight was, and look where it got you. Do you really want to do all this, Cami? What's the point?"

"It's the right thing to do," I say.

"You don't sound so certain."

My lip quivers as I suck in another breath. "Please, Evan. We don't have time for this."

"I just want to know that you're doing this because you want to. Haven't you been manipulated and had your decisions made for you long enough? You can't tell me that you just gave your soul to that guardian of yours. I know you, Cami. Your soul was the one thing you'd rather die with than hand it over to someone else to take care of. If you can look me in the eyes and say that everything you do, you do by your choice and not because you've been cornered, then we'll go get your sister's soul. I'll also stop fighting with you about the side you've chosen. But if you can't, then we're turning around and leaving. Heaven can have your soul, but I'll be damned if they're going to take your life and freewill now, too."

A million responses fly through my mind, but none of them sound convincing, even to me. Because he's right. I've spent the last few months being pushed around, broken, trapped, lied to, manipulated—but it wasn't all by Heaven. The whole world has never really been on my side. Would I have chosen this life? No. I would've never agreed to be a demon. I'd have never agreed to be Hell-bound. I don't know if I'd have joined the angelic army either.

But there is one thing I do know. I'd have done everything I'd done again to help people. For the brief moment in my life, the one where I was in Moonlight Shores hoping to help the werewolves, was the one time I actually had chosen what I wanted to do. It was before I relied on Malicevile and had sparked a relationship that wasn't based on survival. And because of that, is why I'm making this choice now. Not because the world needs me or because it's expected, but because I can't help others otherwise.

I meet his ocean blue eyes. "I might have been manipulated into giving my soul to Zach, but I'm doing this for me. I need to possess heavenly light. I need to feel its goodness in my soul even if it battles with the rest of me, because it reminds me that I might be a demon, but that's not all that I am. It reminds me that the whole world isn't tainted and evil. It reminds me that no matter what happens, that in the end, I did what I could to live with myself."

Evan stares at me for a moment before pressing his lips against mine. His hands move from the wall to my neck, and he pulls me closer to him. "Now if only you could accept my decision to transform."

Over and over again. "Evan," I say. "You know why."

"Because you don't want to lose me. But Cami, I'm going to die no matter what. Why shouldn't I take the chance?"

I rest my head on his. "Because I'm afraid."

"Of what? That it would change me? Don't you think that would be hypocritical of you considering that you just said being a demon isn't all that you are?"

He's right on both accounts. No matter what, he'll die, and as for changing, I can't really know for sure. But as I look into his eyes, feel his arms around me, I know that I don't want to lose him—I can't lose him. I just don't see a way.

I stand on my tiptoes and kiss him. "If this is what you really want, then I support you. But I can't help you, Evan. I'm not putting an angel at risk, and don't you even think about trying to use my guardian."

"The guy that abandoned you?"

I shake my head, letting my hair fall into my face. "He didn't abandon me, but he probably won't talk to me for a few centuries for the cruel things I said to him."

"Might be sooner than you think, princess." Zach appears at the end of the hallway. "Trouble's arrived."

Before I have a chance to prepare, Evan falls against me, causing my head to slam into the wall. My knees give out on me, and I drop to the floor with starbursts dancing in my vision. A man with razor sharp teeth grabs Evan by the back of his shirt, tossing him a few feet down the hallway. He collides with the floor, sliding a few feet before stopping.

The man grabs me by the hair and yanks me from the ground, the smell of boiling asphalt assaulting my nose. A flash of light zooms right behind him, sending his back smoking, but he doesn't move.

All he does is grin at me with irises so white that he only has tiny diamond shaped pupils. "What a pretty little thing you are," he says, holding me up against the wall.

I struggle for a second before I ignite blue fire in the palm of my hand.

"Uh-uh. I don't think you want to do that." His eyes flick from my hand to my chest, and I realize he has the dagger-like nails of his free hand spread evenly around my heart. He could rip it out before the fire would even leave a blister on him.

"Let me go," I say.

"And why would I do that?"

I stare at the man's face. He looks odd with his eyes too far up on his forehead, his mouth splitting his face from ear to ear, and his nose with its missing nostrils. It's a poorly put together human façade for a mid-level demon, but it doesn't mean he can't kill me.

"Because Malicevile will send you to Hell for hurting me. I'm his daughter."

His grin widens, nearly reaching his temples. "Well then, that makes this much more fun."

STRONG ENOUGH

THE DEMON SHOVES his hand into my chest just below my ribcage, cracking a few of my ribs. Pain explodes through me when he grabs upward to lace his grimy fingers around my precious heart. My head pounds with every beat, my eyes watering and my whole body convulsing, while my life rests in the hand of this monster.

My levitation kicks on, taking away some of the weight. He holds me midair, keeping me up only because he's impaling me. His hand untangles from my hair, and he reaches into his pocket and pulls out a cell phone.

Movement flickers in my peripheral vision, and fire lights the dim hallway as Evan launches to his feet.

The demon holds his hand out, waving the cell phone. "You don't want me to accidentally rip her heart out now, do you?"

Evan freezes in his tracks. As he realizes the demon isn't lying, horror crosses his face. Blood trickles down my shirt, staining the soft blue of the fabric. Zach appears behind the demon, his eyes meeting mine, but he doesn't move either. He's shielding himself from everyone but me, and I think it's his way of showing me that he's here even though anything he could possibly do would result in my death.

Tears brand hot streaks on my cheeks. "I'm sorry," I say to him.

The demon rolls his eyes, thinking I'm talking to him. He doesn't respond as he holds the cell phone up to his ear. A smooth, familiar voice echoes through the line, but I can't hear more than the annoyed greeting.

"I'd greet me a little nicer than that, Mal," the demon says. "It seems that I've had a visitor tonight. Maybe you know her..." The demon flicks his gaze to me. "Go on. Say something."

"Hey, Dad."

Malicevile roars through the line.

The demon laughs. "Be careful what you say next. I'm holding your daughter's heart in my hand. Surprisingly, it's softer than I would've imagined your spawn's heart to be."

The line is utterly silent.

"Good, I'm glad you're listening. I want to make a deal. You have ten minutes to get here because my hand is getting a bit tired. It might just slip—" He tugs his hand a little, causing a wave of excruciating pain to explode in my chest.

I scream, long and loud, so loud that it leaves my ears ringing.

"Princess, stay calm," Zach says. "I'm not going to let him rip your heart out."

"What are you going to do?" I ask.

The demon tilts his head as he looks at me. "I never thought an opportunity like this would ever come up, but you're going to make me quite the powerful demon. I bet I could get a few hundred souls in exchange for your life."

Clearly, he isn't aware that my guardian stands behind him. And of course this is about souls. They are the ultimate power source on this plane. I bet it'll help him better his disguise to find his own souls. Humans are vain—they'd make a deal with someone like Malicevile over this poor excuse for a demon any day. He probably scares them off more often than not. The souls he does collect probably come after a Hell-bound person dies, and even then, he might not be strong enough to collect it instead of sending it to Hell.

"Tell him he doesn't need your father for souls. Tell him you can get them for him," Zach says.

Thank God Zach is here. I feel really guilty for calling him the worst guardian ever.

"You don't need Malicevile," I say. "I can get you souls. More than he'd probably get you. But you have to let go of my heart."

"Your father would never allow me to walk away with them. I need to make the deal with him," he says.

My hope dwindles.

"Princess, if your father gets here before you get to your sister's soul, we'll lose the opportunity," Zach says.

"You don't think I know that?"

The demon narrows his eyes and squeezes my heart again. I grind my teeth through the pain. He still thinks I'm talking to him and probably assumes I'm an idiot with the way it sounded like I was admitting that he was right.

"I have an idea, princess, and I need you to remain as calm as you can, okay? This will be tricky."

Oh, unholy Hell. I don't like the sound of that.

Slowly, Zach moves next to me and reaches for the dagger at my belt. I tense, my heart racing harder in the demons hand, and the demon gulps in a breath of my fear. He shifts his gaze down, and I panic and spit in his face. The last thing I need is for him to see some invisible force remove the weapon from my belt. It's not blessed, and Zach can't show his angelic light, so it can't effectively kill him. It'll still hurt, though. I'd like nothing more than to hear him scream.

"You're making it hard to keep your heart in your chest. Your fear, it's mouthwatering. Who knew a demon could even be afraid. Maybe I'll just keep you for myself."

Ugh. Nope. Not happening. I'll rip my own heart out if he thinks he's going anywhere with me.

Zach shuffles past the demon and sneaks up to Evan's side, who has been standing there with fire in his hand, probably thinking of a million ways to save me. Demons never show him much attention because he's not like them, but this gross monster is about to realize that Evan is a million times better than he could ever imagine being.

Evan's fire glints off the dagger as Zach hands it over. Surprisingly, Evan takes it from my guardian without protest. They share a few whispered words, but the demon is too lost on the scent of my fear to realize that Evan has moved a few feet closer—so close, he could reach out and touch him.

I open my mouth to say something, but Zach shakes his head.

He sneaks up behind the demon and smiles at me from over his shoulder. "Listen carefully, princess. When I count to three, I want you to latch your hands around this guy's wrist and hold it in place as tight as you can. Think you can manage?"

Yes? No? Maybe? Holy crap. Instead of answering, I subtly nod. It's not like I have a choice. It's either wait for my father and find out how much my life is worth to him or find my sister's soul to help myself.

"Good," Zach says. "Don't look so scared. I promised to always take care of you. Have a little faith."

"You should try having faith when this monster has your

heart in his hands."

"What did you say?" the demon asks.

Shoot. The demon shifts to look behind him and sees Evan has closed the distance.

Without counting, Zach says, "Now!"

I reach my hands up and grip them as hard as I can to the demon's wrist as he tries his hardest to rip his hand—and my heart—from my chest. Zach stands behind him, grabbing him by the arms, and holds him in place. The demon can't back up and move.

Evan raises the dagger before slamming it down on the demon's arm that holds my heart. The demon wails, and blood splatters over all of us, but his arm doesn't come off right away. Evan whacks down two more times until I'm left holding onto the demon's arm, now severed just below the elbow.

His fingers twitch, still holding my heart. Commotion erupts before me. Evan uppercuts the demon before kicking him in the stomach, sending him down the hallway. He's hurt and pissed off, and now more determined to hurt me than ever.

My vision darkens, and I slowly tug his hand from my chest, leaving five holes circling my heart. Blood pours from my wound, but I'll live. The demon launches forward, crashing into Evan. He wraps his good arm around my boyfriend's neck.

Power erupts in my hand, and I blast him with an energy orb, sending him reeling back. Rage coursing through me, I stomp closer, gathering all my demonic power. He'll be nothing but a puddle on the floor when I'm through with him.

Still holding his severed arm, I swing it out and smack the demon across the face. He growls, swiping his good arm out, trying to steal his arm back from me. Instead of letting him have it, I toss it down the hall before shooting a ball of acid slime at it.

Applause erupts at the end of the hallway when the demon's arm disintegrates. The scent of cinnamon cuts through the nastiness of the mid-level demon, and I back up a few feet when Malicevile strolls into the hallway. The demon remains on the floor between us, and I wish he'd get up and try to fight my father. Because I need a distraction. I need to get to the vault.

The stupid demon cowers instead.

"Camilla, out of all the places in the world, you just happened to come to this one," Malicevile says, ignoring the demon. He turns his gaze to Evan. "I'm assuming she offered something you couldn't refuse to disobey me like this?"

I hold up my hand to Evan before he can talk. "Leave him out of it. I didn't give him a choice."

"And why are you here?"

"Princess, enough talking. Run! We have minutes before you get sucked into the daylight realm." Zach's words echo in my ear, but he remains invisible.

I do the only thing I can think of. Opening my mouth, I release a huge gust of tornado breath, sending the bleeding demon at my father, knocking them both to the floor.

Turning on my heels, I grab Evan's hand and pull him in the opposite direction. Zach remains ahead of us, turning wherever Evan commands. We easily navigate the confusing hallway. Electricity lights up behind us. My father chases us, but I throw everything I have in me behind us to slow him down.

My boots thud on the polished concrete, my breath ragged as the injury to my chest threatens to consume me with pain, but I don't stop.

"Up ahead," Evan says, pointing to a thick, wooden door at the end of the corridor.

I reach into my pocket and pull out the set of keys he had given me earlier. There are at least a dozen, and I'm afraid I won't have time to get through them all before my father catches up. And then what? He'll try to kill Evan before unleashing his wrath on me.

I hand the keys to Evan. "Open the door. I'll hold him off."

Letting go of him, I spin around and summon a slime ball before chucking it at my father, who comes into view from around the corner. He stops and drops to the floor, letting the slime fly right over his head.

He retaliates by hitting me with a bout of energy so strong that it knocks me back. It ends up slipping through my fingers and smacking my sore chest. I gasp, the air knocked from my lungs.

It doesn't stop me from summoning more power, though. Blue fire explodes in my hands, and Malicevile stops dead in his tracks, seeing the power in my fingers. His angry face morphs to curiosity, but I don't have a chance to study his reaction because

Evan grabs the back of my jacket and yanks me through the door.

I slam it shut and spin to face a huge wall of souls—more than I've ever seen before. They hum with an energy that awakens every nerve in my body, and when I step closer, I can hear a symphony of quiet whispers—the voices of those lost.

"Melanie," I say. "Where are you?"

Something thuds against the door and it shakes. I don't look at it though. I follow the wall of souls, listening to each one whisper to me, until I reach a cutout with a wooden box inscribed with the name I've yearned to see.

Melanie Wright.

As I pick up the box in my hand, the door crashes open, flying off its hinges. Malicevile charges into the room, heading right for me.

"Camilla, give that to me," my father says, stopping short.

I shake my head, clutching the box. "I can't. I'm sorry."

With trembling fingers, I lift the lid and stare at the crystal vial with my sister's soul swirling within it. I take it into my hands and feel the heat emanating from glass that should be cold.

Malicevile sneers, electricity erupting in his fingers. "Give me that or I'll kill your boyfriend."

My gaze flicks to Evan as Malicevile aims his power toward him. My heart clenches in my chest, and I clutch the very thing I need while gazing at the boy I want so desperately.

"Do what you have to do, Cami," Evan says.

"Zach," I whisper. "I can't lose him. Please, I'm begging you. You can save him."

"I'm sorry, princess. You can't have both."

I sniffle, meeting my father's gaze. Slowly, I hold the vile up. Evan means more than Heaven or Hell to me. If Zach won't save him, then I will—even if it means giving up the part of me that's good. I just pray that my soul is strong enough to survive.

"Cami, no," Evan says from behind me.

As his words echo through the air, the vile slips from my fingers and shatters on the concrete floor. Swinging out, I clip Malicevile's arm as he tries to shoot power at Evan. Sparks cascade around the room like glorious, white fireworks.

At the same time, Malicevile and I both look at my sister's soul swirling through the air. The room grows hazy with the rising sun, the earth realm melting away. In one quick motion, I shove Malicevile back and grab my sister's soul.

A beam of heavenly light blasts through the air, blinding me, and the last thing I see is my father disappear from the world a moment before I do.

ALWAYS AND FOREVER

"I NEVER IN a million years thought a nephilim would ever grace me with its presence again," a feminine voice says, pulling me from the bright recesses of my mind.

"I'm quite surprised to see you myself."

I blink the haze from my eyes and stare at Dylan standing before me in a halo of sunshine. His ethereal wings flicker in and out of view as he flaps them, sending the spicy scent of cinnamon candy in my direction. The scent's similar to Malicevile's but not as potent.

I sit up, rubbing my eyes. "Please, tell me I'm not dreaming."

Dylan draws his attention to me. "Of course you're dreaming, love, but I'm totally real."

I point at the girl next to him. "And you?"

"I'm not sure."

I get a good look at my sister for the first time, and tears prickle in my eyes. I've seen pictures of her, but nothing compares to her soul standing before me. Her curly hair, the same shade as mine, cascades down her back in soft tendrils. Her bright green eyes light up from within, and she offers me a smile that makes me start bawling my eyes out.

"I can't believe it," I say, covering my hands with my face. "You're Melanie. I never thought I'd ever get to see you like this. I'm Cami. I'm your—"

"Sister," Melanie finishes for me. "Your soul resonates with mine. I'd recognize you anywhere."

Dylan helps me to my feet, and I stand in front of Melanie. "Dad is going to murder me for stealing your soul from him."

"So you were successful?" Dylan asks.

"Uh, I think so, unless he actually already murdered me and put my soul with Melanie's. I don't know. Everything happened so fast and then the sun came up." I blow strands of hair from my face. "Either way, I'm so happy to finally get to meet you. I just wish I had gotten to you sooner. Malicevile's a monster for not letting you move on."

Melanie smiles sadly. "Can you blame him? It's not so easy letting go of those you love."

"Love? No. He doesn't know love. And you don't blame

him?"

She shakes her head. "I've always known what would happen to my soul. It was never a surprise."

I frown. "And you were okay with it?"

"It is what it is."

Another stream of tears escapes from my eyes. How can someone just accept the fate of my father's choosing? I already can't stand the lack of control I have in my life, and because of it, I fight relentlessly to try to make things how I want despite everyone else. Melanie, she's come to terms with who she is as Malicevile's daughter.

"But what if it doesn't have to be like that?" I ask.

"Is that why I'm here? You want your nephilim to usher me to the afterlife?" she asks. "Because if you really think that your life is in danger at the hands of our father, I want you to know that I'm okay with my fate. You don't have to sacrifice yourself on my behalf. I don't want that from you, Cami."

Her response surprises me. She wants me to return her to Malicevile so he won't hurt me.

"That's not exactly the reason I stole you," I say. I feel like such a jerk knowing that she'd spend the rest of eternity stuck for me when I'm here to ask her for her help.

She frowns for a moment before forcing her mouth to smile. "Okay, then what is it?"

"Nothing. Never mind." I glance at Dylan. "I don't think I can do this."

"But, love."

I shake my head. "Can you move her on to where she's supposed to be? I'll figure out another way."

Melanie reaches out her hand and touches my shoulder. "Hey, wait. What's going on? If there's something I can do for you, just ask me. You're my sister, Cami."

"You don't even know me though," I say.

She frowns. "I wish I did."

"Me, too," I whisper. "More than anything. I could really use your help."

"Just name it. I don't know what I can do in this state, but I'll try."

I swallow the lump in my throat before I recount the last few months. I tell her everything—about my time on the run, about the Hunter's Alliance, about Evan, about the werewolves and hellhounds, about Faith. All my memories spill out of my mouth, some with smiles but most with tears. I tell her about my death and journey to Hell, and about what Dylan did to save me.

Her face softens and she peers at Dylan for a long moment. He blushes under her stare, pushing his black curls from his face.

"This is all so incredible, Cami," she says, interrupting me. "With how your soul feels, I just assumed that Dad got you to turn to Hell's side. He constantly pushed me to turn my back on humanity, though he never forced me. That's the fun thing about freewill. He can manipulate you as much as he wants, but in the end, it will be your decision to make."

She's right. "That's why Heaven encourages me but doesn't force me into doing anything."

"So, you're a demon with a Heaven-bound soul?" she asks. "I bet that's driving Dad crazy."

"He's optimistic that I'll swing back toward Hell one way or another." I suck in my bottom lip for a moment. "And I'm afraid he might be right. The more power I take, the harder it is to allow Heaven in."

"Are you sure that's what you want?" Melanie asks.

"More than anything. But I can't do it on my own. I need another Heaven-bound soul to balance out my demonic power."

"And she won't take mine," Dylan says.

Melanie smiles at him. "I don't blame her. How would you expect her to live with herself if something happened to you? I was devastated when my father killed Zachariel. He was my best friend in the whole world."

My mouth falls open. "Zachariel? Your Demon Watcher was named Zachariel?"

Her bottom lip pouts as she nods. "I was the only demi-demon around with her own personal nephilim Demon Watcher. My father hated him, though. Thought he'd take my soul. I told him Zachariel was just trying to protect me, but he wouldn't even listen."

As her words sink in, I connect the dots. Could it be possible that Zach was half-human? That after his death, he ascended as a guardian? It'd make sense why he took the job to protect me. Malicevile stole his life and was ultimately the reason for my sister's murder since the alliance blamed her for his death. But why wouldn't Zach mention something so huge to me?

My breathing quickens as I clench and unclench my fingers.

"Princess." A cool hand slides over my shoulders as Zach appears in my dream. I had wondered where he was and why he wasn't here like the last time. "I know what you're thinking, and I know you're upset, but please, give me a chance to explain."

"Zachariel?" Melanie's surprised expression, which immediately turns to delight, confirms my suspicions. Zach was her Demon Watcher. "You're here. I don't understand."

She closes the distance and wraps her arms around Zach's shoulders. He slowly lifts his arms to hug her back, but his eyes never waver from mine. "Cami is my charge," he says. His black wings unfurl on his back, and he stretches them out toward the sky.

Melanie reaches out and touches his wings. "Oh, Zachariel. You've come a long way since the last time I saw you. I've always known that even death couldn't stop you from greatness." She turns to me. "You're the luckiest demon to have such an angel by your side, Cami."

"If only he told me about your history," I mutter.

Zach cringes. "Princess, please."

I shrug. "It's whatever, okay? I shouldn't be surprised."

Melanie comes over to me and pulls me away from both

Zach and Dylan. Her green eyes stare into mine for a long moment, and then she says, "Don't be too hard on him. People do what they think is right. Whether or not he told you doesn't matter in the grand scheme of things, does it?"

"He wants me to kill Malicevile. What if it's for revenge?"

Tears line her eyes. "If what you've told me is true, it's more than that. Dad is too powerful for his own good. If he's putting humanity at risk..." Her voice trails off.

"So you're okay with this?"

"I didn't say that. But I understand where he's coming from. I spent years fighting in the name of humanity. It's such a beautiful, precious thing that I was lucky to be a part of and to fight for."

"Even though humans killed you in the end?"

"I can't hold that against all of humanity, Cami. There were people who fought for me, who tried to save me. I'd hate to see those people succumb to the world Dad imagines. One Hell is good enough for me." She takes my hands. "And because of that, I want to help you. I'll never be able to do so in our father's care, or even in the afterlife. Not like this."

My lip quivers with her words. "Are you sure? You don't want to find peace or something?"

She laughs, her musical voice ringing in my ears. I tuck away the sound to keep forever. "Giving you my soul is my way of finding peace, Cami. What better way to spend my eternity than spending it with my sister?"

"You want me to hold your soul for eternity?" I ask in surprise. I was only planning on doing so until I figured things out.

She nods. "You need me to balance Heaven and Hell. This isn't only to do what you need to do now. What do you think will happen if you let me move on? You'll be exactly where you are now. I know you don't want that. I can feel it even now. And if I move on, that's it. There's no coming back for me. So, let me do this. Let my soul mean something to the world."

"Thank you," I whisper. "You have no idea how much this means to me, Melanie." I turn to Zach. "Can you help me wake up so I can sort all this out? I need to relocate Melanie's soul so Malicevile can't get to her again."

Zach's jaw twitches for a split second, but he doesn't say anything.

Instead, Melanie grips both my hands in hers. "Cami, that's not necessary."

"I don't understand."

"Here, let me show you." Her whole body engulfs in a shimmering light comparable to Heaven, lighting my dream world brighter than the imaginary sun shining overhead. She squeezes me tighter, heat pulsating between our fingers, and then a second later, her fingers disappear into mine.

A shock zaps through me when our souls connect, and everything that is Melanie rushes through me. Her love and devotion, her hopes and dreams, even her fears and uncertainties. Everything that made my sister who she was now seeps into me as she merges her soul with mine.

Her entire life flashes before my eyes, and I witness what it was like for her growing up in Malicevile's care, and then her life at the academy. I see familiar faces—a young Aston, who Melanie holds with such love, with his mother and Cadence's grandmother, Vivian, by his side. I see a bunch of faces I don't recognize but know that Melanie cared about them. And then I see Zach in his half-human glory. He looks exactly the way he does now, but his wings are sheer and golden, not unlike Dylan's. The next few memories leave me breathless and in tears as I watch Malicevile electrocute Zach and watch Melanie cry over him before she runs into Aston's arms.

All the moments leading up to my sister's death sit heavy in my heart and soul. The fear and betrayal she felt standing up to those she thought were on her side. How they forced her hand to fight against them. The pain and bloodshed. The fire. Her death wasn't the ultimate sacrifice. It wasn't glorious. It was tragic and heart-wrenching as a hunter stabbed her through the chest and left her to die alone in the dark. Her last moment creeps into my mind, watching as she held onto life until Malicevile came for her. He took her soul before she died in his arms. Then he left her body in the dirt.

I blink through my tears. "Melanie."

"Sorry you had to see that."

"I—"

"It's okay. A terrible ending doesn't ruin the rest of my life."

"She's right, princess," Zach says, coming up to us. "I should know."

Melanie turns her gaze toward my guardian. "I trust that you'll take care of my sister, Zachariel."

He puts his arms around both of us. "Always and forever, Lanie."

A second later, Zach wraps us in his enormous black wings, and Melanie disappears as her soul merges completely with mine. It's unlike anything I've ever felt—she doesn't feel foreign or intrusive, but like she fills a part of me that I didn't know was missing.

"How do you feel, love?" Dylan asks from behind me.

"I don't know," I whisper. "I feel—"

Before I can finish my sentence, my dream world explodes in blinding light—a light that doesn't swallow me whole or rip me apart. It fills me, soothing every crack in my soul while taming the demonic power that rolls through me.

"Cami?" It's Evan. "Cami, please. Come back to me."

Holding onto his voice, I pull myself from the light. Hot arms wrap around me as pain radiates through my body. I can't believe I found Melanie's soul and that now she's a part of mine. I can't believe I'm alive.

"Cami," Evan whispers again. "It's okay. You're okay." He brushes his thumb over my cheeks, smearing my tears.

I suck in a small breath. "For now."

LIVE ON

"HE CAN'T COME," Zach says, hopping out of the backseat of the Mustang.

I fly out of the front seat and spin to face him on the sidewalk. He stands tall, shoulders straight and jaw clenched. His chestnut hair sticks down in the front while it stands up in the back, and he's just as dirty as I am. We could both use a hot shower and a meal, but there's no time to waste. Zach's power barely keeps me holding on to the earth realm. It wasn't even enough to sear the five bleeding holes around my heart so I could attempt to heal.

I jab my finger into his chest. "But he risked his life for me.

What if we don't make it back in time? My father will kill him without question."

"We didn't force him to help us. He knew what he was getting into," Zach says, folding his arms to stop me from poking his taut chest.

"But—"

"Cami, he's right. I can handle myself." Evan slides his hands around my waist. I didn't even hear him get out of the car.

Leaning into him, I relax just a little. "Sure, but you can't handle my father. If he hurts you—"

"It wouldn't be the first time," he says, cutting me off. "Plus, I know you'll be back in time."

I spin in his arms and stand up on my tiptoes instead of levitating. "I will. I promise."

His lips meet mine in a gentle kiss, one so soft and short that I find myself craving more. But I don't have all day, and even traveling by air will cut things uncomfortably close.

"Ready, princess?" Zach asks from behind me.

I open my mouth to ask for another minute, but my stomach flies into my throat as Zach grabs me by the waist and launches us into the air without giving me a chance to say goodbye. Maybe that was his point. I shouldn't treat this like a goodbye, because I will see Evan again. I won't fail him. Because tonight, I have to face my father. As much as I want to run, I won't. This isn't over. Too much is at stake, and I refuse to waste the gift my sister gave me.

On the flight to Seraphim Rock, I practice my meditation techniques, breathing in and out in rhythm with Zach's breathing. Neither of us speak, just enjoying the silence of being away from everything. I rest my cheek against his cool chest, listening to his heartbeat. I have so many questions piling up in my mind, things that I didn't get to see when Melanie merged her soul with mine. Only Zach can answer these questions, but I don't know how to ask or if I even want to know the answers.

My stomach sinks to my feet when Zach descends toward the small island in the middle of the Pacific Ocean. My body zings when we enter the sacred air, and I shiver. It's been weeks since I've made this trip. I don't really want to be here now, but apparently I need more heavenly light than ever, and Zach's usual sidekicks have returned to the island since Zach never went back to our church.

His feet skid across the ground, and he comes to a stop outside the enormous sacred building. I'd call it a church, but it's not meant for worship. It's the closest angelic army headquarters and completely demon free—the perfect sanctuary for the winged ones.

"Cami!" Cadence rushes toward us from the arched doorway. I had no idea that she'd be here, but I guess Remi or Dani brought her. They'd never admit it, but my BFF has grown on them. It's impossible not to love such a badass demon hunter. She stops in front of us before she swings her arm and clocks Zach in the shoulder. "You're on my shit list, Zach. How dare you hand Cami back to Malicevile with a bow! Some guardian you are, you jerk."

I step between the two of them. "Cadence, calm down. Zach might be stupid secretive and manipulative, but I think what he did was the right thing."

He grins when I admit it. "So you take back what you said?"

"Considering you stopped a demon from ripping my heart out, I guess."

"What?" Cadence asks. Her eyes flick to my bloody shirt, and her face turns red even through her makeup. "You two kill me. You shouldn't be so cool about that."

"That's the least of her worries," Dylan says, appearing on the threshold of the building.

A smile tugs at my face as I race over the manicured lawn and into his arms. He lifts me off my feet, spinning me around, and then he takes a long hard look at me.

Reaching up, he runs his fingers over my cheek. "It's amazing."

Huh? I frown, pulling away at his sudden weirdness. "What are you talking about?"

Dylan flashes his wings once before he drops his hands to his side. "Your soul."

Oh. "Can you see hers?"

He shakes his head. "It's not hers anymore. It's all you."

The way he says it strikes a nerve within me. I can't explain why, but something about knowing that it's like my sister never existed at all bothers me. *She does exist. Her soul will live on for-*

ever through you.

"Don't look so sad, love," Dylan says.

But I can't help it.

"Come on, princess," Zach says, drawing my attention away from Dylan. "We have things to do."

Both Cadence and Dylan stroll with us as we make our way inside the building. A dozen scents hit me, and a few angels turn to gaze in my direction. I let Zach lead the way through the scents—cherry blossom, grapefruit, lavender—I could get used to this goodness. Too bad I'll be suffocating on demon stench by tonight.

Brilliant golden wings expand from a few angels' backs as they greet me with somber expressions. I force myself to smile and wave, because unlike them, I actually try to be friendly. I still don't know if it's because I'm a demon or because they're expected to trust a demon's daughter to save the world—who knows—either way, I don't feel welcome. It reminds me of what my father has said about not belonging. I sure as heck can try though.

"Hey, Zach," I say, striding up to walk next to him. "Why don't any of these angels have awesome wings like you?"

"You think my wings are awesome?"

I roll my eyes. "What can I say, the black feathers appeal to my demon side."

He chuckles. "It's a sign of status."

"I'd think the top angels would get the cool black wings."

"Who says I'm not on top?"

"You were born a nephilim."

"So?"

"You were assigned to babysit a baby demon."

He raises an eyebrow. "Did you just call yourself a baby demon? And I wasn't assigned this position. I volunteered."

"Because of Melanie?"

"Princess, we don't have all day. Can't these questions wait?"

I stop in place and put my hands on my hips. Dylan and Cadence stop behind me, quietly listening to me interrogate my guardian. My sudden movement doesn't go unnoticed among the angels either, because a dozen faces stare at me and Zach, and I bet all of them want to know the answer to the question I just asked.

"No, I want to know why you volunteered to protect the daughter of the demon who killed you. Is this about revenge? You can't kill my father so you make sure I can?"

His face remains expressionless, and he doesn't answer.

"Were you in love with Melanie?"

He sighs. "It's a little bit of everything, Cami. But you're not going to like the truth, so can we just drop it? I promise I'll tell you later when we're out of here."

"Tell me now."

"Because I asked him to," Dylan says from behind me. "After your transformation, I sought guidance on what to do. I wanted so badly to save you, Cami, to figure out how to change what I had done. In trying to save you, I had damned your soul.

But in asking for help, I didn't get the answers I wanted to hear."

"My father was right, wasn't he? He was concerned that the angelic army was after my soul."

"But they didn't want to save you," Dylan says.

Zach closes his eyes briefly, like he wishes Dylan hadn't said what he did. The room goes silent so that the only thing I hear is the occasional flapping of wings from the onlookers— the angels who I'm here to help, who wanted me dead and gone from this world.

I raise my finger at Zach. "Were you going to end my life, Zach?"

"If I felt it was necessary."

Hurt sweeps over me. I shouldn't be so surprised, but it doesn't sting any less. "That would've really stuck it to my fa-ther, huh?"

"Cami, I didn't take this position to send you to Hell or to get revenge on your father. I took this position because no one else would've given you a chance. And if it wasn't for Dylan, you probably never would've gotten a chance."

I have no idea what to say. I regret bringing this up so pub-licly, because now I have to swallow all the ugly emotions sneaking up on me. I have to pretend that it doesn't eat away at me knowing that the side I'm fighting on wanted to destroy me just for existing. It was bad enough that the alliance pushed me toward Hell, but this? Is this how my sister felt when the alli-ance murdered her? She wanted to fight with the alliance despite the alliance wanting her dead. She wouldn't turn her back on her convictions. But me? I don't know.

My lip trembles as I turn my eyes away from everyone and direct them to the floor. "How do you expect me to fight for the side who wanted to doom me?" My voice is so soft that I'm not sure anyone heard me.

"Princess," Zach whispers. He sounds as defeated as I feel. "Please."

A gentle hand touches my shoulder, and I turn to face Cadence. Tears line her honey-brown eyes, and looking at my best friend and seeing how much she hurts for me is the answer I've needed all along. It's not about what side I'm fighting on. It's about what I'm fighting for. And right now, I'm not fighting for Heaven or Hell. I'm fighting for my best friend. I'm fighting for those who need me. Those who don't stand a chance otherwise.

Straightening my shoulders, I turn and face the gaping angels. "Make no mistake. I'm not doing this for any of you, and when this is all over, you're going to leave me alone. I'm not going to stand by and have to prove my usefulness over and over again. I'm not going to fear for my life."

No one reacts. It's infuriating. So infuriating that I accidentally reveal my true body. The angels turn their gazes away from me like it physically pains them to look at me. Who knows, maybe it does.

"Clearly, people's thoughts still haven't changed," I mutter to no one in particular.

"That's enough, princess," Zach says.

"You're right. Do what you have to do so we can leave. I'm sure any one of these guys will be happy to blast me with their heavenly light."

"You want to do it right here?"

I nod. "Why not?" I turn to the angels. "Any volunteers?"

Three men and a woman step from the small crowd of angels, already wielding their heavenly light in their hands.

I gulp. I didn't expect so many angels to throw themselves at the opportunity. *You asked for it.*

Without warning, all four angels release a wave of light at me, hitting me squarely in the heart. Flying back, I hit the wall without absorbing the sudden influx of power being shoved at me and instead, feel my true body explode with pain. Tears swell in my eyes, and I drop to the floor, so overwhelmed by the light that it takes me a long time to stop resisting before I allow it into me.

"Cami!" Dylan calls, but Cadence and Zach hold him back while my vision turns white. The angelic power fills me to the brim, threatening to drown me, but the angels don't stop. My demonic power ignites within my soul, swirling around the angelic light, caging it in, allowing me to gasp for a much needed breath.

It's not until the edges of my vision darken that a rush of warmth flows through me, and a familiar presence seeps into my core. My body convulses as my demon blood fights with my Heaven-bound soul. Just when I think Hell's going to win me back, something shifts inside me. My sister's soul seeps from mine, latches onto the heavenly power and wraps around it, protecting it. The battle within me sputters out and the pain dissipates, leaving me breathless and shaken on the cold marble floor.

My vision clears, and I watch Zach expand his black wings on his back, creating a barricade between me and the other angels. His hazel eyes shine with an intensity unlike anything I've ever seen. It's not until this very moment that I realize how fierce and brave my guardian is.

His voice booms through the room, creating a stunned silence as he yells, "Enough!"

And just like that, the angels back away.

I force myself back to my feet, my knees quivering. My chest smolders where the gaping holes were before, and my glowing skin fades while I get myself under control and hide my true body.

Dylan and Cadence rush to my side, helping me stay on my feet. Dylan scoops me into his arms when I stumble on the way to the door. Cadence holds it open, and Dylan rushes me outside. Zach slams the door shut behind us.

While Dylan still holds me, Zach touches my cheek. "Princess, I'm so sorry. Are you okay?"

I groan. "What happened in there?" I manage to spit out. My skin might be tender from the blinding light, and my body feels like it's on the brink of shutting down, but my soul feels stronger and brighter than ever. I feel like I'm in perfect control.

"Did you just stand up to Heaven to make them stop?"

He releases a long breath. "I'm your guardian. They took it too far."

"But Heaven."

He pokes my nose with his finger. "It's not just Hell I swore to protect you from, Cami."

"Isn't that against the rules or something?"

He shrugs. "Well, I haven't lost my wings yet."

THE ROMANTIC

"FLY FASTER!" I yell, watching the glowing sun dip into the horizon. "We only have minutes."

"I don't see why your boyfriend just didn't go on the run for a bit."

"Running would be an automatic death sentence. You don't know my father. Evan means nothing to him. So pick up the pace, Zachy-poo. If I don't make it on time, I'm going to break your wings and ground you myself."

Zach nose dives back to earth, wind whipping through my hair. The aroma of salty air mingles with his jasmine scent, and I brace myself. He soars a few feet over the ocean until land comes into view.

The twilight sky sends dread through me, because we're still a few minutes away. Zach flies us above the houses, shielding us from view. A spark of light draws my attention to the road in front of us.

I'm too late.

My heart nearly stops when I spot Evan, standing tall before my father. Malicevile throws an energy orb directly at him, but when it plows into his stomach, Evan doesn't even move. He wouldn't dare fight against my father—it's why he chose to return to the house, knowing Malicevile would more likely return there. He knew we wouldn't stay at his hellacious compound, but I'm also sure he wasn't expecting Evan to be here.

"Let me go!" I yell to Zach.

Malicevile readies another energy orb. The only hope I can count on is that Malicevile wants Evan to suffer. A swift death would be unlike my father.

I squirm in Zach's arms until he hangs me out before him, his fingers digging under my arms. I dangle a few dozen feet above the ground, but Zach still doesn't drop me. Instead, he flies me closer and closer to Malicevile.

"Get ready, princess. The only way you're going to save your boyfriend is if your father doesn't see you coming."

With his words, I summon blue fire into my hands. I want Malicevile to suffer as much as he wants Evan to suffer, and this might be my only chance. Zach zooms closer, his black wings blending with the darkening sky, and when I'm within a few dozen feet of Malicevile, Zach swings me forward, shooting me through the air.

Malicevile spins on his feet to face me a moment before I collide right into him. I slam the blue fire into his chest, causing him to roar, and then he flips me onto my back. We both skid across the asphalt, forcing me to take the brunt of the fall. If it weren't for my leather jacket, my entire back would have been grated off onto the road.

Strong hands lace around my neck. Malicevile digs his sharp nails into my throat, cutting off my air supply. His vibrant green eyes flash red as he looks down on me. His true body juts from his forehead in a flash of deep crimson skin that looks coated in blood, and his sharp crown of horns threaten to impale me if he decides to head-butt me.

Grinding my teeth, my own true body breaks free. I summon another burst of blue flames, burning the skin on his wrists. He still doesn't let me go, even though the scent of burning flesh wafts around us.

I can't die by suffocation, but he could knock me out and ready me for the worst form of torture for stealing his most precious soul. He presses his weight into me, crushing and suffocating me before he releases a spark of electricity to add to my misery.

"Camilla, you're going to wish you'd died by the hands of the angels," he says, his voice rumbling deep in his throat. "You had no right to hand her over to them. Your sister's soul was mine!"

It takes everything in me to open and close my mouth. If I could just get the words out, he might not tear me limb from limb. *Fight, Cami! Make him see!*

The voice that swirls through my mind isn't my own will to survive. It's my sister pleading with me to fight back.

But I can't. I'm outmatched. Even with all my new power, I still can't manage to knock my father back. Hope slides out of me like water through a sieve. I'm failing.

Malicevile moves one of his hands from my neck to my chest, and in that small moment, I gasp for air. Electricity expels from his fingers but the shock doesn't hurt me. It doesn't have a chance. Blinding light erupts from my heart, knocking Malicevile off his feet. I'm not the one controlling the power, though. It comes from deep within my soul, straight through all the demonic evil churning through me.

Malicevile looks startled, surprise morphing his expression, smoothing out his sharp features. The light blinks out, leaving me on the ground, and my father stands over me and looks down. "Melanie?"

I swallow the ache in my throat and push to my elbows. "No."

"I don't understand."

"Of course you don't. You just assumed I wanted to give my sister to Heaven. Well, I didn't."

"Obviously. But how on earth is she—"

I raise my hand and cut him off. "I'm not saying anything until you agree to spare mine and Evan's lives. You must understand. I did what I did because I had no other choice."

"I wasn't planning to kill you, my dear. Not with that Heaven-bound soul of yours. Your boyfriend on the other hand—he had no business taking you to Hellshire Estate." Malicevile swivels at his waist to glower at Evan.

I zap him with his own power to draw his attention back to me. "Don't even think of it, Dad, or I'll take Evan and you'll never see either of us again. You might think you can control me, but you can't. Not anymore. If I have to spend eternity serving the angels to keep Evan from you then I will. Don't doubt me."

He crosses his arms. "I don't doubt you. I just don't see why you haven't already. Something made you stay. Now don't make me fight you to get it out of you."

My eyes shift to Evan's. He sits quietly on the curb, his shirt burned, revealing his abs. I could give a million fake reasons why I came back—like he was right about the angels or how I'm tired of being used—but none of those feel right.

Instead, I say, "I stay because even after how horrible you were to Evan, even after you put us both through Hell, he wants to stay. The angelic army—they don't care about him. They wouldn't even think twice about what happens to him. But I care so deeply for him that I'll risk everything to make sure he survives in the end."

"My daughter, the romantic. Control your heart, control you. Love leaves you weak. It causes you to make poor choices. It'll be what destroys you, you know."

Malicevile offers his hand to me and helps me to my feet. Draping an arm over my shoulders, he half hugs me, surprising me. The moment doesn't last long, though. Because before I realize what's going on, his fingers lock into my hair, and he lifts me off my feet. I squeeze my hands around his blistering wrists and try to pry his hands away without using my power against him.

"Dad, please," I beg, failing to summon my levitation. With all the other power swirling in my soul, it's hard to pull out one of the powers I was born with.

"Your excuses are rather pathetic, Camilla. You say you stay for love, but that's not the reason you stole your sister's soul from me. Now, tell me." He raises his free hand and holds it out at Evan. "Or you better call one of your angel pests to pull your boyfriend from Hell."

One look in his demonic eyes shows he's not bluffing. "I needed her," I whisper. "I can't handle both angelic and demon power. I needed a Heaven-bound soul to balance me out, and Melanie thought she would serve me better if she merged her soul with mine. She would rather spend eternity with me than trapped on your shelf."

He shakes me once before dropping me on my back. "I can't believe after everything she had gone through, she still chose them. And you, Camilla. I'm disappointed. You crave power so much so that you ask angels for it, even if that power weakens you. All for what? A walk in the daylight? I thought I taught you better."

I sneer from my place on the ground and summon every power I hold. One at a time, I blast Malicevile with each one. I can't help it. I want him to take back his words and choke on them. I'm tired of him seeing me as a weak little demon who needs her father to survive in this world. I'm tired of him not taking me seriously. I want him to see me at his level. I want him to fear me.

"Angelic power doesn't make me weak," I snap. "It makes me a better demon than you'll ever be. You think this world is yours, Dad? It's not. It can't ever be. Not like it is for me."

Instead of cowering or stepping back like I expect, Malicevile grins, his smile widening as I ruin his suit and mar his skin with power. He doesn't even turn away when I blast him in the face.

"Come on, my dear. Show me what you got!" He rolls his shoulders, taking another blast of blue fire. His smile ignites rage in my soul, and I scream a long, high-pitched wail, knocking him back a few feet. "Can't you do better than that? You can borrow as many powers as you want, but you're going to run out. What happens if I decide not to give you mine? What then? Is that angelic power enough to save you?"

With wild eyes, I launch a stream of blue power so intense that it engulfs Malicevile in flames. As the fire sears his skin and leaves him blistering, all he does is laugh. It's enough to get under my skin.

"Princess, if you continue down this path, you better plan on finishing him off right now, and then get ready to take on the entire demonic world." Zach's calming voice is enough to stop me in my fiery tracks. He's right. Because the moment Malicevile realizes what I can do, he won't hold back. And if he can still stand tall in the state I put him in, I'm pretty sure he can survive anything I throw at him.

I drop to my knees, covering my face in my hands. The exertion of power leaves me exhausted. Warm hands wrap around me, pulling me to my feet, and I hide my face in Evan's chest while he holds me.

The scent of burnt cinnamon and clove permeates the air, making my eyes water, and then hot, blood red hands rip me free of Evan. Malicevile holds me against him, his true body showing off his terrifying demonic self. Tendrils of smoke swirl from what's left of his tattered suit. His pure black eyes bore into me, like at any second he'd rip my sister's soul along with my own directly from me.

"Are you through with your tantrum, Camilla?" Malicevile asks, his hot breath hitting my face.

I can only nod.

"Good. Now it's my turn."

The world slows as Malicevile shifts me into one of his muscular arms, and then uses the other one to send a blast of energy directly toward Evan. My boyfriend drops to his knees, closing his eyes for a brief second. He opens them in time to see Malicevile blast him again.

And then again.

And again.

My heartbeat thuds in my ears. Evan falls forward, landing face first on the asphalt. My eyes blur with tears, making it hard to watch for Evan to gasp for a breath that takes what feels like forever to come.

"Get up!" Malicevile roars at Evan.

Evan doesn't move, and Malicevile raises his hand to shock him again. Before my father blasts him, I watch as Zach appears next to Evan and forces him to his feet. He remains hidden from Malicevile as he steadies Evan.

Tears burn my cheeks when I meet Zach's sad eyes. By protecting Evan the best he can, he's protecting me.

Malicevile tightens his hold on me. "Let this be a lesson to you. Choose Heaven again, and I'll kill him."

"And me?"

He bares his teeth. "I'll do everything in my power to break you. I'll make you suffer."

His words seal my decision. There's no turning back now. Whatever relationship we had shared is gone. This demon can't charm me anymore.

"Go to Hell," I say, grinding my teeth, half expecting him to smack me.

"Better yet, how about I bring Hell to us?"

THE WORLD FALLS APART

THE CRIES OF strangers echo through the dark room as I rest my head on Evan's lap. We've been locked away for hours in the vault at Hellshire Estate, which is impossible to escape from, the metal door impenetrable. Malicevile keeps me hidden away like one of his possessions.

A soft glow appears next to me. Angelic light radiates from Zach. It's not powerful or blinding like when he summons power but radiates from within him. It's subtle like he's turned himself into an angelic nightlight. The cries suddenly stop, leaving the room in utter silence.

"Princess, I think we've overestimated your father's devotion to you," he says, patting my knee.

I sigh. "You think? He's going to keep me in here until I beg for his mercy and turn my back on Heaven."

"So I guess we should get comfortable."

"No." Evan shifts, brushing his fingers through my soft hair. The chain around his neck moves to rest heavy on my arm. "I don't have all eternity."

He ignites a small flame in his fingers, lighting the room even more, and I shift my gaze to peer around us. The variety of scents stopped me from looking when we were first thrown in here, but now I force myself to assess the situation.

Chained to the walls like Evan are four figures. The demi-demons huddle together, their backs pressed to the wall with utter hopelessness crossing their faces. The oldest man, a seasoned hunter who looks familiar, but who I've never formally met, shifts to protect a girl who hides behind her hair. The two others, a teen boy and a man in his twenties, don't meet my gaze.

Zach climbs to his feet and crosses the room. Bending down, he inspects each demi-demon. They can't see him as he shields himself, but something in their expressions change as they sense his godly presence. Unlike the dread the presence of a demon brings, angels bring peace and comfort.

"These poor souls," he whispers, sending an ache into my heart. "If the consequences weren't too great for you, I'd consider saving them."

His pain, knowing that to protect me means others must

be sacrificed, is enough to bring tears to my eyes. Sitting up, I pull away from Evan and use the wall to get to my feet. My legs wobble as I cross the room to stand by Zach's side.

I drape my arm around his shoulders. "You should save them. Their lives are not worth less than mine. Plus, it'll teach my father to lock me away like this. I could use something to get his attention."

My guardian looks at me. His expression gives nothing away as he considers my words.

His eyes turn dark. "I can't take their souls without giving myself away. You'd have to extract them."

My eyes widen. "But I've only extracted souls my father had claimed."

"You'll have to murder me before you take my soul, demon," the older hunter says, only listening to my side of the conversation.

"This could work," Evan says from his place against the wall. "You're a demon, Cami, and he might not have traded his soul to Malicevile, but he's Hell-bound. Just look at his soul. I can kill him and you can do it."

I narrow my eyes, concentrating on peering into the man's soul. Sure enough, black streaks cut through the soft golden color, proving that Hell staked its claim on his eternity. I wonder what he has done to have his soul bind itself to Hell, but I don't ask.

I reach my hand toward him, and the man stiffens. His soul calls to me, begging me to try to stake my claim on it. I don't need a deal to usher his soul, only to keep it—and I've never sent a soul to Hell before. I bet I could if I tried. Guilt hits me at the thought. Could I damn him before his time? Could I do it if there was a possibility that Zach could redeem him?

"Princess," Zach whispers. "Be careful. Demons don't have their own souls for a reason. If you send him to Hell, you could jeopardize yourself. Are you willing to test the strength of your soul to send your father a message? I think letting him go on his own would be okay."

"I need to show him who he's dealing with, Zach."

Closing my eyes, I run my hand over the man's chest. All it would take is a swift bout of Evan's power to snuff his life out. The man stiffens under my touch, and the girl behind the seasoned hunter whimpers before she starts bawling her eyes out.

"Wait, please," she begs. "Don't hurt my dad."

I draw my gaze to the girl, my brows furrowing, and recognition sets in. I knew the hunter looked familiar, and it was because I'd seen him with the girl during my stay at the Hunter's Academy. It's been so long since I've seen Ella that I almost didn't recognize her. She was in a few of my classes and only a quarter demon. I'm actually surprised to see her here considering she's mostly human.

I open my mouth to say something, but the loud beep of the vault door sends me flying toward our only exit. Igniting my new favorite power in my hands, I ready myself as the door swings outward.

Without hesitating, I launch from the vault and collide into the rock-hard chest of a demon who isn't my father. It surprises me enough to make me pause, opening myself up for an attack. The demon slams his hands over my ears, sending a shooting pain in my head that feels like my brain is expanding against my skull and about to explode at any second.

As the insufferable pain washes over me, my senses suddenly cut off as something pushes into my head—not something physical—but like the man's power allows him to climb into me to kill me from within. It's unlike any power I've ever felt and as much as I try to absorb it and deflect it, I can't figure out how. I can't even touch it. I absorb tangible powers, not ones like this. Even good old George, a demon whose power felt like a magnetic pull, could be felt. I guess I'm not all-powerful after all. I have my limitations.

Fight, Cami. Don't hold back. All you have to do is break his concentration long enough to get him out of your head.

My sister's thoughts push me forward, and I concentrate on pulling power out from within my soul. I can't feel my hands, hear, or see, so I just blindly expel the power. Like being pulled from icy, dark water, I thrash as my senses come back all at once. Stars flicker through my vision as I scramble to get to my feet before the demon can get to his and latch his hands on my head again.

He's powerless if he can't touch me. No wonder my father doesn't consider him a threat and allows him access to the vault.

I hold the blue fire out as he scuttles to his feet. "Don't

move or I'll send you to Hell."

He freezes in his place and glowers at me. "Don't make this more difficult than it has to be, Ms. Hellshire. Your father only wants me to retrieve a half-breed. No harm will come to you or your little boy-toy if you let me do my job."

I step closer, preparing to blast him. "You can't make such a guarantee."

"I can't, but your father can. Kill me and you'll spend the next century in here. That's a promise." I'd like to see my father try. He only controls the night.

I flick my gaze to the dark vault once before I chuck the power at the demon. The blue light speeds through the air and hits him directly in the chest, sending blue flames through the room. The demon drops to the ground, the fire eating away at him, but he doesn't scream. As the blue light dissipates, I rush forward and slap my hand to the demon's chest.

"Camilla," Malicevile says, his voice sneaking up behind me. "Release him."

I snap my head up and glare. "No."

Malicevile summons power in his hands. "Do it now or I'll chain you up."

Summoning blue fire, I push it into the demon, hard and fast, strong enough to quickly eat through his skin and bones.

Malicevile roars as he throws his energy at me, but I don't stop. Instead, I smash my hand through, burning the demon's heart to dust. My knees hit the concrete floor as he explodes under me. I slide on the guts, trying to get to my feet while I absorb Malicevile's power. A set of keys jab into my palm, and I curl my fingers around them. Malicevile hits me with more power, closing the distance between us. I don't even have a chance to summon my own power before he kicks me in the stomach, launching me at the wall. My head cracks against the concrete, black bursts spotting my vision.

I sink into the warm darkness that attempts to protect me from the pain radiating through me. Malicevile yanks me by my hair from the floor and drags me back into the vault. Cold metal sears my skin, and he clamps a shackle on my neck.

"Is Heaven still worth it, my dear?" he asks, pinching my chin in his strong fingers.

I respond by flicking hot power into his face.

Swinging out his arm, he backhands me. Blood trickles from my mouth and onto my dirty shirt, but I don't wipe it off. I glower at him, though my body threatens to collapse to the ground.

He wags his eyebrows. "You'll thank me for this one day, Camilla. Once I get that Heaven out of you, you'll make the best ally. You won't be able to resist. I know how much you want the world."

Without you on it, I think to myself.

Leaning down, Malicevile kisses the top of my head before turning toward the demi-demons across the small room. His shoes tap against the floor, and he inspects each one of them. "It's getting a little crowded in here, isn't it, Camilla?"

"No," I whisper.

He ignores me, pulling a set of keys from his pocket and unlocks the shackle around Ella's neck. She cries as he drags her to her feet and then tosses her over his bent arm. The seasoned hunter, Ella's father, summons fire similar to Evan's in his hands and throws it at Malicevile.

Malicevile drops Ella to the ground with a thud before turning his gaze on the hunter. A bright flash of light barrels through the air, lighting the dark room, and the hunter wails when the electricity shocks him.

Ella screams, but I snatch her by the arm before she can launch herself at Malicevile. It's too late for her father. His soul already seeps from his body. Letting Ella attack Malicevile would mean her father died in vain. He sacrificed himself to try to save her.

I push Ella over to Evan and crawl forward, focusing on the hunter's soul.

"Heaven and their love of self-sacrifices," Malicevile mutters, gazing at the soul. "Costing me a potential demon. That half-breed would've served me well."

I blink in surprise. He's right. Ella's father's soul is no longer Hell-bound. Trying to save his daughter pushed him back into good grace. It's impossible for Malicevile to take a good soul. It should be impossible for me, too. But something about the pretty soul in front of me calls to me.

Stretching out as far as I can, I run my fingers through the hunter's soul. It swirls from his body and into my hand.

I'm so concerned about the soul that I don't notice

Malicevile glaring at me. In one quick motion, he ignites power in his hands and shoots it out at me. I crash back into the wall, the breath rushing from my lungs, and then I succumb to the light—the light of holding onto another Heaven-bound soul.

<hr>

"Cami, love. It's time to let him go." Dylan's voice wraps around me, pulling me from the depths of my mind. It seems I'm unconscious more often than not, and it's getting on my nerves.

Blinking my eyes in the bright sunshine, I stare at two figures hovering over me. Dylan meets my gaze with sad eyes, and the hunter—I now know is named Harrison—stands tall with his arms crossed over his chest.

"I—I'm so sorry," I say, wiping the back of my hand across my cheek. "I didn't know what to do."

"What you did was surprising and amazing. Demons can't take Heaven-bound souls, but you can. Now let him go."

"I don't know how," I say. Confusion creases my forehead as Harrison stares at me silently.

Dylan laces his fingers through mine and pulls me closer to Harrison. Covering his hand over mine, he presses our hands against Harrison's chest, his ethereal wings expanding on his back. A subtle chill rolls through me, and I feel energy pulsate through my fingers, but it's not demonic power. The energy is pure and good and sacred.

"Feel that tingling sensation?" Dylan asks.

I nod.

"Release it."

"I'm afraid."

"I won't let anything happen."

Following Dylan's lead, I slowly pull my hand away from Harrison's chest, imagining releasing the pure energy that hovers between us. Warmth blossoms through my core, and a cool sensation crawls down my arm and out my hand. And then I set it free completely.

The moment I release Harrison's soul, I drop to my knees with a feeling unlike anything I've ever felt sliding through me, pushing the darkness away. Like a blend of love, joy, peace, contentment, hope, and strength, the feeling fills me up and seals the fissures in my soul. Zach mentioned what would happen if I ushered a soul to Hell, but he never mentioned Heaven. I didn't even know it was possible. Yet, here I am, straddling the line between Heaven and Hell and able to touch both places.

The moment my thoughts turn to Zach, I jerk my head up and stare wildly into Dylan's eyes. When he sees the sudden despair thrusting away everything good I just experienced, the smile melts from his face.

"Oh, God, Dylan. Can you send me back? My father—he—" I groan into my hands. "I need to go back now! I need to protect Evan. I need to protect the others." I wouldn't put it past my father to slaughter them all to teach me a lesson.

Cool arms embrace me, pulling me from the ground. "Calm down, love. We'll figure this out."

I smack Dylan's chest. "You don't know that! I've already been here too long. Returning to my father was a huge mistake. He's going to break me. I can feel it. I can only hold on for so much longer."

"Sunrise isn't far away." He brushes the knotted strands from my hair.

"I can't leave Evan or the others."

"Then I'm coming to help you."

"No. Stay away, Dylan."

"I'm not useless, Cami. The angels will back me."

"It's dangerous."

"It's my decision."

"I'd rather die than put any more people at risk."

"And I'd rather you live."

As my emotions run rampant, the world around us cracks and splinters. I fight hard to wake myself up. Dylan holds me tighter against him, pressing his lips to my temple, and I struggle in his arms, breathing in his apple scent.

"Cami, hang on a little longer. I'll gather the angels. We'll scope out the place and see what we can do," he whispers, flapping his wings.

"No!"

He disappears a second later, and there's nothing I can do as my world falls apart.

INCREDIBLE THINGS

"EVAN!" I SCREAM, levitating to my feet only to jerk against the shackle around my neck. The metal cuts into my neck and I gag before sprawling across the floor. Coughing, I dig my fingers into the space between the shackle and my skin, but it doesn't budge.

A hot hand grabs onto my wrist and drags me from the floor. Evan's patchouli scent drifts to my nose, and he hugs me against him, kissing my forehead. He tilts my chin up to meet his soft lips.

"Oh, God. Are you okay?" I struggle to sit upright to peer around. "Zach? What about everyone else?"

No one responds quickly enough, so I summon angelic light in the palms of my hands. I don't want to awaken any of my demonic powers while I still cling to what's left of the feeling that touching Heaven released in me.

The soft glow lights the room, and my gaze rests immediately on Harrison's discarded body. Ella cries silently over her father. Anger rushes through me—Malicevile left the body here to torture us and remind us of what he's capable of. The other two demi-demons remain in the same position I remember. At least I distracted my father enough to leave them alone for now.

"You saved them," Zach says, appearing beside me. He pulls me from Evan to get a look at me. "Whatever you did with that man's soul was enough to send Malicevile fleeing."

"I—" I take a deep breath, settling my shaking nerves. "I ushered Harrison to Heaven."

Ella gasps, blinking through her tears. For the first time since I've laid eyes on her, I see hope. It's a small flicker, but it's there.

"I touched Heaven," I whisper, like I can't believe it myself.

Zach studies me, a smile crossing his face. Reaching out his hand, he gently caresses my cheek before pushing my hair behind my ear.

"You don't look surprised," I say, grinning back at Zach. If we weren't in this room, sitting in front of these tortured demi-demons, I'd probably hold my hand up for a high-five.

"I've always known you were capable of incredible things,

princess. I've never doubted your awesomeness." He boops my nose with his finger, and I automatically flick his hand.

Evan clears his throat, drawing my attention away. It's not until now that I realize how silent the room is. The demi-demons are watching and listening. They probably think I've gone mad, because I'm clearly not talking to Evan.

I shift uncomfortably, glancing at Evan before turning back to Zach. I don't respond to their curious gazes. It'd put Zach at risk. I can't afford for my father to know that an angel has been in my midst since he stole me away. He'd surely try to use Zach to complete his plan.

Zach chuckles as my cheeks flush. "Want me to use a little angelic power on them?"

I nod. "Please do. We need to come up with a plan, and it's better if they don't know."

"That's a good idea, Cami," Evan says speaking up. "Because Malicevile will be back. You can count on it."

"Oh, I am."

Zach gets to his feet and expands his huge black wings. They take up the entire room. The three demi-demons startle when he appears before them, but none of them scream. They don't even move when he touches their foreheads. Within a minute, all three demi-demons rest quietly on the floor.

Zach turns to me. "Now what?"

I shift my legs to stand and knock something heavy with my knee. I reach out and feel the set of keys I had scooped up from the dead demon. Lifting my hands, I jiggle the keys in front of me.

"First, we take these chains off," I say.

"Then what?" Evan asks.

"We wait."

~∾∾~

"Dawn is approaching, princess," Zach says, pacing the small vault.

Night might keep me in this prison, but there's one thing I can count on. A different kind of prison. While the angelic light anchors me to earth, it doesn't chain me down and lock away the key. I can still enter the demon realm with Zach. I can move in and out without an issue. It'll give me the chance to walk right out of here.

I press my face into Evan's chest, clinging to him like if I can just hold on tight enough, I can take him with me. I will it with my very being for it to happen. If I could have a miracle, I'd waste it in this moment instead of on the world. Because Evan is my world.

Without having to see the sky, I can feel the sun deep in my blood. "Less than a minute," I whisper.

"I love you, Cami. If you can't get me out of this vault, I want you to leave, okay?" Evan says, breathing into my ear.

Tears prickle in my eyes. "I'll get you out. I'm not leaving you."

"You might have to. I don't want to be the reason you're forced to turn your back on everything you've fought for."

"You're here because of me."

"I knew what I was getting into the moment I decided to trade my soul and then decided to stay. I'm here because of the decisions I've made. Don't ever blame yourself for my actions, and don't you dare give up your chance to live the life you want because of me. I've damned myself to Hell. I'm not going to be the reason you damn yourself again, too."

"Evan..."

He cups my face in his hand. "I love you, Cami. I'll love you no matter how things end for us."

"Don't say it like it's goodbye," I whisper.

He bends down and brushes his lips against mine. "But it might be."

"Just a few steps," I tell Zach.

He nods.

The air shimmers around us, and the dark vault fades into the dusty light of the prison realm. The tidal wave of emotions that threatened to drown me now drains away, leaving me preciously numb. I had almost forgotten how blissful it could be in moments that threaten to tear me into a million pieces before scattering me on the wind.

I blink, adjusting to the change in my vision. The space where Evan stood is now filled by Zach. He unfurls his black wings for a moment before they disappear. He offers me a sad smile but doesn't say anything. It'd be too easy to say that everything is going to be okay when we both know that it's never so simple. No matter how hard you wish and pray and beg, some things just won't happen.

The crack of a tree branch catches my attention, and I spot a familiar figure standing a few dozen feet behind Zach. Malicevile steps from the dead brush he appeared in, smoothing his suit jacket.

Something in me unravels.

Without thinking, I shove Zach out of the way and rush toward my father, going against the plan to move far enough away from the vault to escape it. We'll have until sundown to figure out how to open the vault for the others, while also dealing with Malicevile's minions. Even then, there is no guarantee.

But now that I see Malicevile before me, I want to attack him in the one place neither of us can die. I want to show myself, show that I can escape his little prison—and this one, too. I want to rub it in and piss him off. He'll be seething for the next few hours.

"Princess!" Zach yells from behind me.

But he's not fast enough to stop me. I collide into Malicevile, knocking him off his feet. The moment I touch my father, the protective shield that makes me invisible and untraceable disappears.

I straddle my father and he jolts me with power, but it doesn't knock me off. The energy barely fazes me. When our eyes meet and he smiles, I do the only thing I can think of. I sucker punch him in the nose. His smile is enough to pull bitterness from my soul, pushing it through the numbness of the world. Being Heaven-bound leaves me susceptible to my emotions—even here. Something as little as a wrong look brings my emotions brimming to the surface.

"Are you happy?" My voice bellows through the gnarled forest. I latch my fingers onto his shoulders and shake him. "Look at where I'm at! This is your fault."

"This is where you belong, Camilla. You can try as hard as you want to grow a pair of wings and ascend, but you're wasting your time. You're a demon. My blood runs through your veins. We are connected for eternity whether you want to be or not. You're just making things hard on both of us. And for what? Because you can't have your way? Because you think you know what's best? Because some heavenly manipulators showed you the light? That light blinded you."

I shake him again. "That light helped me see you for the monster you are."

"We are no different," he says, refusing to react to the pain I inflict on him.

"You don't think I know that? I see the way the world looks at me. I can smell the fear and mistrust. The judgment."

"This is why you need to realize that your place is by my side and not with them."

"You think being among our kin is any different? Demons try to murder me every chance they get. They want to use me as much as the angels do."

"I can protect you."

"I don't want your protection. I can't just forget everything that you've done to me. You left me chained to a wall. You threatened the boy I love. You torture me, abuse me, push me to the brink of destruction—all in the name of molding me into something I'll never be. I'm not like you, Dad. I have your blood, but that's it. There's no fixing what you've damaged. I'm never going to change."

"I'm not trying to mold you into something you're not. I'm pushing you to show you exactly what you're capable of and how strong you can be. You've spent so much time living in the human world that you desire to be mundane. You're my daughter. I refuse to let you settle for less. I want you to want more. I want you to want to take the world. And if I have to take everything from you and destroy everything that you were, I will!"

Slamming his fists in my chest, he thrusts me off him and into a tree. The wind whooshes from my lungs and my back cracks against the trunk, breaking the tree in half and raining dead leaves down on me.

I blink, and Malicevile's on his feet. I scramble away, crawling backwards, because I'm afraid that if he touches me, I'll be stuck here for the rest of the day. If Zach reveals himself, there's no turning back. I was such an idiot. I let Hell control me.

"Run, princess," Zach says from next to me. "I can't shield you unless you get out of view. Now move it!"

I levitate to my feet only to get shocked in the back. Turning on my heels, I race away, weaving in and out of the trees. For the first time ever, Malicevile runs after me. His footsteps ring in my ears as he charges behind me, making it impossible to get much distance between us.

"Camilla! Stop right now." Malicevile's voice booms

through the air, and he draws closer and closer to me.

"No! I'm not getting locked up in that vault again."

"Camilla, if you don't stop, the first thing I'll do when the sun sets is send Evan to Hell."

"He's bluffing, Cami. Keep running. Fifty feet. We can lose him in fifty feet," Zach says, urging me on.

"Kill him, and I'll have nothing left to lose," I say, forcing my legs to work harder. "I'll send you to Hell myself."

"I didn't say I'd send him personally. He's going to send himself. You can't fault me for a choice he'll make on his own."

My heart sinks into my stomach at his words. "He wouldn't."

"If it's possible he'll return better than ever, he might."

I slow down. I can't help it.

"Princess, he's lying. He's trying to trick you."

"It seems a nephilim was spotted near my estate just before sunrise."

My fiery blood cools and my steps falter. Hot hands grab me by my shoulders, spinning me around. I face my father's demented eyes head on. One look shows me he's telling the truth. I can feel it to my very soul. I knew Dylan wanted to come to my rescue. I knew he was going to take advantage of the sunlight. But what I didn't expect was for him to be careless enough to get caught.

"No," I whisper. "He'll never do it."

Malicevile shrugs. "If he doesn't, then both of them will die."

WHAT'S AT STAKE

ANGER WASHES OVER me and power ignites in my fingers. Not my demonic power but the angelic light. I shove my hands at Malicevile's chest, pushing him back. The force of the light knocks him off his feet, but it doesn't keep him down long.

Cool fingers latch around my arm, yanking me away, and I meet Zach's wild eyes. His chestnut hair flies around his head. He flaps his wings, and then he launches us into the air before Malicevile can get his hands on me.

As we ascend into the brown sky, a spark of electricity blasts right into us, hitting Zach hard enough to knock us off course. We freefall for a moment before my guardian catches his bearings, but Malicevile attacks again. Electricity ripples over Zach's left wing, and a few black feathers scatter through the air. The only thing that stops us from smashing into the ground is my levitation. I hold Zach's weight against me with one arm and summon blue fire in my other hand.

But I'm too slow. Malicevile throws another bout of energy, hitting my guardian hard enough to separate us. Smoke billows through the air. Malicevile latches onto Zach's wing, and my heart stalls.

"I should've known you'd try to steal my daughter from me again, Zachariel. Didn't you learn your lesson the first time?" With a flick of his wrist, my father twists his hand, snapping the bones in Zach's wing.

Zach yells out, blasting my father with angelic light, but it does nothing but make Malicevile smile.

Fear washes over me in a freezing wave, the edges of my vision darkening in crimson red. Pain mars Zach's angelic face, and tears sparkle on his cheek as he grinds his teeth. Malicevile kicks him to the dirt to stand on his back. Seeing the odd angle of Zach's eerily beautiful wing, my stomach churns.

But Malicevile doesn't stop there.

To my horror, he grabs Zach's other wing and grips it between his hands.

As Malicevile starts to twist it, I release a long, loud scream and fly forward. Heavenly light erupts from my core, and I tackle my father. Black feathers drift through the air, falling around us in the most heart-wrenching shower I've ever seen.

The air shimmers around me, heavenly light consuming my vision. The light prison realm thrusts me away, and I'm left kneeling in the middle of a vibrant green lawn in front of an unfamiliar house. We're nowhere near the vault. I groan as sun beams warm my skin. I grip my knees, gasping for breath.

"Princess," Zach whispers from behind me.

Tearfully, I scramble to his side. His broken wing hangs crookedly, the tip grazing the grass. "Oh, God. Your wing. This is my fault."

Zach gazes up at me and rolls his shoulder. "It's not, princess. This was your father's doing."

"If I hadn't—"

He reaches up and touches his finger to my lips. "Shhh. It's only a broken wing."

"But you've been grounded."

"And I have two legs."

I close my eyes for a second to compose myself. "You need to call one of your sidekicks to pick you up. I'm not going to let my father force you to fall."

"If I do, they'll make you come with us."

"But I can't go. I can't allow Malicevile to give Evan the option to transform. He'll take it. I know it."

"Dylan won't go to Hell for him," Zach says. "You don't have to worry."

I frown. "They're going to die then."

"I want to talk you out of it, but I can see your mind is set. Are you willing to risk the world in the name of love, Cami? Are you sure it'll be worth it?"

"Make me feel guilty, why don't you?" I say. When he puts it like that, I feel like crap. My legacy will be the demon who destroyed the world in the name of love. But what if I can save the world, too?

"That's not my intention. I just want to make sure you understand what's at stake."

"Do you trust me, Zach?"

"Yes."

"Then trust that I know what I'm doing."

"I guess we better start walking."

⁂

The time we spent in the daylight realm has already eaten away over half our day because of how quickly time moves there. It doesn't help that I've run a few miles from Hellshire Estate, since the realm doesn't reflect the earth world either. At the pace we're moving, we'll never make it before dark.

"I don't think we can do this alone, princess," Zach says as we pass a gas station on the long stretch of road that'll lead us out of yet another sprawling city. "I think we should call for backup."

"You said the angels would force us to go with them so you can recover," I say, scrunching my nose. I'd hate to have to fight the beings that are already suspicious of me, but I'd do it to make sure the people I love don't get hurt, or worse.

"I wasn't talking about the angelic army. You know, there are people better suited for demon slaying."

I suck in my bottom lip at the thought. "You want me to call Cadence?"

He nods. "I have great faith in her skills."

"But she could get hurt."

"Or she could help us."

He's right. Cadence would be pretty peeved if she discovered that I didn't call her when I needed help. We're best friends. We fight together. She'd been hunting with me for weeks. As long as I can take care of my father, she could handle the part I really need help with—saving the others.

Finally, I nod. Zach motions for me to follow him to the gas station, where a man chats on his cell phone at one of the gas pumps. I remain behind, lurking near the street, while Zach takes the lead. He's much more of a people person than I am. I'm more likely to send them running despite wearing my imaginary honorary halo.

Zach returns a moment later, the phone already ringing, but it goes to voicemail. He dials another number and when the line clicks, Alana says, "Hello?"

"Alana, can I talk to Cadence?"

"Cami, where are you? Cadence is supposed to be with you."

"What?"

"She went with Dylan when the angelic army deemed a rescue mission too dangerous on such short notice."

Oh, God. I'm so upset at my friends. Of course Cadence would never let Dylan go alone. If they were here, I'd be screaming my lungs out at them for jumping on a suicide mission to save me when I wasn't on the brink of death or anything. Their lives are worth more than losing my soul to Hell. I could lose them altogether.

My chest clenches. "What were they thinking?"

"They were only supposed to assess the situation."

"Well, they got caught right before sunrise. I had no idea Cadence was with Dylan. I was calling her for help. Zach's wing is broken, and we're running out of light. What do I do? Malicevile will kill them." I cover my face with my hand as Zach rubs my back. It's been a long time since I've asked Alana for advice. I miss the days where she was always with me. I could use her strength now.

"We're not going to let that happen. Tell me where you are. I'm coming."

"Are you sure? It'll be dangerous."

"I want to do this. I *need* to do this. You guys are all I have left. Malicevile has stolen enough from us, hasn't he? He can't have them."

I smile as I nod, though she can't see me. "Thank you, Alana."

Jacie's final words sneak up on me, touching my heart. All this time I've been trying to face my father alone. I had planned to kill him alone so no one else got hurt. But that's where my fault lies. I don't have to do this alone. Not when people are willing to stand up with me. Because together, we're stronger. Together, we might just make it out alive.

NO MERCY LEFT

"YOU BROUGHT BACKUP," I say, sliding into the backseat of the Jag to look at Alana's partner.

Alana and Aston shift in their seats to peer at me. Alana offers a sad smile, and I force myself to keep it together even though I'd rather just curl into a ball and cry my eyes out. It helps that Zach touches my knee, emanating enough hope and faith for both of us. Even a broken wing can't keep him down. I still feel guilty for calling him the worst guardian ever, when in reality, he's been the best. Not many people would let me drag them into a battle to save so few when so much more is at stake. But it's the little things that matter. It's the individuals that make a difference to me. It makes the stakes higher, because I have to save the world for them.

"Cadence is my family," Aston says, hoisting up a duffle bag to hand to me. It's filled to the brim with so many weapons that I doubt we can carry them all.

"She's mine, too." Obviously, she'd do the same for me. I don't mention it, though. Aston probably blames me for all of this. I'm the girl whose demonic father destroyed the Hunter's Alliance, and now I'm a demon, who's supposed to be his worst enemy. I never thought I'd see the day I'd be fighting beside him. Mutual enemies do that to people.

"We're going to get her back. We still have two hours to sunset. Light is on our side," Alana says. "Malicevile's going to regret hurting you, Cami."

"I'm going to make him regret having me at all."

Zach chuckles next to me, somehow lightening the somber mood. He's a lot like Cadence in a way, finding humor in the most dire moments—not only laughing at danger, but making fun of it as well. If Zach wasn't beyond mortal relationships or my guardian, I'd try to set them up.

As Alana speeds down the road, I run through my make-shift plan with both hunters. If everything goes as planned, we'll get the others out with plenty of time to get to a safe house. What I don't mention is my other plan. The one that involves me staying behind to make sure Malicevile doesn't try to go af-ter my friends again. Because he was right about me—control my heart, control me—and every person I care about in my life holds a piece of my heart. It doesn't sit heavy in my chest. My heart is scattered through the world I desperately want to hold on to.

Tonight, I'm going to show my father what he's wanted all along. I'm going to show him just how powerful I really am. The demon world will beg for mercy. But I have none left. They can thank Malicevile for that.

The wrought iron gates that lead to the road that'll take us into the compound come into view. Alana accelerates, picking up speed, and I brace myself. She smashes into the gate, and we barrel through. The front of the Jag is crushed, but miraculously, it still drives. I direct her straight to the front door.

There's no point in sneaking around. If people are going to come after us, I'd rather they charge us head on. It'll be faster to sever their souls from my father and direct them where they'll be spending eternity.

When I reach the front door, I twist the knob and kick it open. I chuck a bout of electricity into the entryway without even checking to see what I'm about to face. The last time I entered the front door, Elora, Malicevile's witchy minion, tried to cast a spell of some sort on me. In this moment, she's my biggest threat, and I won't let her take me by surprise.

"Subtle, Cami," Alana whispers from behind me.

"Watch out for the witch," I say over my shoulder.

No one says anything, and I stride into the foyer with power blazing in my hands. "Try to sneak up on me, and it'll be the last thing you do!" I scream into the grand entrance.

A loud pop echoes, and a bullet ricochets off a bulletproof window. Both Alana and Aston duck behind a decorative table as another gunshot sounds out. Zach remains by my side without flinching. The bullet clunks into the wall behind us.

Winding my arm, I expel a stream of blue fire in the direction of the gunshots. A deep wail reverberates through the air. My power washes over a tainted man who tries to shoot me again, even though my power consumes him.

I dash forward and stab my dagger straight through his chest. I'm a demon, but I'm not cruel. There was no need to make him suffer longer than he had to. He drops to the ground, the overwhelming stench of burning flesh and fabric clouding my senses. His inky soul drifts from him, but I don't touch it.

Zach shakes his head when I meet his eyes. "Unless you want to send him on his merry way to the gates of Hell, we need to leave him. There's no redemption for his murderous soul. Your father sure knows how to pick them."

I bare my bottom teeth in a grimace. "Yeah, not really in the mood to test my luck."

Leaving the man's soul and body behind, I motion the others to stay close behind me. Zach mirrors my every move, his wings now invisible, though I can see him occasionally clench his jaw at sudden movements.

"This place is too quiet," Alana whispers, turning her back to me to check behind us for the millionth time. "Malicevile would never leave his possessions in the hands of one tainted soul. Something's up."

She's right about that. Dread seeps into my stomach the deeper we make our way into his maze of a compound. Without Evan, I'm going off my memory, and it seems to be failing me. I swear we've passed the same picture twice though we haven't made any turns.

Sliding my dagger from its sheath, I carve a huge X into the cream-colored wall before striding forward again. A wave of nausea washes over me, and I shake the sudden confusion from my mind when the X appears a few feet in front of us.

An earthy smell of pine and sandalwood sneaks up on my senses, and I spin in place, looking down the hallway in both directions. Iridescent smoke trickles through the air, seeming to come from every crack and crevice, surrounding us in a blanket of hazy air I hadn't noticed when we were moving.

"Crap," I say, stabbing my blade into the wall. "We're being spelled. I thought I'd see Elora coming."

Zach rubs his chin as we stand in the hallway. We've wasted at least ten minutes, and the longer I stand here, the more nervous I get. What if we're stuck here until sundown, and Malicevile comes to collect us? Then what?

"Elora!" I scream, releasing a long gust of wind to clear the hazy air with my tornado breath. It's a stupid power, but it does come in handy—like my extra sensitive sense of smell. "Face me!"

Elora shimmers into view, her long black skirt shifting around her ankles in an imaginary breeze. She doesn't smile when she meets my annoyed expression. All she does is stand there with her wavy dark hair veiling half her face.

I blast a bolt of electricity in her direction, and it zaps right through her, disappearing into the never-ending hallway.

Freaking fantastic. How on earth am I supposed to stop her if I can't even touch her?

"You little witch! Why are you doing this? What does my father have on you?"

She sways as she moves closer. It's easy to be fearless in the face of a demon when they can't actually hurt you. A smile pulls up one side of her lips, because in this moment, she's more powerful than Malicevile's own daughter.

"You should've run when you had the chance. And now, you've returned with a gift. This angel is much more suitable than the half-breed. Your father will be pleased with me," she says. Her gaze flickers to Alana and Aston. "If you leave the angel behind without a fight, I won't tell him about your two little hunters."

"Are you kidding me?"

She shrugs. "You're wondering why I'm willing to make a bargain? You don't respect your father's demonic contracts, and mine doesn't expire for a long time. I know you'll kill me if the opportunity arises, and Malicevile won't protect me."

I clench my fingers into fists. "I'm not running. So either stop this magic or you can bet that I'll not only kill you, but I'll also take your soul."

She shakes her head. "No."

Shifting on my feet, I lean closer to Zach. "We need to

cross planes for a second. Her magic can't follow us."

"That's a huge risk. What about the others?" he whispers.

I grab Alana's arm and pull her to me. "I know we haven't had the best few months, and in no way do I deserve your help, but I need you to trust me."

She tilts her chin in agreement without revealing too much to the powerful witch. "I do."

"Grab Aston and drop to the floor the moment I disappear, and don't get up, okay?"

"Okay."

Turning to Zach, I hug him against me. His wings expand on his back, and he groans with the movement but doesn't stop while his heavenly light drags us into the light prison realm. The hazy brown air swirls around us for a moment, and then electrifying light hits my back. Malicevile's voice rings through the air, but Zach engulfs us in ethereal light, protecting us, and a second later, we cross back to the earth plane.

The shimmery air clears, and I yank myself away from my guardian, shooting a wave of blue fire through the hallway and setting the whole place ablaze in demonic light. The second I took to cross planes was enough the break the enchantment. My dread disappears, and my blue flames eat at an invisible barrier, revealing Elora standing behind her protective magic.

Her eyes widen, realization about what I've done smacking her hard. She holds her hands up, screaming something in a language I'm unfamiliar with, but she's too slow. I thrust out my hands, sending an orb of energy directly at her chest. She flies backward, skidding across the ground. Her skirt smolders with power, but she's not dead.

"Let us go and I won't finish you off," I say. "Use magic on me again, and I will keep your soul. If you think my father is scary, you're going to realize you've been sorely mistaken." With my words, I unveil my true body, flashing my horns and blood red eyes.

The witch remains in her place, and I close the space between us. I pull her from the floor before binding her wrists behind her back with a set of blessed cuffs Alana had among her supplies. I notice a glowing amulet around her neck and rip the chain free. Elora glowers but doesn't say anything.

"You can have this back after I get my friends out of here," I say, pocketing the necklace.

"You're making a huge mistake," she says when I turn away from her. "Heed my warning and get out while you can."

I glance at her from over my shoulder. "I'm not leaving my friends behind."

"Friends or not, what you're about to face will be the cause of your undoing. You can't remain in purgatory forever. You will have to make a choice."

"I already have," I say, motioning the others to move. "I'm not picking Heaven or Hell. I'm picking humanity."

FINISH THIS

THE MOMENT WE step off the elevator and into the nearly pitch-black hallway, the sounds of the damned whisper through the air, slicing through my skin to crawl inside me. Dozens of tainted people voice their sorrows—some praying to God, some crying, some yelling their anger. As we pass each grate-covered window, I stop to peek in.

"Save me!" a woman screams, popping into view through the grate.

Her high-pitched voice startles me, and I fly back, smacking into Zach's hard body. He steadies me on my feet, holding me like I need the extra support.

This tainted woman is the first person to confront me straight on. "I don't deserve this!" she yells.

Straightening my shoulders, I step forward. "How long have you been in here?"

The woman stumbles back in shock. I guess no one ever responds to her. "You shouldn't be here," she says after a moment.

"Yeah, I keep getting that," I mutter.

"It's not dark."

Oh, that's what she meant. Once you've been tainted by demons, it's easy to figure things out. "I'm different."

"You can help me," she says.

"Probably not."

"You're looking for someone." She sticks her fingers through the grates.

That grabs my attention. "How would you know?"

"You're not bringing those hunters in to lock up, which means you're after the hunter who was brought in this morning." She holds one arm across her chest. "Being trapped here gives me nothing better to do than watch the hall, and it's been so long since the demon brought in a human hunter. I knew she was special."

I keep my face steady. "Is she here?"

"Can't answer that."

"You can't or you won't?"

"You're wasting your time, Cami," Alana says. "She's not going to help us."

Zach digs his hands into his pocket and pulls out the set of keys I stole. "I think she might."

The woman sucks in a deep breath, hitting her hands against the door when she sees the keys. "Open the door, and I'll tell you anything you want!"

Alana shakes her head at me, but I tug the keys from Zach and go through five of them before the lock clicks open. If this woman has information about Cadence, then I'll give her what she wants for it.

I push the door inward to allow the woman to step into the corridor. Her whole body trembles as she exits the cell, like she's gulped a few gallons of coffee. Her jittery nerves make me anxious, and I take a step back when she reaches out to touch me.

I summon a small burst of my father's power in my hand. "Where did they take the hunter?"

Her dull blue eyes twitch, and she points to the end of the hallway. "The vault."

I blow out a frustrated breath. "I was in the vault."

Her mouth drops open for a second at the realization that I've caught her in a lie. She dodges past me with wild eyes, colliding into Alana. The two of them hit the wall. The woman catches us all off guard and manages to swipe a blade right from Alana's hip holster.

"Come any closer, and I'll kill her," the woman growls. "The demon will change my contract for capturing another hunter."

I laugh. I can't help it. "You seriously think that's how

things are going to work out for you?"

She scrambles to pull Alana against her. Alana's steely gray eyes hold mine. She's not even fazed by the tainted woman. Her serious expression keeps my own nerves under control.

"You're just wasting your time. Plus, if you kill her, I'll just put you right back in that cell for my father."

Her eyes narrow. "Don't test me."

The power in my fingers lights up the dark hallway, drawing the woman's focus to my hand. Aston sneaks up on the woman, his shadow crawling across the wall. She was incredibly foolish for assuming she had a fighting chance. Her desperation got the best of her when I was going to let her go.

Swinging his arm back, Aston punches the woman in the face while Alana grabs for the blade. The woman screams and stumbles to the floor away from the hunters. There's a reason she's locked up in one of these cells—she's completely useless. Only those useful can serve my father in the outside world.

The woman raises her hands protectively. "Wait! I'm sorry! I can help you. Let me make a deal with you."

It takes everything in me not to let my demonic blood control me. I'd like nothing more than to snuff out this woman's life. But one look at Zach makes me hesitate. A line puckers between his eyebrows as he watches me. He won't stop me from doing what I feel is right, but he'll make me question why. I'd rather act now and think later.

"Tell me what you know about the hunter," I say.

The woman huffs. "And then you'll help me?"

"This isn't how it's going to work. You're going to tell me what you know without any promises from me. If you can do that, then I might be able to work something out—but I also might not."

"No. I need a guarantee."

I turn to Alana. "Put her back in the cell."

"No!" the woman screams. "Please! The girl you're looking for was taken to the kennels. You have to turn right at the end of the hall. I always hear the howling at dusk."

What? Why on earth would Malicevile take Cadence to the kennels? She's not a werewolf. She's—*oh, God.* No. No. No. Cadence would never make a deal with Malicevile, and there's no way for him to get his hands on her Heaven-bound soul. He put Cadence in the kennels as her death sentence. He wants her last moments alive to be the most horrible thing possible—death by hellhound is a horrendous way to go.

"We have to hurry," I say. "If we don't get to her by dark, she's dead. She'll be burned and eaten alive."

Aston swears, his voice booming through the air. In one quick motion, he rips the woman from the ground and smashes her back to the wall. "If you're lying..."

"Aston, stop. We don't have time." I turn to the woman. "Since I can't trust that you're not lying or setting us up, here are your options. One, you can leave and try to escape, or two, you can go back in your cell and see if we make it back alive, and we'll take you with us."

"You forgot option three, princess," Zach says, speaking

up.

I frown.

He reaches out and touches the woman. "Cami can break your contract, but with that, your mortal life will end. I can assure your redemption, though."

I blink. I hadn't even bothered to look at her soul. I just assumed that she'd done some atrocious stuff to wind up in this position. Not many of the souls Malicevile possesses have the option of being saved.

The woman studies Zach for a moment. "I—"

Aston shakes her. "Decide now!"

"Save me," she whispers.

Sucking in a deep breath, I shock the woman's heart with my power, killing her in an instant. Aston catches her body as she falls and gently sets her on the ground. Her soul shines brightly with one single streak chained around her heart.

I close my eyes, my fingers grazing her soul. Her life flashes before me. This woman has been in here for years—since she was my age. She didn't murder people or cause harm. She was a victim. This woman traded her soul to Malicevile so he'd punish the vile man who was a monster and not a father. She did it to save her little brother and two sisters.

Tears prickle in my eyes, and I hand her soul over to Zach. Even with a broken wing, he manages to wrap them around us, his heavenly light radiating from his very being. A moment later, the woman's soul is gone, and Zach's jasmine scent is stronger than ever.

"It's done," he says.

Heaven's grace clings to him, sending an ounce of jealousy through me, because I wasn't the one who got to touch Heaven by ushering her soul. But we're running out of time, and I don't think I could've done it fast enough.

Zach offers his hand out to me. "Time to go, princess."

I race next to him with Alana and Aston behind us. When we reach the end of the corridor, I fly right like the woman said. We find ourselves in another long, dark hallway. I stop at the end where it breaks off into another hallway, and fear sneaks into me.

"Which way?" I ask.

"We can split up," Alana says.

I squeeze my eyes closed for a second. "It's too close to dark."

"Then we—"

A symphony of low howls cuts through the silence of the dark hallway. With wide eyes, I spin to face Zach. We're too late. The sun has set. I can't believe we've come all this way to fail. And what's worse is that the hellhounds are the least of our problems.

"This way!" Alana yells, shoving me forward and to the right.

Half-levitating and half-running, I break away from the others and run as fast as possible. The stench of burning flesh clouds the hallway, pushing me toward the very last door. A scream rips through the air, cooling my fiery blood, and I can't stop my own scream from unleashing through the air.

A string of curse words sound out, and I recognize Cadence's voice. I reach the door and summon electricity into my hands, shooting it through the grate-covered window cut-out. A high-pitched whine blares in my ears, and then a dozen growls erupt. I swear the whole place vibrates as the hellhounds circle the door, sensing our intrusion.

Zach fumbles with the keys until he finally opens the door, and I rush in without thinking. The hellhounds are my father's—they're loyal to him. It could go either way with me.

Over a dozen flaming beasts turn their coal eyes on me. I quickly search the kennel and spot Cadence chained to a pipe from the cement ceiling. Her foot rests on the chain, keeping her off the ground but still in reach of the massive hellhounds. She remains in her place when our eyes meet—and then she smiles her radiant smile.

"About time!" she yells.

"We ran into some problems," I say.

The hellhounds slink closer, herding me back to the door while ignoring Cadence. Alana, Zach, and Aston all remain in the hallway. I face the broken wolves alone. As long as one of them doesn't lunge, the rest will stay in line.

"Back off!" I yell, shooting a blast of energy around the pack. I can't show any weakness. They'll tear me apart if they think I'm no match for them. The hellhounds don't move so I blast them again. "I said, back off!"

A monstrous-sized hellhound releases a throaty growl. My

muscles tense at the sound, and the beast takes that as a sign of weakness. It lunges forward, crashing into my chest. My back hits the floor, and I scream. I zap it with energy, and a few more broken wolves follow suit, dragging me a few feet.

A hellhound yelps when a sparkling blade sinks deep into its neck. It gives me the moment I need to summon power. I expect more electricity to radiate from my core, but instead, heavenly light blasts from my fingers, sending the hellhounds scrambling. I propel to my feet, swinging my hands, shooting the light through the room. One by one, the hellhounds' flames die out as the heavenly light consumes them.

"I'm sorry," I say, tiptoeing over the convulsing bodies of the hellhounds. "I know this wasn't your doing. I'm sorry you've been forced into servitude."

With my blue fire, I weaken the chain enough to snap it. Cadence drops to her feet and flings her arms around me, hugging me for a minute as the others risk coming into the room. It's not until the loud crack of shifting bones echoes through the room that I realize what I've done. I not only put out the hellhounds' flames, but I triggered something deep within them. Like I did with the one hellhound I created, my connection to Heaven and Hell has reversed the transformation my father cursed them with. Angelic light alone can't heal a broken wolf. But angelic light with my father's demonic blood? That seems to have given this pack a miracle.

"Princess," Zach says. "We need to go."

I turn to him with tears in my eyes. Thirteen naked and

bald men and women lie on the floor across the kennel along with two dead hellhounds. There are too many of them for us to take, but we can't leave them behind.

Alana and Aston help a few of the reborn werewolves to their feet. If they're anything like Greg, the boy who stood up to his pack to protect me and was transformed into a hellhound as a thanks, then these wolves won't have any recollection of what has happened. Unlike the half-broken wolves, these people won't be haunted for the rest of their lives by my father's torture.

Cadence looks between me and Zach. "Where's Dylan?"

I hug myself. "I was hoping he was with you." I knew he wasn't, because the tainted woman didn't mention him, but I was hoping anyway.

She grimaces. "Oh, God. You should've gone for him first."

"And let you get eaten alive?" I ask.

"Well, yeah. I'm not the one who can transform demi-demons into demons. Don't ever tell him I said this, but he's kind of important."

Running my hands through me hair, I spin to look around the room. "Think you can get them out of here?"

Cadence nods. "Give me your weapons."

I load Cadence with every weapon I have, and she runs across the kennel to a door opposite from the one we came in. It would have to lead directly outside. Cadence turns the handle, showing it's unlocked, and then she rushes back to us.

"The perimeter isn't far. We can climb the fence," she says.

"Just hurry. I want you nowhere near here when my father finds me."

Hugging my best friend once more, I wait a moment to watch as she leads the others to the exit. Before she opens the door again, a strange scent wafts through the air, sending my heart racing. The sweet, grape cough syrup scent sends my stomach churning. It's strong enough to taste, making me cover my mouth.

As Cadence's fingers touch the knob, the door explodes off its hinges, sending my best friend flying back. She skids across the floor and knocks into a reborn wolf, sending him to the floor with her.

A demon with long silver hair blocks the exit to the outside. He narrows his eyes, taking in the dozen of naked werewolves before his eyes turn to the hunters. With a leering smile, he raises his hands in front of him and claps. The entire room shakes, forcing everyone to fall to their knees.

If my levitation didn't kick on, I'd have been on the floor myself.

I don't even give the demon a chance to take a step forward before I fling my hands out. Utter shock freezes my heart when nothing happens. I had intended to use my father's power, but it's gone. It's finally run out.

The demon takes advantage of my sudden failure to attack and crosses the room at lightning speed. Cadence doesn't even have time to scream when he latches his fingers around her ankles and pulls her off her feet upside down.

As I summon blue fire into my fingers, the demon raises his arm to hit Cadence in the chest—a blow I know will be lethal. A crimson haze clouds my vision, rage rushing through me, taking over and sending my true body slicing through my human façade.

"No!" I yell, throwing power at him.

All it does is make him side step out of the way.

My knees buckle. I hold my breath, willing time to stop. I'm too far away to absorb the shock of the demon's power.

The demon swings his arm back, and a figure launches from the ground, cutting between Cadence and the demon's hand. The whole room quakes as he smacks his hand into leather, and the roof overhead cracks. Cadence falls from the demon before rolling and jumping to her feet.

The demon lifts his chin to find his next victim, and I launch across the room. Blue fire blazes in my hand. I slam my palm against the demon's chest. Fire rolls over him, eating away at his clothing, sending a putrid cloud of demon stench into the air.

But I don't stop there.

I pop the demon in the face, knocking his head back hard enough to hear a bone crack. We fall to the ground at the sudden motion. The room quakes again, the demon colliding into the cement. My vision shadows, darkening until I can only see the demon. I pummel him over and over again, smashing his nose so much that you can't even tell he had one. He wails under me, digging his hands into my shoulders, but I absorb every bit of power he tries to rattle me with.

I want nothing more than for him to feel my wrath, to suffer for working with my father, for threatening my best friend, for just existing in this world. When the demon stops fighting, I raise my hand back behind me before jabbing it down. My fist rams though his chest, shattering his ribcage, pulverizing his heart. My knuckles crack against the concrete ground underneath him, the motion enhanced by his own power I've borrowed. The room shakes once more, a few of the reborn wolves crying and screaming, and then the demon melts underneath me as I send him back to Hell.

My chest heaves, and I force my true body to hide itself before I scare the werewolves anymore. A cool hand touches between my shoulder blades, rubbing small circles. I take one more deep breath before pushing to my feet while shaking demon guts off my hand.

I turn to face my friends.

Cadence and Aston kneel on the floor, hovering over a body, and it feels like my whole world falls apart. Rushing forward, I slide across the slippery floor and drop next to my former protector. Blood runs from Alana's nose, ears, and mouth as she shudders on the floor. Tears well in my eyes. I can't stop the high-pitched scream that rips from my throat.

Pulling Alana to me, I cradle her on my lap, pushing her blond hair from her bloody face. Her watery eyes meet mine, and her bottom lip quivers as she tries to speak.

"Shhh," I whisper. "It's going to be okay. We're going to get you out of here."

All she does is smile with her sorrowful gray eyes—they look exactly as I remember them when she lost David—when she lost me.

"Just hold on, okay?"

Zach slides his arm over my shoulder. "Princess."

With the sound of my nickname comes a reminder that this isn't it. That I have more to do. But I can't leave Alana. I can't.

I sniffle, wiping my face on the cleanest part of my disgusting sleeve. "I can't leave her, Zach."

Alana squeezes my fingers in her hand while she opens and closes her mouth before finally saying, "You've made me so proud, Cami." Her words barely come out a whisper as pain washes through her with every word.

I thrash my head back and forth. "Stop. Stop talking like this is it. I need you, Alana."

She swallows, closing her eyes for a second. "You haven't needed me for a long time. But the world needs you. The rest of our family needs you. You need to stay strong."

"Alana, you have to stay. You can't go. Your soul—" As the words come out of my mouth, her soul flickers into view. It's so bright and beautiful and Hell-free. It's the prettiest thing I've ever seen, and while it shatters everything within me seeing it, it also leaves me feeling peace. She sacrificed herself to save Cadence, pushing her soul back to Heaven, back to David.

My whole body shudders watching the life leave Alana's eyes. A million words fly through my mind—all the words I left unsaid—all the stuff I still had to share with her, to tell her. But it's too late.

"No," I whisper. My gaze turns to Zach. "Zach, do something. You need to bring her back. She can't be gone. She can't. Please."

"I'm so sorry, Cami. All I can do is usher her soul."

I snatch his hands before he can touch Alana. "Help me do it."

His wings appear into view, and he wraps us in them. I hold Alana's soul in my hands. Her entire life flashes through my mind. Every secret she's kept from me, all the times she was protecting me, all the mysteries that surrounded my former guardian are unveiled before me. For the first time in my life, I know exactly who Alana is and how amazing she truly was. How selfless she was. She didn't return to the alliance to betray me; she did it to change things, to make sure another demi-demon wasn't hurt again. Every decision she made was for me and because of me.

If only it didn't take her death to truly know her.

A blinding light erupts through the room, and as my eyes adjust, a figure stands before me. Alana wraps her ethereal arms around me and wipes the tears from my cheeks. She places her hands on my shoulders and smiles

"Don't cry, Cami. I'm okay."

I blink away more tears. "I'm not ready to say goodbye."

"We never are, but you're needed there."

"I'm sorry," I whisper. "I'm sorry for everything. I've ruined these last few months. I've ruined your life. I've ruined everything."

"Oh, stop it. You were the best thing to ever happen to me. You gave me a purpose that I never knew I needed until I met you. The only regret I have is that I let Hell get between us, and I'm sorry. I love you, Cami. I want you to always remember that."

I squeeze her against me again. "Don't leave. I can't ever follow you."

She pets my hair. "But that doesn't mean it's the end for us. Our paths might be different, but I'll always be here for you, Cami. I'll always be your protector. Now, I need you to let me go. You're strong—the strongest person I've ever known and the world is a better place with you there."

But the world isn't a better place without Alana. Once again, my demonic heritage has stolen another person from me. Malicevile's getting what he wants. What do I have left if I lose all those I love? Nothing but my demonic self.

The guilt is enough to eat away at me and burn me to my core.

Alana hugs me again. "You can do this, Cami. Don't let him win."

I slowly nod my head. "He won't."

"Princess," Zach says from behind me. "It's time to go."

Tears burn my cheeks as Alana's soul disappears. A wave of

heavenly emotions washes over me, pushing away my grief and heartache, and the pain of losing the person who spent her life saving others until the very end.

When the blinding light dissipates, I blink a few times, and the world comes back into view. Everyone remains exactly where they were, like time stopped when I ushered Alana's soul. Maybe it did.

Straightening my shoulders, I turn to face Cadence. "Do you think you can take her?" My voice comes out low but even, and I imagine channeling Alana's strength.

Cadence nods. "Yes, of course."

Zach helps me pick up Alana, and one of the reborn wolves takes her from him, leaving Cadence and her father free to fight. I wipe my hands off on my dirty jeans and stroll to the exit that leads outside.

Taking a deep breath of unscented air, I peer over my shoulder and say, "There aren't any demons. But hurry." Zach helps the others get ready to leave, and I turn to Cadence. "Be careful. I can't lose you, too."

She hugs me. "You better do the same."

I turn away from her to face my guardian. We stare at each other while the others make their way into the night. Zach looks utterly exhausted, and I can tell that his broken wing bothers him by how he keeps reaching for his shoulder.

He holds out his hand for me. "Let's go finish this, princess." I only look back once as Zach leads the way. It's time to face my father.

HEAVEN WAS WRONG

WE RACE BACK the way we came, my heart pounding in my ears with each step. My senses buzz on high alert, and I listen for anything out of the ordinary while taking deep breaths so I don't miss any new scents.

But everything is exactly the same as we pass the cells. Even the tainted woman's body remains on the floor. Slowing down, I reach out and grab Zach by the hand. Something feels so utterly wrong that fear washes over me in wave after wave. The vault is up ahead, but there still isn't any sign of my father.

Why hasn't he come searching for me? Why hasn't he sent some of his demonic minions to face me? I don't like this one bit.

"Look," Zach whispers. "It's open."

I release a shuddering breath, staring at the half-open door leading to the room with the vault. I swing the door the rest of the way open. Only the faint scent of cinnamon hangs in the air. I spin, taking in the built-ins that line the walls around the metal door that leads to the makeshift prison where my father keeps his most prized possessions.

The thousands of cylindrical crystal vials hum with the energy of the damned souls, soft whispers drifting through the air around me. Nothing has been touched or moved, and I'm surprised they remain unguarded.

"It's a trap," I whisper. "This is too easy."

"We're shielded," Zach says, refusing to let go of my hand.

"He'll expect that."

"He still can't see us coming."

As I peer around the room, my heart slides into my stomach. The vault door is cracked open. I force my legs to work, shuffling closer. I lock my fingers around the heavy handle. What if I open it to find everyone dead? What if my father killed Evan and stole my chance at goodbye?

I don't open it. I can't.

I turn away, covering my face with my hands.

The door whines as Zach opens it for me. "Princess."

"They're dead, aren't they?"

"No, they're gone."

Spinning to face the vault, I squint like it'll give me the

ability to see something that isn't there. Everyone, including Evan, is gone. Only the stench of filth and the hint of demon blood remain.

"We're never going to find them," I say.

Zach circles the room, peering at all the cylindrical vials holding souls. "Have some faith. While sneaking up would've been ideal, maybe we just need to make a little noise to bring them to us."

I smile at my guardian. "Destroying my father's possessions always puts me in a good mood."

Zach slides his hand across one of the shelves of souls, knocking the glass vials to the floor. They shatter at our feet, spraying shards across the small room. The air hazes with the sudden release of Hell-bound souls, though neither of us touches them.

I cross the room to Zach's side and scoop up a few vials. Each vial explodes to pieces as I chuck them one by one at the metal door of the vault. It could take hours to break all the vials, but I'm sure my father will realize soon enough that I'm destroying his pretty, tainted possessions.

I roll another soul in my fingers to read the name etched in the glass. "Be free, Malory," I say, smashing it to the ground.

"Be free, Richard," Zach says, crushing another vial under his boot.

The air thickens with the black streaked souls waiting to discover their fates. There's no time to usher them all over, but someone will have to take care of them. My father has quite the mess to clean up. It'd take the whole army of angels to sort through them to see whose contracts could be broken to be saved. I could do it myself, but most will be heading to Hell, and that's the last place I want to connect myself to at this moment.

The sound of footsteps erupts in the quiet hall outside. I stiffen as Zach turns invisible. My father already knows he's with me, but it doesn't mean we'll make things easy on him. He already has Dylan—he'll have to kill me to get to Zach, too.

The scent of sugar and nutmeg hits me before Raphael appears in front of me, his arms crossed over his chest. He looks into the hallway behind him for a second before returning his gaze to mine. "I had hoped you'd be a better influence on my daughter, Cami," he says. "Look at the mess you've made. And for what? Revenge? That's a little childish for someone your age isn't it?"

Blue fire explodes in my palms, and I hold my hands up. "Tell me where he's taken them," I say without responding to his comment.

"Or what? You're going to send me to Hell?" He takes a step into the room. "I'm not your enemy."

"If you're working with my father, then you are," I snap, increasing the power in my hand.

He leans his back on the wall with a sigh. "It's a mutual understanding. You know I'm not in it to take over the world."

"You do realize that Faith doesn't want to be like us, right? Even if she could, she wouldn't." I move closer.

"Her mind can change."

"But her soul would have to as well."

He combs his hand through his blond hair, his cheek twitching. "That's enough about my daughter."

"Then tell me where Malicevile took Evan," I say.

"How about I show you instead?"

He strolls across the room, closing the distance between us, but I back off before he can get his hands on me. He doesn't stop until I hit my back against the built-in shelves, knocking more souls onto the ground.

"Get away from me!" I yell.

He latches his fingers to the front of my shirt and yanks me forward.

Without hesitation, I use the motion to ram into his chest. He stumbles, and I keep pushing him until he hits the wall on the other side of the room. Levitating, I rise to meet him at eye level and press my hand to his chest. The last thing I want to do is send Raphael to Hell, but I'll do what I have to.

"Do it, princess," Zach says, appearing next to me. "If he's not with you, he's against you. We have enough enemies."

"Cami, wait!" A familiar voice rips through the room, stopping me from sinking my nails deeply into Raphael's chest. "Please. You can't take him from me."

I tense, but don't lose focus on Raphael. He'll overpower me the moment I give him the opportunity.

"Faith, I'm sorry. I didn't want things to end this way," I say.

My heart races at the sound of her small cries. She doesn't see Raphael for the demon he is. She's too close to him. It's too easy to overlook the evil surrounding him when it's not directed at her.

"I love you, Faith," Raphael says, surprising me.

"Do it now, Cami," Zach says.

Gathering my strength, I prepare to rip Raphael's heart out. He holds my gaze, his blue eyes shining, but he doesn't fight. He doesn't even resist.

"No!" Faith screams from behind me. Heat explodes in my back, knocking the wind from me. My clothing smolders from the red orb she attacked me with. I can't deflect her power while using mine against Raphael.

She slams another bout of power into me, and I jerk forward and fall into Raphael. His arm strikes out, grabbing my hand, pulling it from his chest, but he doesn't let go. Instead, he holds me in place and head-butts me.

Stars burst in my vision, pain radiating through my head. Raphael slams his fists into me, forcing the air from my chest, and I fly across the room. He races forward, hitting me with another lava bomb.

I glimpse a flash of heavenly light behind him, and terror slithers down my back as my guardian reveals himself. "Zach, hide! Don't let him get you!"

My guardian disappears.

Raphael swivels to look behind him. I summon blue fire, but Faith attacks me again from the side with a lava bomb and knocks it from my hands. For being a young demi-demon, she's incredibly strong with her power.

"You're going to damn yourself, Faith!" I yell. "Is that what you want?"

Raphael hits me with another lava bomb, stopping his daughter from responding. Wave after wave of his red power rushes into my soul, filling me up to the point where I don't think I can take anymore. He's taken a lesson from Malicevile when it comes to stopping me. Even I have my breaking point.

Tears rim my eyes. "Stop."

"I'm sorry, Cami. I can't make an enemy of your father."

"Please."

My head spins. Fire lights up his blue eyes, unveiling his true body as he tests my limits. My skin glows with red light, and it feels like I might explode at any minute.

"Dad," Faith says. "That's enough."

Exhaustion steals away my will to fight. Doubt blankets me in iciness, and I think about what I've gotten myself into. Heaven was wrong about me. I'm not the girl to save humanity. I can't even save myself.

"Dad," Faith says again. "Stop."

My back arches with the last wave of power Raphael sends into me. The moment it stops, I hit the floor with a thud, my very soul stinging with his demonic power. I blink a few times, struggling to hold onto my consciousness.

Hot arms wrap around me, and Raphael pulls me from the floor, cradling me in his sweet smelling arms. He shifts me to his shoulder, and then reaches into his pocket to pull out his cell phone and make a call.

"I have her. Want me to lock her up?" Raphael asks into the phone.

A warm hand touches my arm, and I glance at Faith standing next to her father. I should be so angry and upset at her after everything, but I'm too defeated to think. To even care. We both had our reasons for doing what we did. It's more obvious than ever how powerful love—no matter the form it takes—can be. Faith's love for her father is what saved him.

"Okay, will do," Raphael says before hanging up. He shifts me in his arms again to look me in the eyes. "I'm sorry, Cami. I truly am." In one quick motion, he covers my eyes and blasts power into my head.

As red sparkles cloud my vision, I spot Zach's form standing behind Raphael before he disappears. Knowing I'm not alone is the only thing that keeps me together as the rest of my world crumbles to dust.

NOTHING ELSE TO LOSE

"LOVE." DYLAN'S SOFT voice circles around me, pulling me from the darkness clinging to my soul. "You should've left."

I snap my eyes open and stare at Dylan's ethereal wings. He hovers over me, the dream world blurring in and out. I try to blink past my splitting headache. The hazy air hangs between us, and every few seconds, Dylan disappears.

His black hair hangs limply on his forehead, and black and purple bruises decorate his handsome face. I scramble to my feet to close the distance between us. Reaching out my hands, I try to hug Dylan. My fingers brush right through him, leaving me feeling empty and alone in this suddenly devastating nightmare world.

I swallow the lump in my throat, swiping my hand through him again. "God, please. Tell me you're alive."

His sad eyes hold mine, and he slowly nods his head. "I wish you didn't have to be here. I'd trade my soul to make sure you weren't in this place. I don't want you to see me like this."

I stifle a cry. "I came to save you."

He presses his lips together for a long moment. "It's too late for that, Cami."

He disappears from my view with the words, sending me to my knees as grief rushes over me. It can't be too late. I refuse to believe it.

Dylan reappears. "I'm sorry. It's hard to stay. Your father, he—"

"He's not going to get away with this."

"Cami." The sound of my name on his lips pushes me to rise back to my feet. "I just—I want you to know how sorry I am. You have to know that I have nothing against Evan, and as much as I want to do everything I can for you—" He pauses, swallowing. "I can't do this."

"Please," I say. "This isn't about Evan or me or even my father. I can't lose you."

His ethereal fingers caress over my skin, but I can't feel his touch. "I love you, Cami. I love you with every bit of my soul. Now be strong, okay?"

Dylan flickers from existence as the ground opens up and swallows me whole. Pain radiates through my body, swelling from my core to travel down my legs and up to my head. Both fire and ice swirl through me while power churns in my soul, stirring me from my mind.

The scent of cinnamon overwhelms my senses, and reality yanks me back. Thrashing, I flail my arms and kick my legs, expelling power to ease the discomfort caused by Raphael. Hot hands release me, and my stomach rises into my throat before I hit the ground with a thud and open my eyes.

"Princess, stop. You're going to hurt an innocent." Zach's voice whispers from behind me, but I don't move to look his way.

Instead, I train my eyes on Malicevile. He stands a few feet away from me, a wicked smile crossing his face. Raphael stands in front of him, holding the power I expelled in his hands before it disappears. The two demons watch me for a long moment, and I gather my bearings to get myself in control.

Inhaling a deep breath, I pick up several familiar scents in the air—all of which threaten to obliterate my heart into dust. Though I can't see them, Evan and Dylan are nearby, along with Ella and the other two demi-demons. Faith's vanilla scent also mingles with others in the air, but I hold my gaze as expressionless as possible. Malicevile will not get the satisfaction of seeing me break down.

Forcing myself into action, I press my hands into the cool marble floor of an unfamiliar room. Sparkling chandeliers hang down from the vaulted ceiling and murals of Hell on earth decorate the walls. Even without furniture, the place is still impressive. It reminds me of a grand ballroom that can be readied for any occasion. Just hopefully not for what my father has in store.

"I was beginning to think you'd miss the show," Malicevile finally says, moving past Raphael to close the distance between us.

I summon blue fire in my hands and hold it out without a word.

He holds up his hand. "Do it and the nephilim will pay."

His gaze darts behind me, and it takes all my willpower to shift in place to look over my shoulder. A scream threatens to rip from my throat when I see Dylan beaten and bruised, slumped against the wall, with his hands and ankles bound with chains. His chocolate eyes remain focused on the floor, and he refuses to meet my gaze.

Extinguishing the fire in my hand, I push from the floor and rush to Dylan, though I don't make it within five feet of him. Malicevile snatches the back of my shirt and jerks me away, sending me skidding across the marble floor.

"Absolutely not, Camilla. I don't want you messing things up. You'd sure enough push me into accidentally killing you trying to protect that half-breed. But don't worry, he doesn't have to die. All I want is for him to perform a small task and then he's free to go." Malicevile smiles as he says it. "And I know he'll do it, because he doesn't have it in him to break your heart."

I gasp small breaths of warm air. The whole universe seems to close in on me, threatening to suffocate me with the evil emanating from my father. He's the one thing that stands between me and Dylan, and I won't let him force Dylan's hand.

Pressing my fingers into the cool tile, I summon the strength to fight. I raise my hands a few inches above the ground before smacking my palms down, making the whole building shake as my newest power explodes from my hands.

Faith slips on the tile, falling to the floor, and Raphael scoops her up. I pound my hands down again. Malicevile spins, levitating a foot above the ground, and glowers at me. I don't stop what I'm doing though. I'd rather the whole building fall on us than let my father get his way.

Electricity erupts in my father's hands, and I brace for the sudden rush of power that never comes. Dylan yells from his place on the floor as Malicevile's power shocks him, and for the first time since I woke up, his gaze falls on me.

I freeze, his hopelessness burrowing deep inside me.

"That's what I thought." Malicevile points his finger in my face. "Don't test my patience again."

Zach appears next to me on the floor, but he doesn't reveal himself to Malicevile. I hope he has some brilliant plan to get us out of this mess, because I'm all out of options that don't involve people dying in the crossfire were I to really go after my father.

"Brace yourself, princess," Zach whispers from next to me.

I tense under his words when the sound of heavy footsteps draws my attention to a doorway that leads to who-knows-where. Evan pushes the three demi-demons forward in our direction. He's unchained and free, and I shouldn't have expected anything less, though I was hoping for more. Evan wants to transform as much as my father wants his new army, and his Hell-bound soul won't even consider what this—using Dylan—will do to me. What it will do to us. Because if Evan does this, I can't ever forgive him. I can't sit by and watch him stand by my father's side, even if he's doing it for an eternity with me.

Tears prickle in the corners of my eyes when Evan moves from the demi-demons and kneels by my side. I rein in my tears as he touches my chin, forcing me to look into his oceanic eyes. Studying my face, his jaw twitches, and I'm sure my expression screams a thousand words.

"Cami, you have to understand," he says, his voice low. We're both aware of everyone watching us, but it's not like we can leave the room to have a private conversation. "I'm doing this for you."

Without thinking, I raise my hand to slap him. He catches my hand and twines his fingers through mine, holding me so tightly that I can't let him go.

"I will *never* be with you if you go through with this. Do you understand? Is eternity worth that much to you?"

"I'm sorry, Cami. I'm willing to risk it. I know you, and I know we're supposed to be together."

"Not like this!" I scream. "Never like this!"

This time, I do slap him. His head turns sideways at the force, and he brings his hand up to his reddening cheek. I shove him away, putting space between us, and all he does is apologize again as he gets to his feet. He strolls away, leaving me on the verge of falling apart on the floor.

"He's made his choice," Zach says. "He'll have to live with the consequences."

But that's just it. So will I. Because Dylan won't risk his wings to go to Hell for him, and I wouldn't expect him to. With this decision, Evan isn't choosing an eternity together. He's choosing one apart from me. That's what devastates me the most.

"They're going to die, Zach," I whisper. "Please, you can do something. You're strong. This is how you're supposed to protect me. Protect my heart. Because I don't think I can survive this. I don't want to."

Zach doesn't say anything. My eyes remain locked on Dylan's as he mouths, "Stay strong."

A spark of electricity forces my eyes to what's happening before me. Malicevile zaps the young boy, causing him to yelp. Like the predator he is, my father circles the small group, looking for the weak link, the link that'll succumb to his will.

The boy doesn't stand a chance when he flinches before Malicevile even does anything. My demonic father stands before the young demi-demon and Evan holds out a small dagger. Ella remains stiff and guarded by the brave older demi-demon at her side. I think both would rather die than break. And I shiver at their fates, because that's exactly what'll happen if my father doesn't get his way.

"Do you want a chance to live, half-breed?" Malicevile asks, slapping the flat side of the blade against his palm.

The boy furiously nods.

"Then you'll have to do something about that pretty little soul of yours—and it doesn't involve me binding you to Hell. It must be at your own doing."

Malicevile hands the blade to the demi-demon, who takes the knife with a shaking hand. He peers at the other two, a dark expression marring his face. He doesn't think long before he lunges, aiming the knife directly at Ella. She screams, throwing a ball of fire in his direction, but it only slows him down.

Faith screams when the boy charges Ella again, and Raphael grabs hold of his daughter by the shoulder before she can run forward. She might love a demon, but she is as horrified by the atrocious acts as I am.

My father points at Raphael. "Get her out of here before I make her go next!"

I expect Raphael to stand up to my father, to threaten him right back, but all he does is drag Faith away. He's not going to risk his daughter's life. If there's one thing I know about Raphael it's that he's protective. Something Malicevile is not toward me.

"Come on, boy! You're wasting my time. Bind your soul to Hell or die."

The boy closes the distance to Ella, holding purple electricity, not unlike my father's, in one hand and the dagger in the other. Ella screams as the electricity shocks her, sending her to her knees. The older hunter jumps into action, racing toward the boy. He's inhumanly fast, his ability completely physical instead of manifested power like Ella's or the boy's. The hunter rams into the boy from behind, knocking him off his feet. But the boy doesn't stop. He spins midair, throwing the dagger, before landing on his back.

Ella screams out. The hunter drops to his knees, blood splashing onto the pristine marble floor. A second later, the hunter falls forward.

"How could you?" Ella yells. "Ollie was our friend!"

The boy summons more power in his hand, but Malicevile zaps him before he can use it. "Enough. Let's not be wasteful."

The boy's chest heaves, and he spins around to face my father, a look of pure anger and defeat frozen on his face. He strolls forward, keeping his fingers clenched at his side, before he meets my father's icy gaze.

"Let me go," he says. "I did what you wanted."

Malicevile raises his hands and rests them on the boy's shoulders. Peering into his eyes, he says, "I asked you if you wanted a chance to live. I said nothing of letting you go."

"What?"

Malicevile chuckles. "And your chance lies on the wings of a nephilim. Good luck." With his words, Malicevile sends a huge burst of power directly into the boy's chest, stopping his heart.

The boy's body slumps to the floor, and the room falls utterly silent. My eyes turn to Dylan, who refuses to look at anything but his own hands. He's not going to attempt to rescue the boy. What my father did was just to get under my skin.

"Time's ticking, nephilim." Malicevile kicks the boy's body. "Or do I have to get my daughter involved?" Malicevile motions for Evan to move closer, and he does as my father says.

"Zach," I whisper. "Please. Please, I'm begging you."

He reaches out and touches my hand. "I'm sorry, princess."

I nearly lose it when Zach denies me the one request that will surely save my world. I shove him as I hop to my feet and run toward Evan. Malicevile is quick to move, blocking me from reaching him, and grabs me by the arm.

I burn him with the blue fire, yanking away to stand in front of Evan. He clutches a dagger in his hands, staring at the sparkle of the blade in the bright lights hanging overhead. Tears shine in his aqua eyes when I reach out and touch his cheek.

"Don't do this, Evan. Don't you see? Dylan won't help you. If you do this, you'll die. You'll seal our fate apart." I stand on my tiptoes and kiss him, sliding one of my hands around his neck and the other to the hand that grips the dagger. "I know you want to spend eternity with me, but it can't happen like this. You're going to die. Do you know what that's going to do to me? Do you want to destroy me?"

"Cami," he whispers.

"Evan, do it," Malicevile says. "That nephilim loves Camilla too much to watch her suffer. This is the only way you can live forever. Think about all the power I have to offer you. Think about all that you can do."

My lip quivers. "He's lying. Even if Dylan goes to Hell to

bring you back, you'll be nothing to my father. You won't have his power." My heart races, banging so hard against my ribcage that I'm sure it'll bust through and splatter on the ground. "Don't do this. Don't break my heart."

Evan's fingers slowly release the knife, and it clatters to the floor between us. I release a breath and embrace him. Closing my eyes for a second longer, I pull away from Evan, fire swirling in my palms. I turn to face my father with all my wrath.

Rage crosses Malicevile's face, his horns ripping through his skin as he unveils his true body to me. Jumping into action, I raise my hand and thrust my power at Malicevile. He jerks his hand forward, but electricity doesn't sparkle from his hands. A dagger flies straight for Evan, sinking deep into his stomach. Surprise crosses Evan's face. I release a long wail, watching the blood pour through his fingers as he touches the hilt of the blade.

"No!" I scream, charging forward to attack my father.

I expect him to face me head on. I expect him to attack me with all he has. I expect to die at any second.

But Malicevile doesn't come after me. He strides the few feet to Dylan and forces him to his feet.

"Are you really going to break my daughter's heart by letting her boyfriend die?" he asks, shaking Dylan. "Just look at her."

He holds Dylan out to me, and I meet his chocolate eyes. Tears pour down my face as Evan sinks to his knees before falling on his side. Dylan stares at me for a long moment, giving me his answer without having to say it. My heart shatters to dust.

"Do it or die!" Malicevile roars.

My whole world stops when Dylan elbows my father before flashing his brilliant wings. They sear Malicevile's face as he expands them, fighting against the chains. Running closer, I ignite angelic light in my hand. I thrust it at Malicevile as hard as I can.

He hollers, blisters sprouting over the skin on his face, and I keep a steady stream on him. He has already forced the hand of Evan; there's no way I'm going to let my father hurt Dylan, too. I blast more power at my father, sending the ground shaking as I stomp closer.

Malicevile strikes me with a bout of electricity that I immediately absorb. Anger pushes me forward, but love is what keeps me fighting. Love is what pulls every single power from the depths of my soul so I can use it against my father the way he tries to use my love against me.

I plow into Malicevile's side, knocking him away from Dylan. Blinding light flashes from behind me. Zach is readying himself to fight by my side. Malicevile shocks Zach with his power, smoldering the feathers of my guardian's black wings. I take the small opening to latch my hand to Malicevile's shoulder to aim my hand over his chest.

Fire lights in his demonic eyes, and he snatches my wrist in his hand and twists, snapping my bone. I scream out in pain, my vision blurring. I fall back to the floor. Malicevile kicks me, his heavy foot colliding with my ribs, sending me a few feet away.

I blast him again with power, grinding my teeth from the pain radiating up my arm.

His eyes narrow, and the corners of his lips pull up as he leers at me. Power glows from his fingers. "This is your nephilim's last chance. He either brings Evan back from Hell, or I will kill him."

A flash of brilliant wings expand out behind Malicevile, and Dylan launches at my father. The same time my father turns, I throw all of my power at once at him, but he doesn't stop. He grabs Dylan by the front of his shirt, presses his hand against his chest, and shocks his heart.

My ears ring with the sound of my screams. Dylan's eyes widen for a split second before the light disappears from them. I sway on my feet, shock and horror threatening to knock me unconscious as another piece of my heart crumbles to the floor.

Cool hands grab my shoulders, and Zach pulls me back when Malicevile turns away from Dylan's discarded body to face me. Murder shines in his pure black eyes while he summons more power into his fingers.

"It's over, Camilla. It is time you realize that your place is by my side. If you join me now, I'll spare your watcher's life."

Zach pulls me farther away from my father. "He's lying, princess. Come on, we have to go. There's nothing more we can do tonight."

But I can't turn away. I don't care if I'm not as powerful as

Malicevile or if he can murder me before I could even touch him. Because I'm not leaving until this is over. It's me or him. He's already taken my whole world from me. Because of him, everyone I love is dead.

I shake my head, pulling away from Zach. "I'm sorry, Zach. Save Ella and go while you still can."

Malicevile smiles as I take a step forward.

"Cami." The voice comes from neither Malicevile nor Zach, and my bottom lip quivers as I watch Evan's black streaked soul hover around his body.

Shifting to look behind him, Malicevile watches Evan gasp one last breath, giving me the most precious gift in the entire world.

I fly forward, my hand raised. With Evan's death, he's made it possible for me to surprise my father.

He's made it possible to fight.

With his death, he's given me nothing else to lose.

ETERNITY

I CRASH INTO my father, power blasting from my hands, knocking him off his feet and onto his back. With everything in me, I unleash every power that swirls in my soul straight into his chest. His vibrant green eyes startle as pain washes over him, searing his skin, and threatening to explode through his ribs to destroy his heart.

His fingers latch around my neck, squeezing so tightly that starbursts dance in my vision, but I don't stop. I can't. The moment I do, Malicevile will overpower me. He'll see to it that I fall by his hands. But if I fall, I'm taking him with me.

As my power sears his flesh, blistering the skin under his

ruined dress shirt, he roars, blasting his own power into me. His fingers slide from my neck to my chest, and he digs his sharp fingernails into the skin around my heart.

His own heart thrums under my palm, the beat in perfect sync with my own, and it makes me wonder how deep our connection is. His blood runs through my veins. His power through me. Killing him could lead to my own demise, but it'd be worth it if it saves the rest of humanity in the end.

Power sparks in his palm, and he shocks my heart, leaving me breathless. The flow of power from my hands slows as he does it again, stalling my heartbeat for a second before it picks back up again.

A wicked smile pulls at the corner of his lips. My head lolls forward, exhaustion threatening to knock me out before he can murder me. It's almost wishful thinking that I could somehow move into the next world in peace.

"You're wasting your time, Camilla," Malicevile says, digging his nails deeper into my chest. "The sun is rising. Can't you feel it?"

I can't. All I can feel is the beating of our hearts and the power flowing between us.

"All it will take is one little tug," he says, squeezing.

I grind my teeth through the pain, forcing more power into my father. The scent of burning cinnamon wafts through the air as my hand slides into my father's chest, and his eyes widen. I blast more power at him, finally breaking through all the demonic energy that has been protecting his life for most of time.

My vision blurs, pain ripping through me. Malicevile tugs on my heart, fire lighting his eyes as his hand slides its way out of my chest. Memories of my life flash before my eyes. My soul hums over my skin, it's golden color shining bright enough to make Malicevile shut his eyes, and then a heavy body lands on my back, pushing me down at the same time Malicevile tries to steal my heart from me. But what he doesn't know is that he's already taken it and smashed it.

And now, I'm going to do the same.

The scent of jasmine clears all the pain and anguish from my mind as my warrior angel weighs my body down. Zach reaches his hand around and locks his fingers around Malicevile's, burning his flesh with his heavenly touch. It's enough for Malicevile to loosen his fingers on my heart.

I bury my fingers into his chest, his power shocking me, trying to force me out before I can reach the thing that'll send him straight to Hell.

"Camilla!" Malicevile roars, and for the first time I smell the sweet scent of fear. Fear he wouldn't have ever had to experience if it wasn't for my being born. Fear strong enough to wipe away everything else I feel.

He thrashes under me, but with Zach's extra weight and the intensity of all our power, he's outmatched. Even his own electricity fizzles out the deeper I slide my fingers. Boiling blood soaks my hand, coating me in the blood I share with Malicevile. Blood that I yearn to spill. Blood I'd die for not to share.

His heartbeat thrums against my fingers. He locks his fingers around my wrist, attempting to break it like my other, but my power blasts his hand away.

"Camilla," he says again, pleading with me. "Don't do this. I'm your father. I'm your family."

I suck in a ragged breath, hesitating. "You killed my family."

"They would've died anyway. But us? Our bond is eternal. Please, my daughter. My blood. We can make a deal."

"Princess," Zach says.

I tense at his voice but don't take my eyes away from Malicevile's. "I can't let you destroy the world, Dad."

"Okay," he says. "Whatever you want."

My fingers loosen around his heart and tears blur my eyes. This has been the moment I've been preparing for, and I never thought my father would ever ask me to show him mercy. Mercy I refuse to give.

"I never wanted any of this," I whisper.

His jaw clenches. "I'm sorry, Camilla, but look how strong I've made you."

"You didn't make me strong." My voice comes out surprisingly even. "My real family did. My humanity did. My soul. You've done nothing but ruin me. And this all ends here."

"You'll be nothing without me!"

"I'm nothing with you either!"

I press my lips together, watching his eyes flicker. Electricity ignites in his palms, and he jerks his hand free to blast it at me. I absorb his power one last time as I release my own power at the same time into his heart. My nails dig into the soft flesh, and I jerk my arm back and pull his heart free from his chest. Malicevile's eyes widen, watching his black heart beat in my hand. I throw it across the room, splattering it on the wall.

The air shimmers around us, and the first rays of sunlight push the darkness of the night away. With a silent scream, my father explodes into a dazzling light show. His power sears straight into my heart before his body crumbles into dust. Everything that Malicevile was sinks into me, his blood and power coursing through my veins and in my soul. My skin lights up, glowing from within, and I arch my back, accepting my father's existence.

It's in this moment that I know I didn't send Malicevile to Hell. I've taken all of his essence, and it now lives within me.

I will now reign over his kingdom. The earth, humanity—it's mine.

I can finally set things right.

But I refuse to do this alone. I refuse to accept such a fate.

I push to my feet and turn to Zach. "I did everything you've asked. Now, I need you to do something for me."

He gets to his feet and takes my hands. "Anything, princess."

I point to Evan's body. "Save him."

Tears shine in his beautiful hazel eyes, his black wings expanding on his back. "I wish I could, princess. I'd give you anything, but something like that isn't in my power. You know that. You know that you're a precious rarity."

My hair smacks my face as I shake my head. "Zach."

He pulls me into a hug. "I'm so sorry, Cami."

But I can't accept it. I won't.

"Then hold onto my soul, okay? Promise you won't let me go."

He opens and closes his mouth for a second. The energy of the daylight realm hovers around us. I'm running out of time.

Finally, he nods.

Rushing to Evan's side, I focus on his tainted soul. It fades in and out, fighting against Hell as it tries to take it. Because he's unbound from a demon, he doesn't need to be ushered. Hell will welcome him with open arms. But I refuse to give him up.

Reaching out, I touch Evan's soul as it disappears, aiding him the best I can. I expect his soul to feel awful, like the worst parts of myself reflected onto him, but all I feel is everything that made Evan who he was—his strength, his confidence, his power, his loyalty.

I hold onto his soul with everything in me. Hell rushes over us, pulling us together to the side Evan chose. An inky darkness seeps into me, and the world falls away, leaving me standing in front of the fiery gates of Hell. I can't get over how welcoming it feels as the voices of the damned call my name.

Evan's soul stands before me. He doesn't look at me but stares at the fire that'll grab onto his soul and hold him for the rest of eternity. But I can't let him go. Hell can try to take him from me, but I refuse to allow it.

When Evan takes a slow step forward, I reach out and grab onto him. "I don't think so."

He spins in his place to face me, surprise crossing his handsome face. "I don't understand."

"I'm a demon, Evan. Hell is my home away from home. You opened the tunnel, and I followed."

"You're giving up your eternity for this?"

I blink away my tears. "No, you are. I want you to give me your soul." It's my last ditch-effort to save him. He might've died, but he doesn't have to leave me. I can't let him leave me. Not like this. Not for Hell.

His brow furrows. "It's always been yours."

"Forever?" I ask.

"Always."

Evan pulls me against him, kissing me in front of the place neither of us belongs. The world around us shimmers, and the fire disappears and leaves us hovering in utter darkness. But even in never-ending darkness, I could survive as long as I hold Evan's soul. As long as I get to keep it forever.

"Princess." Zach's voice slides through the darkness. "Come back to me."

A flash of light flickers in the darkness, and I imagine myself floating toward it. It's exactly how I imagine entering Heaven would be like, heading toward the glittering light and all that jazz. But when my eyes blink open, I'm not greeted by harmonious voices or silver-lined clouds.

A brown sky and hazy air greets me with the pure awesome

numbing sensation that comes with the daylight realm. I stretch my limbs out, feeling the dry grass beneath me. Zach hovers over me, his black wings expanded on his back, blocking the sun from my vision. I never thought I'd enjoy the daylight prison realm, but I can't think of a better place I'd rather be. Because here, the pain and grief doesn't consume me. Here, I can heal.

"Evan's soul? Where is it? I made a deal with him—I couldn't let him spend eternity in—"

"Why do you think we're here?" Zach says. "It seems you've managed to create your own miracle, princess."

I jerk upright and turn my gaze to Evan's body sprawled across the ground next to me. His chest rises and falls as he takes slow breaths. Reaching out, I slide the dagger from his stomach so he can start to heal.

My eyes widen when I stare at my guardian. "I didn't mean to transform him. I just bargained for his soul."

"A demi-demon's soul that touched Hell I might add," Zach says. "And your Heaven-bound soul brought you both back."

Heartache cuts through the numbness as his words sink in. Malicevile didn't need an angel all along—all he needed was me. This could've changed everything. I could've changed the demonic world. I could've saved Dylan.

Dylan.

Sobs grip my chest, awakening every emotion in me despite how hard the daylight prison realm tries to heal me physically and mentally. I might've defeated Malicevile, but in the end, I still failed.

And what now? The whole demonic world will be after me. The angels, too. There's no way in Heaven and Hell that I'll be left alive if I can move from one place to the next. I'm too powerful with Malicevile's essence flowing through me. His darkness lingers deep in my soul. What if it changes me?

"This is bad, Zach. I don't want this kind of power. It's too much." I curl my knees to my chin and rest my head on them while I watch Evan's body adjust to the demonic transformation.

Fear laces around my heart, a million what-if questions fogging my mind. I'm reminded of the first night of my life as a demon and how hard it was—how feeling such evil flow through me was enough to make me shut off my humanity. And if Evan does that, he'll change. He'll allow Hell to rule him. He'll be no better than—

"Cami." Evan stirs next to me, his eyes fluttering open. He blinks in the hazy light before he reaches out for me. I lock my fingers with his, pulling his hand up to caress against my cheek. I had expected to never hear his voice or see his beautiful eyes again—but I didn't expect this. I didn't expect that we'd get our eternity, whatever that may be.

I sniffle, helping him sit up. With curious eyes, Evan looks around the gnarled forest. His eyes peer through the trees, confusion wrinkling his forehead.

"I have something to tell you," I whisper.

"Is this where I'll be spending my eternity?"

"During the day at least," Zach says from beside me.

Unlike me, Evan doesn't absorb power. He can never take in the heavenly light that binds me to the earth during the day. But that doesn't matter to me now. Because I'm never leaving Evan. His soul is mine, and I'll take care of it—I'll take care of him. If it means giving up my days, I'll do it.

Evan licks his dry lips and looks at me for confirmation.

I nod. "You're a full-blooded demon now."

A smile crosses his face. "I always knew you'd be the one to save me, Cami. I owe you my life. I owe you everything."

"I'm glad you say that," Zach says, interrupting. "Because Cami's shifted the balance and will need you. She's done something impossible, and now that Malicevile is dead, she's going to need help putting things in order in the demonic world."

Someone clears their throat from behind us, sending me flying to my feet. Power ignites in my hand as I spin, half expecting to see my father. But Raphael greets me instead. He holds his arms up in surrender, a seriousness in his eyes that I haven't seen before.

Evan stands tall by my side like he'll attack if the demon tries to do anything. My heart swells with his loyalty, something I never imagined possible. Even though Evan's a full demon, he still radiates everything I loved about him as a demi-demon. I didn't think it was possible, but in this moment, I love him even more.

"What do you want?" I ask, keeping my head high.

"I overheard your conversation. I'm here to offer you my services," he says.

I crinkle my nose. "Why? I'm not going to transform Faith if that's what you think."

He links his fingers together. "I felt the shift in power as it fell onto you. I think we can work well together, Cami. Unlike your father, I never lost sight of my purpose, but it's hard to resist doing what I have to, to assure my place on earth. And I like my place in the world. I don't want to leave. Serving you will guarantee it. We can help each other."

I blink a few times. Of course this is about power. Demons crave it. But how do I know Raphael won't turn against me to try to take his place on top?

"Why should I believe you?" I ask.

He lifts and drops his shoulders. "Because I'm willing to make a deal. I'll swear my allegiance to you with the consequence of returning home if I ever go against you."

"And what's in it for you?" I ask. Every deal comes with a price.

"Nothing. That's why you'll believe me. You have nothing to lose."

I turn to my guardian angel for his opinion, but he stands silently at my side. I'm alone when it comes to demonic affairs.

"I think we should trust him," Evan says. "He's never given me a reason to doubt him."

With a shaky breath, I offer out my hand. "As long as the angelic army doesn't decide to take my soul after all this, it's a deal, Raphael."

He shakes my hand. "Then I'm at your service."

REVIVED

I BURY MY head into Evan's chest as the world shimmers around us. We never left the spot where we arrived, and we end up reappearing in the world where we had left it. The comforting numbness that comes with the prison realm wears off immediately, and Evan sucks in a deep breath, his emotions coming back more potent than ever.

He holds me in his arms, breathing into my hair, and I levitate a few inches to bow my head against his and kiss the few tears away that splash on his cheeks. My concern for him is the one thing that keeps me together as the world closes in around me. Even as Evan stands before me, real and alive and stronger than ever, I can't help sensing the darkness left behind by my father. In his last moments on earth, he stole so much from me. My heart hurts with every beat. I force myself to pull away from Evan to face the aftermath of my broken world—the world I have to rebuild even with all the missing pieces.

Evan reaches out and snatches my wrist, stopping me in place. "Let me take care of things. You've been through enough. I promise I'll be careful."

My bottom lip quivers, the realization of what Evan's trying to protect me from sinking heavily into my soul. I tug away from him despite his protests and spin on my boots to take in the bodies of those who've died by my father's hands.

When my gaze falls on Dylan's body, left exactly as he was when my father murdered him, my hand flies to my chest and my heart threatens to stop. His black hair hangs on his forehead, half covering his wide, lifeless eyes. Sobs rake at my chest. I rush forward and fall to the ground beside him, pulling him onto my lap.

I brush strands of hair from his face, leaning forward to cry over my fallen friend—my purest love. Gently, I close his eyes so I can pretend he's sleeping even though death has stolen away everything good about him. I'd give anything to smell his apple and rain shower scent one more time, to hear him say my name, to glimpse the gold of his wings, to see his peek-a-boo dimples as he smiles, wearing his love for me stitched right on his chest for all the world to see.

"God, why?" I ask. Tears brand shiny streaks down my

face, and I tilt my head to the sky, waiting for a response that doesn't come. "I didn't even get to say goodbye." What hurts the most about everything is knowing that I'll never be able to follow Dylan. My place is here on earth. I don't belong to either Heaven or Hell. I belong to humanity. I'm responsible for maintaining the balance in the world just like I do with myself.

I don't understand or know how I know my purpose, but it resonates deep within me. It's like I've always known, though I fought so hard to pull myself from Purgatory—but it's where I've belonged all along.

Zach comes to my side and rests a cool hand on my shoulder. "Dylan wouldn't want you to say goodbye, princess. This is just a body."

"That doesn't make me feel any better, Zach," I say, pressing my warm lips to Dylan's cool forehead. I beg for his eyes to flutter open. I pray that this was all a mistake, and his heart will start beating. But nothing happens. Dylan's soul has already moved on. "He shouldn't be anywhere else but here. This isn't fair."

"I know, Cami," Zach says. "I know."

He doesn't try to comfort me with angelic words of wisdom, or try to put into words what he thinks Dylan would want from me. Instead, he just holds my hand while I cry over Dylan's body until my tears run out and leave me exhausted enough that if I closed my eyes, I could probably sleep for the first time on my own—but that's the last thing I want. Because if I sleep, I'll dream. And my dreams would be utterly lonely.

After Evan takes care of the other two bodies, he returns to my side. He doesn't try to take Dylan from me. He just joins me and Zach on the floor, and we just sit around. I feel like I should do something, announce my reign, tell the world of my success, but after everything, I just want to hide.

Footsteps sound from the grand archway to a massive hallway that leads through the compound, and I pull my attention away from Dylan to meet Raphael's gaze. He'd left us before sunset so he could reappear at Faith's side where he'd left her hidden away on the premises.

Faith steps out from behind him, and I shift to block Dylan's body from her view. She slows down when I raise my hand up to her.

"Stay back, Faith. I don't want you to see Dylan like this," I say.

The young demi-demon covers her mouth with her hand before backing away to return to her father's side. Raphael's brows pinch together, and he thins his lips when he looks at us gathered around Dylan's body.

"My condolences, Cami," he says, wrapping his arm around his daughter's shoulders. "We didn't mean to intrude, but I wanted to give you an update."

I force myself to let go of Dylan. Evan takes his body from me, and I slowly get to my feet to cross the room. With my father's death, I have to fill his place before another demon attempts to do it. The world doesn't stop because I want it to.

"Give it to me straight, Raphael. Is the whole demonic

world about to come after me?" I ask.

"Word of Malicevile's demise hasn't spread, but the shift was felt everywhere. It won't be long before the scavengers start to arrive to get their hands on anything they can. We also have the matter of the demi-demons and your father's living collection." He shifts his gaze to look at Faith who quietly listens. Turning back to me, he leans in and whispers, "I'm afraid you might have a lot of soulless ones to deal with."

I rub my hand down my face at the thought of having to face all those still living who had contracts with my father. Just the thought is too much. Why the heck did all this fall on me? It's tempting to just hand over everything to Raphael and let him deal with it. I could go into hiding, distance myself from it all, and spend the rest of eternity on some desolate island with Evan. *A demon can dream...or not.*

"I think I need to call for reinforcements. I'm not about to take on all this alone," I say.

"The angels?" he asks, flaring his nostrils in disapproval.

I square my shoulders. "They're not our enemies, Raphael. I'm putting an end to this war."

He lifts an eyebrow. "Long live our new queen."

⚬

"Oh, Cami." Cadence rushes over, flinging her arms around me in a hug tight enough to crack my ribs. As she breaks down, tears smear her usually flawless eyeliner. "I wasn't sure if I'd ever see you again. The angels wouldn't let me go back to the compound. Everyone is up in arms."

I lean back, still holding onto my best friend. "I'm glad you stayed away. I wasn't there. I was—"

"Hi, Cadence," Evan says, coming up behind me.

Stiffening in my arms, Cadence shifts her gaze from me to Evan and then back to me. Her mouth falls open in surprise and then she waves her hand in front of her face. A mixture of emotions light her honey-brown eyes.

She jabs Evan in the chest with her index finger. "You're why the angelic army is going nuts like wild birds suddenly shoved into cages. I can't believe Dylan did it after all. He swore he'd never, but I knew he wouldn't be able to break Cami's heart like—"

I stifle a cry with my sleeve. It wasn't Dylan who broke my heart in the end.

Cadence snaps her mouth shut, her eyes filling with tears even though I haven't said anything yet. My grief and despair are obvious enough that I'm sure the entire world can sense it. Evan slides his arms around my shoulders, hugging me from behind, and I sink against him.

"No," she whispers. "He's—"

I nod because I can't bear to hear her say the words out loud.

"Then who—" Her question hangs in the air unfinished as she releases a quiet sob.

"Cami," Evan says, answering.

Cadence rubs her hands over her face before taking a deep breath. "Whoa."

"Tell me about it," I say.

A smile crosses her face through her watery eyes. "I always knew my BFF was amazing, but holy crap, Cami. I don't even know what to say. It's sort of romantic if you don't think about all the Hell and evil." She nudges Evan, having an easier time pulling herself together than I am. "No offense."

He shrugs. "I feel less evil now than I did. Probably because Cami owns my soul."

Leaning forward, he kisses my cheek before resting his chin on the crook of my neck. His patchouli and amber scent clings to me with his soft breathing, and I can't help bask in the relief I feel hearing his words.

"So what now?" Cadence asks.

"I need to right all the wrongs my father's done in the world," I say.

Cadence reaches out and grasps my hand. "And I'm here to help."

I softly smile at my best friend, both of us on the verge of more tears, though neither of us falls apart.

"I'm glad you say that, Cadence," Zach says, appearing out of nowhere. "Because we can use all the help we can get." His attention turns to me. "I've managed to get a few angelic volunteers, but there's still a lot of hesitation. Not many want to enter a demon's lair."

I sigh. "It's my lair now."

"They'll come around."

"As long as it's not to redeem my soul."

Zach's lips curl into an easy-going smile. "Like I'd let that happen. Plus, we don't need them. We've got this under control."

I smile. "Together?"

"Duh," Cadence says. "It wouldn't be any other way."

Holding my arms over my chest, I glance around at what's left of my family. With them by my side, facing the aftermath of my father's demise doesn't seem so daunting. I can face the world knowing that no matter what I'm going through or what happens, no matter what side I'm on, no matter what I have to face, I'll never be alone.

For so long, I had assumed that my life would end by my father's hands. I had never imagined that it would also be him who revived me when I thought it was over. With his blood and power flowing through my veins—his essence—I'm powerful enough to withstand whatever the Veiled Realm throws at me. I'm strong enough to rip the veil free and take charge. I'll finally get to do what I've always wanted—to help those in need.

By taking my father's place, I'll be the change humanity needs to survive. Better yet, I'll be the change that helps humanity thrive.

BIRTHRIGHT

I STAND JUST outside the elevator in the concrete hall that'll take me to the dozens of cells in which my father imprisoned those still living who had made deals with him. An eerie quiet settles around me and I take a slow step forward.

Zach's soft wings expand on his back, brushing against my arm, though one remains tucked in place, still healing from the injury my father had inflicted on him. Beside me, Remi and Dani stand stiff and ready. They're the only angels who agreed to help me—and I think it's only because Zach begged them. Jazmin and Aston follow behind to assist in what might be the worst job yet—taking care of the soulless. Though, none of us has any idea what we're really getting into.

A flash of light glows in the hall as footsteps sound out. Raphael appears from the door that hides one of six vaults my father has at this estate—I don't even have a clue about all his other properties. But according to Evan and Raphael, this one is the largest.

Raphael stops in place when he sees my small army of angels and hunters. Cadence, Evan, and Faith all come out into the hallway behind my new demonic assistant—though, he'd probably throw a lava bomb at me if he heard me call him that.

I step forward. "Everyone needs to chill out. We're in this together. Raphael, this is Remi and Dani. They're with Zach."

"I'm quite aware of who they are," Raphael says.

I grimace and turn to the angels. "Raphael has a deal with me. You aren't in any danger."

Reluctantly, the two angels follow Zach's lead while he strolls behind me, and I close the distance. The scents of Heaven and Hell mingle in the hallway, and it starts feeling a little overcrowded for my liking.

I turn to Raphael. "How bad is it?"

He shifts on his feet to peer through the grate of one of the door cutouts. "It's bad, my queen."

I grimace at the nickname and his assessment. "How many living people did my father have down here anyway?"

Raphael rubs the back of his neck. "It's not the living that's troublesome. It's the departed."

"They're still here? I thought souls followed their demons

to—" I reach up and smack myself in the forehead. "Are you kidding me?"

"You didn't send your father to Hell," Raphael says, peaking his eyebrows on his forehead.

"No," I admit. "All his power and blood—his essence—" I pat my chest. "Yeah, that's all mine."

"Including all the contracts and souls he's acquired," Raphael says.

I release a breath through my nose. "Ugh. Looks like it."

"You say that like it's a bad thing, princess," Zach says.

"Why don't you try ushering thousands and thousands, maybe millions of souls to Hell and tell me how you like it when you're through." Because I'm pretty sure it won't be anything like following Evan.

"You don't have to do it alone. Plus, I'm sure we can find a few to send to Heaven. I'll even let you have dibs. It'll all balance itself out." Zach squeezes my shoulder before pushing past me in the crowded hallway.

"I'm at your service as well, and I'll show Evan how to usher souls so he can help," Raphael says.

"And the rest of us will get snacks," Cadence says with a smile. "Because this is clearly out of our league."

I laugh, the mood lightening as a plan falls into place. Evan laces his fingers through mine and guides me into the room that leads to the vault. It's exactly how I left it, glass shards covering the floor, broken shelves, the opened, empty vault.

The air buzzes with energy as the souls I released from their vials swirl through the air. Soft whispers send goose bumps over my skin, and the voices of the tainted call my name. It's enough to make me take an automatic step back into Evan's chest.

"You're the strongest, most talented and beautiful person I know," Evan whispers into my hair. "You can do this. I'll be right here to help."

I release a shuddering breath, and everyone waits for me to make the first move. Reaching out my hand, I caress my fingers over a soul, feeling its very essence deep into my core. A life that isn't my own flashes before my eyes, and an icy darkness slithers through me as I'm shown the horror this soul inflicted on the world. Without thinking, I release the soul of its contract and the negative energy disappears as I send it to where it belongs.

I shiver as I shake the evil from my bones. "I don't think I can do this."

Zach frowns with sad eyes, but he doesn't argue with me.

It's Raphael who steps forward to face me. "It must be done."

"Says the guy who's been playing with souls for years. I'm sure your collection is just as impressive." I don't mean to snap at one of the few demons who isn't going to attempt to take me out, but I can't help it. "You know you'll have to go through yours next, right?"

"Hey," Faith says, speaking up for the first time all afternoon. "My dad doesn't collect souls. He's been doing his job."

I press my lips together unsure if I can believe it. He had broken his fair number of werewolves—I wouldn't put it past him that he took souls, too. I know he likes deals—he wanted to make one with me and Cadence when we broke into his house the first day we met. *But it wasn't for your soul. He wanted you to work for him.*

"Like using tainted humans?"

A flash of red brightens Raphael's eyes. "I'm not going to lie. I've done some questionable things—but who hasn't?" He strolls closer and slides his arm over my shoulder. "The difference between your father and I is that I work with living souls—souls already on their way to Hell. I don't keep souls when their lives end."

"That still doesn't make me want to do this," I mutter. "I'm not like you. I don't enjoy feeling the wrongness of a Hell-bound soul."

He sighs. "Think of it this way, Cami. You're serving a greater purpose, providing justice in a sense. And for your information, it's not supposed to be enjoyable. I'd be concerned if you found it to be."

"My soul, it—"

"It's strong enough, princess," Zach says. "You're strong enough. "

He's right. They're both right.

I straighten my back and reach out my hand again, feeling the sting of another Hell-bound soul. It shocks through me before I release it.

"I'll never get used to this," I mutter.

"Good," Zach says. "I wouldn't want you to."

I roll my eyes. "Let's just get this over with."

"Sounds like a plan to me."

<hr>

When I toss the last crystal vile into the black trash bag Cadence holds out for me, I drop to my knees and curl them to my chest. We've worked all night, and I can sense the sun readying itself to light the world in its warm glow.

Faith sleeps in the fetal position on the hard floor with her father's suit jacket draped over her, while Dani, Remi, Aston, and Jazmin help Zach with the living in the hall. Every demonic contract in the Hellshire Estate has been voided, and my soul already feels lighter—freer. Because unlike my father, I don't need a bunch of souls to be powerful. My power was my birth-right.

Evan plops down next to me on the floor, resting his head on my shoulder. He plays with a bright white flame in his fingers—the fire different, more powerful than it was when he was a demi-demon, and I reach out and run my fingers over it before snuffing it out by pressing the palm of my hand to his.

"You know, you don't have to follow me to the daylight realm if you don't want to," Evan says, rubbing his fingers against my palm. "If you want to stay here, I won't be mad or hurt."

I offer him a small smile. "Even if I can stay on this plane, it doesn't mean I should. I am a demon after all." It's taken a long time to come to terms with my demonic heritage. I could barely live with knowing how close to Hell I really was. I couldn't handle thinking that being a demon would define me.

But it doesn't.

My thoughts, my actions, everything that makes me who I am is what defines me. I know that now.

"You're more than that, Cami," he says as he turns my face to meet his eyes. "You're brave and stubborn and sometimes infuriating..."

I laugh, kissing him.

"And sexy and compassionate and the most amazing being in the universe," he continues.

"I love you, you know," I say, climbing into his lap.

"Forever and always?"

"Even longer."

Zach clears his throat from the entrance, drawing my attention to the small group of people who I've come to lean on and who lean on me. His black wings flash in and out of existence as he takes in the emptiness of the room.

"The sun is rising, princess, and I still have a few things to do," he says.

I glance at Evan with a smile. "I think we'll manage by ourselves. You can take your time."

"You sure?" he asks.

Cadence slaps his arm. "She's positive."

The air shimmers around us in a brown haze, and I hug Evan, kissing his lips as we enter what is now our own private world—one where it's just the two of us without having to worry about anything apart from what makes us happy.

I never thought I could be this happy.

I never thought I could be this free.

And I never in a million years thought I'd ever be working alongside angels, demons, and humans and more. But there's a first for everything—especially in this bright new world where I'll no longer be hunted, where I'll no longer have to worry about the damage done to my soul or worry about my father. In this new world, I have a future. I have eternity.

And I get to spend it to my best abilities.

WITHSTAND TIME

CADENCE HOLDS OUT a sparkling tiara to me as I sit in front of my vanity table. My curly hair cascades down my back in soft ringlets, and I'm actually kind of excited to dress up in the deep sapphire gown she picked out for me while I enjoyed another day in the light prison realm, though that doesn't bother me nearly as much. It's just my life now. A life I wouldn't trade for anything.

My hand freezes halfway to my mouth before I apply my shimmery brown lipstick. "I don't think so."

She waves it in her hand. "Oh, come on. You got me this beautiful necklace, so I found this crown. You can show them

377

who's queen." She fiddles with the rainbow stone on the platinum chain on her neck, the amulet given to her by my father's witch, whose contract fell into my hands. Even though Elora fought against me, she did try to warn me, and for that, I voided her contract and received her necklace as a gift, along with her offer to help me with anything I need in the future.

It never hurts to have a witch on my side Jazmin said before she and Aston joined some of the angels to rebuild the Hunter's Alliance under new accords, with new mottos and motives. All tailored to fit me. To help me. Even Vivian, Cadence's grandma, agreed to leave her town in Desertville to help change the future she thought was lost. Because now, we're all on the same side.

I pull myself from my thoughts. "You've been hanging out with Raphael too much," I say, snickering when she rolls her eyes. "The angels would throw a fit if they thought I was prancing around, claiming to be the ruler of earth."

"You're right about that, princess." Zach enters my room before Evan, and I tilt my head back and laugh. Only he could pull off wearing a screen-printed tuxedo shirt to a formal affair. At least he's wearing clean jeans and combed his hair.

Evan on the other hand...wow. I push to my feet and spin to face him. He's already crossing the room before I even take a step and pulls me into his strong arms to kiss me passionately on the lips. We linger together, holding each other. Despite everything we've gone through, despite our ups and downs and circles and explosion, I've always known that Evan was my soul mate and that our love was eternal. That our love can withstand time.

"Demons in love," Zach says, musing his thoughts aloud to Cadence and pulling my attention away from Evan. "Who would've thought?"

Taking my hand in his, Evan smiles and leads me across the room to leave Malicevile's house that I took over near Moonlight Shores. My stomach flutters with nerves, but I wouldn't dare mention how freaked out I am about tonight.

It's been six long months since I killed Malicevile and took over the Hellshire Empire as his sole heir. I never knew how much you could learn about someone after their death, and I'm constantly learning every day about the man too cruel to see past his own twisted big picture. He really was an ingenious force in both the human and demonic world, and if he wasn't a cold-hearted monster, I'd be impressed. But one thing's for sure—he left me with so much to offer, and all I can hope for is that somehow I can right all the wrongs my father did. I hope I can ease the devastation he caused humanity, even just a little.

"Earth to Cami?" Cadence says, tapping my shoulder.

I pull myself from my thoughts. "Sorry, what?"

"Zach wants to drive," she says, motioning to my guardian. He stands in front of the Maserati I had given him to replace his piece-of-junk Tercel that Evan set on fire. If I didn't know about his achingly beautiful wings hiding on his back, I'd think he was demonic with his leering, excited grin.

I crinkle my nose. "Maybe if you'd drive like we weren't

stuck in a never-ending school zone," I say, causing Evan to laugh.

"We have precious cargo," Zach says, motioning to Cadence.

Lifting an eyebrow, I say, "I'm pretty sure it's because you want me to remember what Hell is like."

Glorious black wings flash on his back as he glares at me. "Very funny, princess. Now, come on. Let me have a little fun."

I pull Evan forward with me, giving in for a change. "Fine, but you better actually stomp the throttle, because I want to visit someone before I have to face my minions."

Zach shakes his head and chuckles. Tonight will be memorable if anything. With the shift in power created by my father's demise, demons have been gathering in anticipation. Raphael managed to keep things in control, but the angelic army is still on edge about everything. So tonight, I must make my demonic debut. Tonight will be the ultimate test to see what I'm made of and if I can withstand the world like my father.

Ten minutes later, Zach pulls the Maserati into a dark, quiet cemetery which is usually the last place you'd find a demon. We spend our time among the living, not worrying over the dead. But I can't help it. Two parts of my heart rest here, and talking to them gives me the strength I need to face my forever—even if they can't face it with me.

Evan leans against the door while Zach and Cadence remain in the car and watch. I lift the hem of my gown and cross the cemetery. The cool night air causes me to shiver, but all I do is hold myself in the silvery moonlight when I stand in front of the familiar graves I hate that I know so well.

I hike up my dress and kneel in the bouncy grass between Dylan's and Alana's graves, placing my palms on each of the stones like I can suddenly summon their souls to talk to, but that's not possible. Once you've moved on, that's it. They're busy with their eternities while I'm busy with mine.

I inhale a long breath through my nose. "Can you believe this is it? Things are finally coming together. I just wish you were here to be with me." My voice fades as I sniffle back the tears that never seem to go away no matter how hard I try. "I could really use all the support I can get."

I close my eyes, thinking back on all the good memories I have—about all the times Alana and I used to joke around. How much of a badass she was when it came to demons. How much she cared.

And Dylan—

The scent of apples and rain showers wafts around me, sending my heart racing. It's not the first time I've imagined his scent—I can't even handle having apples around—but something feels different.

When I open my eyes, the dark cemetery is lit in a soft glow, like the sun is shining from behind me. I dig my fingers into the grass, bracing myself.

"You know, love, I'm not actually in there listening to you, right?"

My heart stalls at the sound of Dylan's smooth voice. "Am

I—" I gasp in another apple-scented breath. "Am I dreaming?"

"You haven't dreamed in half a year. Why would you start now?"

I propel to my feet and spin around to face Dylan in all of his angelic glory. His skin, haloed in ethereal light, nearly blinds me. I rush forward and fling my arms around him. Tears spill from my eyes and he hugs me with cool arms, keeping me from falling to the ground as my legs give out.

"I can't believe you're here," I say, pulling away so I can look into his chocolate eyes. "All Zach said was that you moved on and were at peace."

He grins, flashing his dimples at me. Against my protests and need to cling to him, he slowly backs up and puts a foot of space between us. A moment later, giant black wings expand from his back, reaching out and up toward the moon, and I cover my gaping mouth with my hand. I reach out and gently caress his downy feathers with my fingertips.

"I've ascended, Cami," he says. "And I've returned to help out with some things."

He doesn't say what, but he winks at me, sending me flying forward again to wrap my arms around him. He laughs as we topple to the soft grass, and I squeeze him against me, not wanting to let him go.

"Be careful, love," he says, pushing my curls from my face. "You don't want to make me fall, now do you?"

A blush crawls up my cheeks as he laughs. "Dylan—I—"

"I'm teasing, Cami. If there was one thing I've learned

from my mortal life with you, it was restraint."

I grin as I smack his chest. "You have no idea how happy I am that you're here."

He helps me to my feet and hugs me once more. Love radiates from his very essence, but it's not the same kind of love I'm used to feeling radiating from him—this love is new. It's pure. It's unconditional. But just like before, it runs soul deep.

"I'm pretty sure I do. Six months was a long time."

"It felt like forever."

He reaches over and runs the pad of his thumb under my eyes, wiping away the dampness from my tears. "Don't worry. You'll never have to feel that again."

The Morningstar nightclub buzzes with life when Zach pulls to the curb for the valet to park the car. Evan helps me from the backseat before hooking his fingers around my waist. He stands tall with serious blue eyes, a five o'clock shadow covering his strong jawline, and a flicker of power in his free hand.

Cadence hooks her arm through Zach's, and they disappear right before my eyes as he shields them from the world. It's better to be safe than sorry in this new world, but there was no way either of them were about to miss a party.

Dylan leans against the wall near the bouncer, and Evan's gaze flicks to mine when I smile at Angel Boy. As quickly as he appeared, he disappears.

"Cami," Evan breathes, leaning close to me. "Was that?"

I purse my lips, stopping myself from smiling. "Yeah."

"When did you—"

"At the cemetery. As it turns out, someone needed their own personal Demon Watcher to appease the angelic army, and it takes someone special to handle the job considering you have a bad reputation, and I'm overprotective—according to the rumors." I study his expression for a reaction.

"He's *my* Demon Watcher?" he asks with a laugh.

"Is that going to be a problem?"

He shakes his head. "It was just unexpected."

There once was a time that Evan wouldn't have accepted it. Dylan once threatened our eternity. He's who I turned to when I felt lost. But he was never a choice for me to make. I'll always love him, and I had dearly missed him in the months after his death—but I love Evan. I'd face Hell every day for him.

Raphael appears in the doorway to The Morningstar, and we waltz right past the gigantic line that travels around the building and head inside with my new right-hand demon. He's proved himself worthy of the position, and it frees up my time to spend it with the people I care about.

Straightening my shoulders, I saunter through the club with Evan by my side. I meet every curious gaze that meets mine. The air permeates with a collection of demonic scents— some sweet, some spicy, some gag-inducing—all of them eager and waiting.

We head to the VIP area, and Raphael steals me away from Evan to face a few demons I recognize from the times my father used to parade me around.

We stop in front of a group of the most beautiful people, dressed in their finest, and Raphael introduces me as Malicevile's daughter.

A man with sharp nails offers his hand to me. "Camilla Hellshire, I've heard the whispers of your power." He doesn't let go of my hand when I try to casually pull away. "But what I want to know is what you intend to do with it. This is a big world for such a young girl to attempt to rule."

Seriously? "First, call me Cami," I say. "Only my father called me Camilla and look where it got him." He squeezes my hand tighter. "And second, I'm not your queen or ruler, but make no mistake, I will be your enforcer."

A smile pulls at his puffy lips as he grins, displaying a mouthful of sharp teeth. "I love a good challenge."

I tense as cerulean liquid seeps from his palm and wraps around my wrist, searing my skin before my ability kicks into action to absorb it. The wind flies from my lungs when he shoves his free hand at my chest, knocking me a few feet before my levitation kicks on. The last person to challenge me was my father, and facing this demon stirs something deadly within me. Evan leaps forward, but Raphael grabs the back of his tuxedo jacket and stops him in his place. As much as I'd love him to fight my battles, I know that this is one I have to do on my own. This is the ultimate test as I stand before the demons I'm expected to control, to make sure they do as they're supposed to, to keep a balance in the world.

The demon charges forward, and something dark sneaks up

from the depths of my soul. Shadows darken my vision, turning the world crimson, and electricity explodes in my palms without even having to summon it. A familiar rush of power overtakes me, taking over my movements. It's almost like possession, but it's all me. I'm not being controlled, but guided. *Show him whose daughter you are.*

Ice rushes through my veins as Malicevile's voice echoes in my mind, but just as quickly, it disappears. It's only a faint memory.

Jerking my hand out, I snag the demon by the front of his shirt and flip him onto the floor. I step on him, digging my spiked heel into his gut while holding my father's—my—power in my fingers.

The demon's sharp nails rip at my gown, splitting the soft fabric. He refuses to back down. I press my lips together for a second before I raise the power over my head to blast it down. The whole room shakes when I release the electricity at a speed fast enough to burn the wicked heart right from the demon's chest.

His body explodes beneath me, and I levitate before I slip and fall on the guts and goo left behind. The last thing I need is to fall on my butt as the demons watch and judge my every move.

I press my lips together to stop from grimacing when all I really want to do is yell because for once in my life I want to wear a gown without ruining it. For once I want to be looked upon as the powerful demon my father's blood created, and the strong demon Heaven helped me to be.

"Let this be a lesson," I say, summoning my new vibrant blue liquid power in my hands. "This world doesn't belong to you anymore. It belongs to humanity, and I'll send you all back to Hell to protect it."

A cool hand touches my elbow as Zach squeezes my arm. "Princess, have I ever told you that you're terrifying?"

I don't smile or react, knowing he's still hidden among the demons, using his shield. I have to face one thing at a time, and revealing the peace I've come to with the angels will have to wait for another day.

"And incredible," Evan says, wrapping his arms around me from behind. Zach never hides from Evan.

Dylan and Cadence appear by my other side, standing with me as I look at the demons who now bow before me in respect.

Zach bumps me with his elbow. "What do you think? You ready for all this?"

After tonight, I won't have to worry about my place in the world. I've fought so hard to be where I am, that no one, no demon, can take it from me. Because I'm exactly where I need to be, exactly where I belong. It's here, standing up for humanity, with the people I care about by my side.

I hold my head high and smile. "I'm ready to face the world."

THE END

I HOPE YOU enjoyed Cami Anders' journey in the Demon Within series! It was such an emotional rollercoaster adventure to write, and I'm so honored that you've joined me for the ride. This series was possible because of you, dear reader, and I'm grateful that you took a chance on me.

If you enjoyed this series, I'd like to ask you a favor. Please leave a review at the retailer you've purchased your copy from. Reviews help persuade other readers find new books and authors, and they're crucial to help boost a books visibility. A review doesn't have to be a book report—a sentence or two about your thoughts and feelings goes a long way. I appreciate any and all reviews. Again, thank you!

THERE ARE SO many people I want to acknowledge, who have put so much time and energy into this series. First and foremost, thank you to my editorial team—Jan, Jamie, and Katie—none of this would've been possible without your help. You three are amazing!

Thank you to my family for all of your support through my writing journey. Thank you for letting me get lost in my own world but also being there to remind me to take a step back and enjoy the real world, too. Eric, I know that sometimes five more minutes turns into a few hours or one more paragraph turns into several chapters, but I'm incredibly thankful that you never complain and let me do my own thing. Mom, Eddie, Dad, and Sue—thank you for your unconditional love. Thank you for believing in my dreams and supporting me anyway you can. Tami, Eric, Shawn, Breanna, Jason, Jacob, Lily, Jakob, Jay, Jadyn, Max, Daphne, Dylan, and Ashley—we don't get to see each other as much as I'd like, but I'm thankful for all of you being a part of my life.

Jazmin, Nikki, Courtney, Renee, Malory, Amy, Sarah, Amanda, Kim, and all my other friends, near and far, thank you for making my life better. I'm so happy you're a part of it.

And thank you to my readers. You always brighten my day. Thanks for the emails and interactions across all my social media platforms. Thanks for being #TeamCami #TeamEvan, #TeamDylan, #TeamZach, #TeamCadence, #TeamInsertFavoriteCharacterHere. I love hearing from you!

GINNA MORAN IS A WRITER from sunny Southern California. She started writing poetry as a teenager in a spiral notebook that she still has tucked away on her desk today. Her love of writing grew after she graduated high school, and she completed her first unpublished manuscript at age eighteen.

When she realized her love of writing was her life's passion, she studied literature at Mira Costa College in Northern San Diego. Besides writing novels, she was senior editor, content manager, and image coordinator for Crescent House Publishing Inc. for four years.

Aside from Ginna's professional life, she enjoys binge watching television shows, playing pretend with her daughter, and cuddling with her dogs. Some of her favorite things include chocolate, anything that glitters, cheesy jokes, and organizing her bookshelf.

Ginna Moran loves to hear from her readers so visit her online at www.GinnaMoran.com. You can also find her on her Facebook page or Group, Twitter, Instagram, and Snapchat. To stay up-to-date on new releases, sign up to her newsletter. You'll not only get a FREE book, but you'll be able to participate in monthly giveaways!

Ginna Moran is currently hard at work on her next novel.

MORE BY GINNA MORAN

PARANORMAL

Destined for Dreams Series
Demon Within Series
Finding Nate Series
Going Ghostly Series
Spark of Life Series
When Souls Collide Series
Demon Watcher Series
Call of the Ocean Series

CONTEMPORARY

Falling into Fame Series

STANDALONES

Life After Lila